RUMOR HAS IT
Cindi Myers

HARLEQUIN®

TORONTO • NEW YORK • LONDON
AMSTERDAM • PARIS • SYDNEY • HAMBURG
STOCKHOLM • ATHENS • TOKYO • MILAN • MADRID
PRAGUE • WARSAW • BUDAPEST • AUCKLAND

This book is dedicated to
the Conroe High School Class of 1979.
Go Tigers!

ISBN 0-373-79122-4

RUMOR HAS IT

Visit us at www.eHarlequin.com

Printed in U.S.A.

1

SOMETIMES THE PAST sneaks up and bites you in the butt. You think you're doing great, planning for the future and then up pops a ghost from your personal history to prove you wrong.

"I hear Dylan Gates is moving back to town."

Alyson Michaels, who taught physical education as if it were merely an extension of her long career as a Cedar Creek Cyclone cheerleader, dropped this bomb as she stood with Taylor Reed and several other teachers on the bus ramp in front of the high school one bright September morning.

For half a second Taylor stopped breathing. She hadn't thought of Dylan Gates in a long time, but the memory of him was enough to bring a hot flush to the back of her neck, even after ten years. She swallowed hard and stared out at the lines of students who slouched up the steps of Cedar Creek Senior High with all the enthusiasm of cattle being led to slaughter. Ah, the joys of high school. How ironic that after enduring her own personal high school hell, Taylor had ended up coming back here to teach. Guess she was just a glutton for punishment.

"It'll be great to see Dylan." Fellow English teacher Grady Murphy sidled closer. "Last I heard, he was out in California."

"He was, but he's moving back to Cedar Creek to open a law practice," Alyson said.

Dylan, moving here? Taylor's stomach flip-flopped. "How do you know that?" she asked.

Alyson bounced on her toes like a hyperactive poodle. As usual, she was dressed in a too tight golf shirt, white shorts and tennis shoes with white anklets. She carried the bus duty roster on a clipboard and her blond hair was pulled back in a tight ponytail. In her more vindictive moments, Taylor wondered if Alyson's whole face would collapse if that ponytail was undone. "Troy Sommers, the real estate agent, is a friend of mine. He said Dylan e-mailed him last week about renting space downtown, across from the courthouse. *And* he told Troy he intended to move back into his parents' old place."

"Who's Dylan Gates?" Mindy Lewis, freshman algebra teacher and Taylor's best friend, joined them.

"Before your time, child." Grady grinned at their younger colleague. "Alyson, Taylor, Dylan and I were all at school together, right here at good old Cedar Creek High." He laughed. "Those were the days!"

"Yeah, right," Taylor mumbled. Days of sheer torture as far as she was concerned. Even Dylan...

"Speaking of our high school days, are you going to the reunion Saturday?" Alyson asked.

"Why do I need to go to the reunion when half our class is still here?" Taylor said the words only half jokingly.

"I'm on the reunion committee and I noticed you hadn't sent in your R.S.V.P." Alyson frowned at Taylor. "I can't believe you'd think of missing our ten-year reunion. *Everyone* will be there."

"I won't," Mindy said. "Of course, I've got *years* to go before my reunion."

Alyson ignored the dig from her younger colleague and pointed a pencil at Taylor. "You don't want to miss out on this reunion. Trust me."

Taylor shrugged. "I guess I'm not very big on reliving old times." In fact, she'd just as soon forget her short career as a student at Cedar Creek High.

"It'll be your last chance to see everyone before you head off to London or wherever it is," Grady said.

"Oxford." In January, Taylor would start a graduate fellowship at the hallowed university, far away from Cedar Creek, Texas, and reminders of the past.

"Dylan will be there." Alyson studied Taylor through lowered lashes. "Maybe you two can pick up where you left off, for old times' sake."

"That's right—you and Dylan were quite an item senior year, weren't you?" Grady mused. "Is it true Coach Nelson caught the two of you in the boys' showers?"

For once Taylor was grateful for the shrill bell that announced the start of classes. Nodding goodbye to Alyson and Grady, she maneuvered past groups of students and headed toward her second-floor English classroom. Only four more months to endure Alyson's and Grady's snide comments and suggestive winks. Four months until she started life over in a place where no one had ever heard of her allegedly torrid past.

Mindy caught up to her. "What was all that about? Who's Dylan Gates?"

Taylor shrugged. "A guy I was friends with in high school."

"Friends? As in boyfriend-girlfriend?"

"No, it wasn't like that." Not that Taylor hadn't

dreamed about the possibility. "There were some rumors about us, but they weren't true."

"Alyson and Grady apparently think they were." Mindy wrinkled her nose in distaste. "Of course, those two are still stuck in high school. I mean, look at them. Alyson still thinks she's the popular cheerleader and Grady is the dumb jock panting after her. It's pathetic, really, when people can't move on with their lives."

"Yeah, pathetic," Taylor echoed. But were they any worse than a twenty-eight-year-old woman who let high school teasing still get to her?

"Good morning, Mindy. Taylor." The principal, Clay Walsh, waved to them from the door of his office.

"Good morning, Clay." Mindy's cheeks flushed pink as they moved on down the corridor.

Taylor nudged her friend. "If you like him so much, why don't you come right out and tell him?"

Mindy's smile dissolved into a look of openmouthed horror. "Does it really show that much?"

"Relax. Only because I know you so well. But seriously, why not let him know how you feel?"

Mindy glanced back at Clay, who was still watching them from his office doorway. She quickly faced forward again. "I've tried dropping hints," she said. "But he doesn't seem interested."

"What kind of hints?"

"Well...I always give him a big smile and say hello whenever I see him in the hall. And when I sent Larry Atwater to the principal's office last week for disrupting class, I walked him down there myself and told Clay I was available to discuss the situation further after school." Her shoulders slumped. "But all he said was that he appreciated the offer, but he didn't think that would be necessary."

Taylor couldn't hold back her laughter. Mindy glared at her. "What's so funny?"

"You! How are any of those things supposed to let a man know you've got the hots for him?"

"Well, what do *you* think I should do?"

Taylor composed herself. Who would have thought usually outgoing Mindy would have such a problem letting a man know she was interested? "Flirt with him," she suggested. "Make it a point to sit with him at lunch. Stop by after work and invite him to have a drink with you."

Mindy's eyes widened. "I couldn't do that!"

"Why not? The worst that could happen is he'd turn you down. And I'd bet money he wouldn't."

Mindy shook her head. "It's complicated, with him being principal. Not to mention fifteen years older than me."

"That shouldn't matter. I think you two would be good together."

"Like I'm supposed to trust the judgment of a woman who hasn't had a serious relationship with a man in how long?"

Taylor switched her book bag from one hand to the other. "It's been a while. Maybe I'm just picky."

"Maybe you're *too* picky. Or a coward."

"A coward?" Taylor glanced at her friend. "Because I have high standards?"

"Sometimes women use that as an excuse because they're afraid of getting hurt." She shrugged off Taylor's glare. "Hey, I may be an algebra teacher, but I minored in psychology."

"I minored in home economics, but you don't hear me telling you what to fix for supper, do you?"

"Feeling feisty this morning, are we?" Mindy laughed and came to a stop at Taylor's classroom door. "Okay, I promise not to analyze you anymore if you promise not to say anything else about Clay."

"Deal." The two friends parted, still laughing, and Taylor prepared to face another day of trying to make classical literature relevant to hormonal teens.

"Wassup, Ms. Reed?" Class clown Berkley Brentmeyer greeted her as he passed her desk. "I had a great idea this weekend. Instead of wasting our time studying all this boring old stuff, why don't we move right along to modern literature?" He held up the latest Stephen King release. "I guarantee we'd all stay awake in class if we were reading this."

"Nice try, Berk. But I'm betting even Stephen King did his time studying the classics."

As Berk shuffled to his place in the third row, Taylor took her seat at her desk and pulled out her roll book. "Open your books to page seventy-six. This morning, we're going to continue our discussion of *Beowulf*. While everyone is getting ready, please pass in your journal entries." As part of the creative writing portion of senior English, students were required to keep a journal. Some days Taylor assigned topics for them to write about; other days they were free to explore any subject they wished.

A tall blonde in the fourth row raised her hand. "Yes, Jessica?" Taylor asked.

"I thought a journal was supposed to be private. But how can it be private if you're reading it and grading us?"

"If there's anything you don't want me to read, don' put it in the journal." Taylor surveyed the class. "Certainly all of you should feel free to keep private journals outside of class. In fact, I'd encourage it. The journal entries you make for class may be completely separate from those."

"Did you keep a journal in high school?" Berk asked.

Taylor smiled. "Yes, I did. My family moved to Cedar Creek from California my senior year and, as you can imagine, it was quite an adjustment. Writing in my journal really helped me."

"Do you still have your journal?" Jessica asked.

Taylor laughed. "It's probably somewhere in a trunk. I haven't looked at it in years. But that's one of the things about journals—the main benefit comes in the writing, not so much the reading later."

Jessica pursed her lips in a pout. "Then why do *you* have to read it?"

"All I care about reading are the assignments. Anything else you write is your business."

"I'm going to keep my journal forever," the class brain, Patrice Miller, announced. "Then when I'm older, I'll dig it out and write a bestselling novel about high school angst."

Uh-huh, Taylor thought. *As if anyone would want to relive high school.*

DYLAN GATES STOOD on the sidewalk across from the Bee County Courthouse and felt the tension in his shoulders ease for the first time in months. He slipped off his jacket and loosened his tie, relishing the feel of the still-hot September sun on his back. Next summer he'd be moaning about the Texas heat along with everybody else, but right now he was glad to be home.

"Hey, Dylan. Sorry to keep you waiting." Real-estate

agent Troy Sommers crossed the street from the court-house, his hand already extended in greeting. "It's good to have you back in town, man," he said, shaking Dylan's hand.

"It's good to be back." Dylan grinned at the man who had played tight end to his quarterback for the 1993 District Champion Cedar Creek Cyclones. "I'm anxious to see this office you've picked out for me."

"Oh, you'll like it." Troy dug a ring of keys out of his pocket and motioned down the sidewalk. "It used to be Pokey's Barber Shop, remember? Dale Hanson turned it into an office a few years ago and it came up vacant about the time you got in touch with me, when Debra Nixon moved over to that new complex by the library."

Dylan laughed. "It's amazing to think that even though I've been away ten years, I know every one of the names you mentioned."

"Plenty has changed since you left, I promise." They reached the glass-fronted office door and Troy unlocked it. "So how was Los Angeles?"

"Crowded. Stressful. Impersonal." Dylan followed him into the darkened office. "Lots of people love it, but I guess I'm not cut out for the big city. I wanted to come back to a place where I can be really involved in a community again."

Troy flipped a switch and flooded the room with light. "You can be involved here, all right. If you don't watch it, you'll be signed up for every committee and club in the book." He moved down a short hallway. "Bathroom's down here and a Pullman kitchen. Private office back here."

Dylan followed him to the room at the back. Sunlight streamed through two windows onto scuffed wooden floors and a massive oak desk. "Don't see how they ever got that big thing in here." Troy shook his head at the desk. "But it comes with the place if you want it."

Dylan ran his hand along the edge of the desk. His father had had one like this. Dylan had spent hours playing under the kneehole, reading adventure stories by flashlight and munching peanut-butter crackers while his father worked above him. Texas Ranger Sam Gates was already a local legend by then, but to Dylan he was just his father who was equally at home with a gun and a typewriter.

He supposed his youngest sister had the desk now. She'd agreed to take most of the furniture when his parents' estate had been settled. "I'll take it," he said.

"Good deal." Troy rubbed his hands together. "We can go over to my office and finish up the paperwork now."

As they walked around the courthouse square to Troy's office, Dylan looked for familiar names among the businesses they passed. The Courthouse Café still advertised a daily lunch special, but the office supply, florist and dry cleaner were all new. "I guess things have changed," he said.

"Yeah, but there's still a lot of us old-timers around." Troy glanced at him. "You seen Taylor yet?"

"Taylor?" He stopped. "Taylor Reed? Did she come in for the reunion?" That surprised him. After the hell they'd put her through, he hadn't thought Taylor would ever want to see any of them again.

They started out walking again. "No, she lives here. Teaches over at Cedar Creek High." Troy grinned. "She's still a hot number, I tell you." He glanced at Dylan. "You two were quite an item, weren't you? Is it true you almost got arrested for making out up on Inspiration Point?''

Dylan frowned. "That never happened."

Troy laughed. "If you say so. But that was a long time ago. You don't have to worry about protecting her reputation now."

He only wished he'd done a better job of protecting it then. Taylor Reed. He'd thought of her a lot over the years. When she'd moved to town, all the way from Los Angeles, California, you'd have thought a movie star had descended into their midst. Taylor was at least as pretty as any movie actress and every bit as exotic with her fashionable clothes and big-city attitude. But underneath all that polish had been a really sweet girl. Someone he'd considered one of his best friends.

Then all those rumors had sprung up and he'd started avoiding her, thinking that would put a stop to the talk. But all it did was isolate her further. She'd been his friend and he'd let her down. Even ten years later, the guilt made a knot in his stomach.

What would have happened if he'd stood by Taylor? If he'd told her how he'd really felt about her—how much he'd wanted to make the rumors about them true? Would they still be together now or would they have both moved on to other relationships?

"We had some wild times in high school, didn't we?" Troy said. "Sometimes I regret not being able to live that way again."

"Yeah. I know what you mean." Too bad you couldn't go back in time and do things over. Only this time, he'd do the right thing. This time, he wouldn't run out on Taylor. He'd let her know he really cared about her. Enough to stick with her, the opinions of others be damned.

TAYLOR ARRIVED HOME a little before six and headed straight to the refrigerator for a glass of iced tea. Summer was hanging on into September and the air conditioner in her car was on the blink again. She drained half the glass, then sagged onto a bar stool at the counter. Why did some days seem so much longer than others?

She glanced at the stack of mail on the end of the bar and spotted the invitation to the Cedar Creek Senior High School Class of '93 Reunion. She picked up the engraved card and studied it. Should she go, or not?

If she didn't show up, Alyson and the others would be sure to talk about her. But if she attended, wouldn't all those painful memories resurface like some nasty, long-dormant rash?

Frowning, she laid the invitation aside. Coming to a small town her senior year, to a class full of students who'd been together since grade school, had been bad enough. The fact that she'd moved from the exotic land of Los Angeles to the dusty isolation of South Texas had made things ten times worse.

Then all those rumors had started about her and Dylan Gates.

Dylan. She smiled, remembering. The moment she'd laid eyes on him, she'd been as infatuated as any other girl. He was the school quarterback and the salutatorian, cowboy-handsome in a way that made California surfers seem like pretty boys. He had thick brown hair, eyes that were almost black and a smile that made everyone like him instantly.

What did he look like now? she wondered. Had those boyish good looks matured to true handsomeness? How ironic that he was moving back to town now, when she'd be leaving in a few months. Several times over the years she'd been tempted to try to contact him, but had pushed the thought aside. After all, Dylan was only a high school crush. He probably wouldn't even remember her and the brief time they'd been friends.

Her smile faded. If he did remember, would it be the good times they'd shared or the bad things everyone had said later?

She pushed aside the memories and opened her briefcase, intending to grade papers. The folder containing the students' journal entries lay on top. If anything could take her mind off herself, these would do it. Despite her permission to keep personal things to themselves, her students seemed eager to pour their hearts out onto the page. She felt privileged to read their secret desires and troubles and was often amused by the minor things they took so seriously.

But that was life as a teenager, wasn't it? You were the center of your own universe and everything that happened to you was new and painfully important.

If she found and reread her own journal, it would no doubt be filled with as many petty worries and moments of high drama. She pushed aside the stack of student papers, distracted by the thought. Had she made too much of the events of her senior year? Had what happened back then been no big deal after all?

She stood and carried her empty tea glass to the sink. There was only one way to find out. Unable any longer to avoid the idea that had nagged at her mind all day, Taylor went into the hall and pulled down the stairs that led to the attic.

Her old footlocker sat under the eaves beneath a layer of dust. She opened it and carefully lifted out a stack of yellowed college dance programs, followed by a shoe box filled with withered corsages, the peppery smell of carnations rising up when she slipped off the lid. Next came the thick, bound volume of the school annual. The *Cedar Sage*. Beneath, wrapped in brown paper, she found the blue leather diary her grandmother had given her the day the family had left California for Texas. "Write all your problems in here," Grandma had told her. "Then maybe they won't seem so bad."

She ran her fingers over the diary, tracing the gold-toned metal heart that served as a lock. Who knew where the key was now; surely she could find a way to open the book. She lay the diary on top of the annual and replaced everything else in the trunk. Then she carried the two books down to the kitchen.

She poured another glass of tea and looked at the books laid out on the bar, reluctant to open them. Thank God no one was here to see her being so silly. Finally she took a deep breath and opened the annual. The plastic cover was stiff with age and the first grouping of pictures, of the freshman class, made her laugh. Had they really worn such awful hairstyles back then?

Quickly she flipped to the back of the book, to the section devoted to the seniors. She found her picture: a pretty young girl with short dark hair who smiled shyly at the camera. Beneath her name were the words "Voted girl most likely to…"

She frowned. Mark Wilson, the yearbook editor, had put that in after she'd refused to go out with him. She closed the book. Maybe digging up all this old stuff wasn't such a good idea, after all.

But the diary beckoned her. In the bright light, the cover looked scuffed and faded. Harmless. Why not revisit her seventeen-year-old self in those pages? It might be good for a laugh.

She found a pair of kitchen shears in a drawer and sliced through the leather flap that held the book closed. Carrying the diary into the living room, she settled herself at one end of the couch to read.

The entries began with her arrival in Cedar Creek.

Well, we're here, and all I can say is it's hot and dusty and looks like a set out of some old Western movie. The only kids I've seen so far are wearing boots and jeans and cowboy hats and they all stared at me when I rode by on my bike and didn't say anything.

Well, I didn't say anything to them, either. Next time I will. We're here and I have to make the best of it. Dad is always saying things like that, as if clichés are going to make everything all right.

Anyway, I do want to fit in here. I want to make friends. I'm sure things will be a lot easier when I start school next week.

She flipped over a few pages, past entries about shopping with her mother and arranging her room. Finally she found an entry written after the first week of school.

I'm really tired of everybody staring at me as if I'm from another planet. You'd think they'd never seen cool clothes before. There's this one particular girl, Alyson. She's a cheerleader and she and her friends think they are so "all that." She makes a face at me every time I go by....

There is one boy, though. He's on the staff of the

literary magazine. His name is Dylan Gates and he is sooooo cute!!! And he writes the most awesome poetry.

She read on, about her growing friendship with Dylan. She and Dylan ate lunch together in the cafeteria. She and Dylan worked on a project in chemistry class. Dylan let her borrow his history notes when she was out sick.

I think Dylan must be the sweetest guy in the entire world! She smiled, the feelings rushing back as if it all happened yesterday. She would never have admitted to it then, but Dylan had been her first big crush. She'd have given anything to really be his girlfriend, but he'd never given the slightest hint that he'd wanted to be anything more than a friend.

She flipped through a few more pages of boring entries about homework, television shows and records. It might be fun to share some of this with her students sometime, to show how things had changed and how much they'd stayed the same.

I hate this place!!!! The words were bold and underlined three times. Apparently the cause of all this angst was the annual senior camping trip. Taylor hadn't wanted to go, but Dylan had talked her into attending. If only she'd listened to her gut and stayed home, none of the rest would have happened.

Today I found out what everyone really thinks of me. Saturday night, after everyone else went to sleep, Dylan and I stayed up talking. It got colder and colder and we kept putting wood on the fire, until we ran out of wood. It was so cold, I knew I'd never sleep, so Dylan invited me into his tent with him. We

*were both wearing so many layers of clothes, it was
completely innocent. We only wanted to get warm.
But the next morning, when Mr. and Mrs. Healy got
up and found us, they had a cow. You'd have thought
we'd committed murder or something. We tried to
tell them nothing happened, but they wouldn't believe us.*

*By the time our parents came to pick us up, the
Healys had calmed down some. Thank God my mom
and dad believed me when I told them Dylan and I
didn't do anything in that tent—or out of it—but
sleep. I figured most of the kids didn't know what
happened and by Monday everything would blow
over. I should have known better.*

She scanned the pages, her stomach in a knot. It was
all there: the jeers from other students, the whispers, the
rude propositions from some of the bolder boys. She
stared at the words at the bottom of one page, the writing
cramped and small. *Dylan wouldn't even look at me. I felt
so awful.*

She closed the diary, blinking back tears. That had been
the beginning of the end. Every day a new rumor developed. She and Dylan had been caught showering together
in the boys' locker room. She and Dylan had been skinny-
dipping at the old gravel pit. By unspoken agreement, they
avoided each other, hoping this would scotch the rumors,
but the gossip escalated. When she left school, everyone
was sure it was because she was having Dylan's baby.

What would have happened if she'd found the strength
to face up to those rumors? If she'd had the courage to
tell Dylan how she'd really felt about him? Would they
have had a normal high school romance and its inevitable

end as they each moved on to other interests? Would she have lived the rest of her life without this sense of having left something back there unresolved?

Instead she'd spent the last month of her senior year in a home schooling program, graduated, gone off to college and gotten her teaching degree. She'd vowed never to return to Cedar Creek.

But four years later, when she'd seen an opening for a teacher here, she'd felt a rush of nostalgia for all the things she had liked about the town: the slower pace of life, the lovely old courthouse square and the sense of being connected to history, the chance to really get to know your students in and out of school. Her parents had long since relocated to Arizona, so Taylor had had no reason to even visit Cedar Creek since she'd left for college.

She couldn't explain why she'd been so drawn to a place where she'd suffered so much, but in the end she'd decided the best way to put the past behind her was to face her demons head-on.

Things hadn't worked out quite the way she'd hoped. Sure, she loved teaching and she'd made a few friends, especially Mindy. But that sense of belonging—of home—she'd hoped to find was still missing. To the town, she would never stop being an outsider with a wild reputation—an outsider who never fit in.

So when the opportunity had come up to study for a year in England, she'd jumped at it. Maybe she'd be happier in a place where the past everyone was interested in wasn't her own.

She looked at the diary again. Would things be any better in Oxford if she took her old problems with her? Had she really faced her demons? All of them? Mindy's scornful words came back to her. *Some people are still stuck in high school. It's pathetic.* Then how pathetic was it that Taylor had let the events of ten years before shape her life? How else to explain her inability to encourage any kind of lasting relationship with a man? It wasn't as if she hadn't had opportunities. She'd dated quite a few perfectly nice men. But none of them had measured up to the ideal she had in her head.

An ideal that had been firmly fixed since she'd developed a crush on Dylan Gates. Whether she wanted to admit it or not, she had spent ten years comparing every romantic relationship with the one she'd imagined she and Dylan would have had.

She might not wear her hair the same way she had in high school or dress like a perpetual teenager, but, emotionally, part of her had never grown past those angst-ridden months at Cedar Creek Senior High.

She set aside the diary and folded her hands in her lap. If she attended the reunion and saw Dylan again, would that break the spell he held over her? Would she be able to see him as an ordinary man and not some unfulfilled fantasy?

Somehow she sensed it would take more than a mere meeting to get her moving forward again. She needed some way to prove to herself that the "might have been" she'd imagined could never have been at all.

Maybe you two can pick up where you left off, for old times' sake. A shiver raced through her as she recalled Alyson's words, followed by a rush of heat. Well, why not? Why not exorcise those old demons by making the rumors come true? Since everyone believed they'd had such a good time back then, why not enjoy themselves now?

The more she thought about the idea, the better she felt. Sure, it would be risky, but maybe she needed a little more risk in her life. She'd been playing it safe for the past ten years. Maybe it was time to take the kinds of chances she'd relished in her younger days. Turning lies into truth would be sweet revenge.

And it might be exactly what she needed to shake Dylan out of her system for good. After all, everyone knew fantasy didn't live up to all the hype. A few days or weeks with Dylan were bound to prove they would never have made it as a couple. Puppy love like that never lasted. Once she'd confirmed her suspicions, she'd be free to go out and find the real love she deserved. She'd head to Oxford with a world of new possibilities filling her thoughts, instead of the same worn fantasies.

But would Dylan go for it? Would he be interested in a sexy fling "for old times' sake"?

2

By Saturday evening, the reunion committee had transformed the Cedar Creek High School gymnasium into a tropical garden with trickling fountains, Tiki torches and banks of flowers. Swags of tiny white lights wound among tall palms and glittered overhead like stars and candles flickered in the center of dozens of small white tables.

The class of '93 and their spouses, dates and significant others moved in ever-changing groups between the buffet tables at one end of the room and the dance floor at the other, the hum of their conversation rising and falling like an idling jet engine.

Taylor paused at the entrance to the gym, heart in her throat. How would she ever find Dylan in this crowd? She craned her neck, trying to see around a group of chattering couples. Dylan could be anywhere. What if she didn't recognize him?

No, she was sure she'd recognize him. She would never forget that smile. The memory warmed her.

But what if he didn't smile when he saw her? What if he didn't want to see her and turned away? She swallowed, fighting sudden nausea.

"Taylor! What are you doing standing there like a deer in the headlights?" Grady Murphy threw his arm around her shoulders and dragged her into the room. He smelled of bourbon and some overly sweet cologne.

"Um, hello, Grady," she said, extricating herself from his grasp.

"Now that you're here, this party can really get going." He grinned, already glassy-eyed, though the reunion had officially started only an hour ago.

She crossed her arms over her chest and glared at him. She'd deliberately dressed provocatively, in a black knit dress that clung to every curve and revealed a generous amount of cleavage. Tonight she intended to begin living up to her reputation as Cedar Creek High School's most infamous girl-about-town. But that didn't mean putting up with ogling drunks.

"Sugar, you look good enough to eat," Grady drawled.

"Too bad, *sugar*. You don't look very appetizing to me at all." Chin up, she strode past him, toward the bar. She needed a little liquid courage for what she was about to do.

A hush didn't exactly fall over the crowd as she passed, but she was conscious of heads turning her way and a few whistles and sly comments. Men grinned and elbowed each other, while women narrowed their eyes and shook their heads. Taylor ignored them all and asked the bartender for a glass of white wine.

She resisted the urge to drain the glass in one gulp and turned to once more survey the crowd while she sipped demurely. As her eyes adjusted to the light, she could make out familiar faces. She spotted Alyson in a belly-baring sarong skirt and crop top, her ponytail and breasts bouncing as she danced to Alan Jackson's *Chattahoochee* with a tall, balding man Taylor recognized as Mark Wilson, the nasty yearbook editor.

Grady had transferred his attention to the buffet table, where he appeared to be having a cocktail-weenie eating contest with a beefy former football player whose name

Taylor couldn't recall. Milly Stefanovitch, another former cheerleader, waddled into view, looking as if she might give birth to twins at any moment.

Taylor shifted her gaze to the tables at the back of the room and her breath caught as her eyes came to rest on a pair of broad shoulders in a gray suit coat. The man turned his profile toward her and Taylor's wine sloshed against the sides of the glass as her hand shook.

Ten years had changed Dylan Gates, transforming him from good-looking youth to heart-stoppingly handsome man. His frame had filled out, his face weathered, with a few fine lines fanning out from his eyes and a firmer jaw. The man with him said something and he laughed, his lips parting to reveal even white teeth and the smile that had won Taylor's heart the very first time she'd seen him.

He stood hip-cocked, his tall frame relaxed, radiating strength and unmistakable sex appeal.

Taylor drained her wineglass and set it aside on an empty table, her eyes never leaving him. Her heart pounded and heat curled through her. She'd imagined all kinds of emotions upon seeing Dylan again, except the one that rocked her now: she wanted Dylan Gates. Wanted him bad.

DYLAN STOOD WITH a group of former football players, listening as Troy recounted the team's attempt to spy on the cheerleaders in the girls' locker room after a game. "Their coach, Georgia Hoffman, found the holes we'd drilled in the shower walls," Troy said. "She waited until someone stuck an eye to the hole, then let loose with a blast of Right Guard."

"I seem to remember your eye watered for a week." Dylan grinned as the group burst into laughter. It felt so good to be back in a place where people knew him and shared his history. In California he'd always felt like a stranger, an outsider. People there commented on everything from his accent to the cowboy boots he liked to wear, but here no one thought those things were odd. Why had it taken him so long to return to this place where he belonged?

Troy launched into another story and Dylan idly searched the crowd, tallying the familiar faces. Almost everyone in their class had made it home for the reunion. Everyone except the one person he'd been most hoping to see.

A movement to his left caught his attention. He turned and for a moment stopped breathing. Taylor Reed was making her way toward him, a vision straight out his most erotic fantasies. She still had the movie-star polish that had captivated him from the first, but her girlish beauty had ripened to womanly curves that caught the eye of every man she passed. She'd let her hair grow, so that it swept her shoulders in a dark brown cascade. But the eyes were the same, big and dark and seeming to look right down into his soul.

She stopped in front of him, her gaze locked to his. "Hello, Dylan."

He sucked in a deep breath, inhaling the spice-and-flowers scent of her perfume. "Hello, Taylor." The shakiness in his voice startled him. He cleared his throat and tried again. "It's good to see you."

The tension in her shoulders eased and she smiled. A wide grin. "It's good to see you, too."

He was conscious of the silence around them and knew everyone was watching. That much hadn't changed since high school. He shifted around to bring her into the group he'd been standing with and lightly touched her shoulder.

"You remember Troy Sommers, don't you? And Ed Offray. Gib Hartsell. Al Proctor."

"Hey, Taylor."

"Hello."

"Nice to see you again."

They fell into an awkward silence, the men staring at Taylor. She reached to tuck a strand of hair behind her ear, then smoothed the skirt of her dress, a faint flush creeping up her neck.

Dylan feared that at any moment she'd bolt. And who could blame her? You'd think these jokers had never seen a woman before. Not that he was any better. He couldn't take his eyes off her. "Uh, would you like to dance?" he asked.

She dipped her head and regarded him through the veil of her lashes. "I'd like that."

The DJ had just put on R.E.M.'s "Everybody Hurts." Taylor moved into his arms and he rested his hands lightly at her waist, as nervous as he'd ever been back in high school. She felt good, her skin warm beneath the thin fabric of her dress. In high heels, the top of her head was even with his nose and his every breath filled his lungs with the exotic scent of her.

He had the disorienting sensation of being cast back in time to the only other dance they'd shared. They'd been in this same gym, after a football game. He couldn't remember the song they'd danced to or whether the team had won or lost the game, but he could remember this feeling of sensory overload, of being filled up and overflowing with the sight and smell and feel of her.

He'd wanted so much to kiss her then, but before he'd even worked up the nerve, the song had ended and she'd moved out of his arms.

"So I hear you're moving back to Cedar Creek?"

Her voice pulled him back to the present. "Yes. I'm opening a law practice across from the courthouse." He smiled. "But how did you know that? I've only been back in town a day."

Her own smile was tight, never reaching her eyes. "You know how word gets around in a small town like this."

Didn't they both know that—too well? "Troy tells me you're teaching here at the high school."

She nodded. "Senior English. I came back three years ago, after a few years teaching in Austin."

"Funny how you stayed in Texas while I went to California."

She raised her eyes to meet his. "But now you're back."

"Yeah. Now I'm back."

The song ended and they stopped moving; still arm in arm, they stared into each other's eyes. He had the feeling she was searching for something, but he didn't know what.

He thought he'd left all that high school awkwardness behind, but here it was, creeping in again. Grasping at any reason to keep her with him, he nodded toward the buffet table. "Are you hungry? Want to get something to eat?"

"Sure."

He kept his hand at her back, guiding her through the crowd to the catered buffet. They filled their plates with canapés and cheese cubes, grabbed drinks from the bar and found an unoccupied table and sat. She unfolded a napkin across her lap and studied him. "You look good," she said. "California must have agreed with you."

He laughed. "Then looks are deceiving. I couldn't wait to get out of there." He took a sip of beer. "It's good to be back home, where I feel like I belong."

"Someone said you moved out to your parents' old place."

He nodded. "We've been renting it out since Mom and Dad died and it's gotten kind of run-down. My plan is to fix it up again."

"I heard about the accident after I moved back. I'm so sorry."

Her voice was soft. Sad. The words more than mere formula. "Thanks." He spoke around the tightness in his throat that always grabbed him when he thought of his parents. They'd died in a small plane crash in the Rockies when he was in his sophomore year of law school. He hadn't been back to town since the funeral. Even before then, he'd pretty much left Cedar Creek behind, visiting only on holidays and for a few weeks in the summer. Now he'd moved back, partly because this was where he felt closest to his parents' memory.

"You really are coming home, aren't you?"

Her words startled him, as if she'd been reading his thoughts. She sipped her wine. "I guess that doesn't surprise me. You always seemed so much a part of this place. Whenever I thought of you, I always pictured you here, settled down with a wife and two or three kids."

So she'd thought of him? The knowledge warmed him. "It took me a few years, but I finally made it back. Without the wife and kids, though."

"Alyson mentioned you were still single." She picked a sprig of parsley from her plate and twirled it between her thumb and forefinger.

"I'll confess I haven't even come close to tying the knot yet," he said. "I didn't see any reason to hurry."

He tipped the neck of the beer bottle toward her. "What about you?"

She shook her head. "No, I haven't come close, either.'' She glanced at him. "My friends tell me I'm too picky. I tell them I'm holding out for the right man.''

Her words sent a quiver through his stomach. Was she trying to tell him something or was he reading too much into her words? "I never would have thought you'd have ended up staying here,'' he said.

She set aside the parsley, avoiding his gaze. "Why is that?''

"I don't know. You were always so…sophisticated. Cosmopolitan.''

She laughed. "I may have *thought* I was sophisticated, but I'm sure I wasn't.''

"Hey, it doesn't take much to impress a bunch of hicks from the sticks.''

She regarded him through the lacy veil of her lashes. "And were you impressed?''

"Oh, yeah.'' He pushed aside his half-filled plate. "I still am.'' Seeing her again tonight had made him certain he'd made a big mistake when he'd never kissed her all those years ago. Did he dare try to make up for that now? He leaned toward her. "About what happened back in high school—''

She put her hand over his. "Wait.'' She glanced around them. "Could we go somewhere else and talk? Someplace with a little more privacy?''

"Sure.'' Suddenly he wanted nothing more than to be alone with her.

They moved apart and he followed her toward the door. They passed Alyson Michaels, who stopped in midsentence to stare. Her voice followed them out of the room. "They certainly aren't wasting any time.…''

They stopped outside, on the walkway between the gym and the main building. A few smokers huddled against the side of the gym, swatting at the June bugs that dove at them from the overhead lights. "Where do you want to go?" Dylan asked.

She glanced around them, then nodded toward the main building. "There's some picnic tables behind the cafeteria. Let's go there."

He walked beside her, putting his hand at her back to steady her as she picked her way around the side of the building and across the gravel lot toward a trio of wooden picnic tables in the shadow of a live oak. They sat side by side on a table, feet on the bench, looking back toward the gym. The faint throb of the music drifted to them.

He turned his head to study her. She still had a certain stillness about her, a calm reserve he'd admired from the first day they'd met. "You haven't told me yet—why did you come back to Cedar Creek?"

"I think…" She stared out into space, silent for so long he thought she'd forgotten the question, then she turned to look at him. "I think I had some unfinished business here."

He let out the breath he hadn't even realized he'd been holding. So they were finally going to talk about that. "You mean, what happened in high school. All those wild stories."

She nodded. "I ran away from them, but I never really left them behind."

He gripped the edge of the table with both hands. "I owe you an apology for my part in that. If I'd said something sooner—"

She covered his hand with her own. "I don't think anything you said would have made a difference. Most people made up their mind about me the first day I walked down those halls. I was the fast girl from California."

"Maybe so. But I still should have said something. Done something."

She leaned toward him, the intensity of her gaze making his temperature edge up a few degrees. "Do you really want to make it up to me?"

He swallowed. "Of course."

She angled closer, her knees brushing his. "I've decided I've let those rumors haunt me for too long. I'm ready to get them out of my system for good."

"How are you going to do that?"

She took his other hand and rested them both in her lap. "That's where you come in." She traced the lines of his palm with one red-painted fingernail, sending a lightning bolt of sensation straight to his groin.

"I want to revisit the past, so to speak, and turn those rumors into the truth."

He blinked, trying to pull his thoughts away from sex to the discussion at hand. "I don't understand. You can't go back in time."

"Not physically." She continued to stroke his palm, so that he ached to reach out and pull her to him. "I want to take all those wild stories and re-create them today."

She lifted her head and met his gaze and his breath caught. Was it only wishful thinking that made him see desire in her eyes, or was she really saying what he thought she'd said? "You mean, you want us to really do all the things they accused us of back then?"

She nodded and wet her lips, the pink tip of her tongue darting out between her teeth in a surprisingly erotic gesture. "Before you say yes or no, there's something else I have to tell you."

Something else? What else could she say that would tilt his world any further on edge? He waited, not breathing.

She looked down at his hands, her touch light as a butterfly's wing as she traced the lines of his palm. "I'm going away in a few months to begin a year-long fellow-ship at Oxford, studying Shakespeare. If I'm lucky, it could turn into a long-term teaching assignment.''

The words landed like a rock in the pit of his stomach. "You're leaving?" Just when he'd found her again?

She nodded. ''So you see, this would only be for a few weeks or months, then we'd both be free to move on with our lives.'' She leaned toward him, her pupils dark and liquid, her lips slightly parted. ''Are you willing to do it? To be my lover for real this time?''

He'd never wanted anything more. Had wanted it ten years ago, but hadn't had the courage to admit it. ''If you're sure…''

''Oh, I'm sure.'' She closed her eyes and leaned toward him, her lips finding his.

Their movements were tentative at first, each gauging the other's reaction with feather touches and gentle ca-resses. But desire quickly overcame caution. He reached for her and pulled her nearer, his lips more demanding, urging her to open to him.

She responded eagerly, pressing her body against him. Her tongue teased him, tracing the outline of his mouth, then plunging in to taste him fully before retreating once more. She kissed the corners of his mouth and along his jaw, lingering at his neck, her mouth warm and moist against the pulse of his throat.

His hand moved down her back, tracing the curve of her hip, the indentation at the base of her spine, the soft fullness of her bottom. ''That feels good,'' she whispered, and wriggled closer.

He scooped her up, into his lap, her thigh pressed against his rock-hard erection. He felt seventeen again, hot and horny, and desperate for relief.

But at seventeen he hadn't known what he did now.

That there was pleasure in waiting, in making the moment last and letting the desire build.

She pulled at the knot of his tie, loosening it enough to undo the top two buttons of his shirt. A shiver raced through him as her fingernails grazed his chest. "Do you like that?" she murmured.

"Yeah, I do."

She laughed, a throaty chuckle, and nipped at his earlobe while she unfastened another button and slid her hand all the way inside his shirt, down toward his stomach.

He pulled her more tightly against him, trying to keep her from going farther. He couldn't believe he was so turned on, so quickly. If she kept this up, he was liable to embarrass himself, and he hadn't done that since he was a kid.

When she tried to protest, he silenced her with a kiss, then trailed more kisses down the satin column of her neck to the tops of her breasts. A breathy moan escaped her as he traced the curve of her cleavage with his tongue and his erection jerked in response. He buried his face between her breasts and inhaled deeply. Her perfumed woman fragrance flooded every nerve with awareness of her.

He slid his tongue beneath the fabric of her dress and found the hard bud of her nipple. She moaned again as he began to lick her and he brought his free hand up her leg, to the silk edge of her panties. He smiled, glad to see he wasn't the only one turned on so quickly. She was soaking wet and ready for him.

As he stroked her, she arched toward him, silently begging for more. He hesitated only a second before laying her back on the table and reaching down to undo his fly.

TAYLOR HAD NEVER IMAGINED that a man she hadn't seen in ten years would be able to make her lose control so quickly. As he kissed and caressed her, every atom in her ached for him. All the doubts and fear she'd battled when she'd walked into the reunion gave way to a flood of want and need. She wanted Dylan to kiss her, to touch her, to stroke her. She needed him inside her in a way she had never needed anyone before.

She cried out in frustration when his hands left her and opened her eyes to stare up at him accusingly. But then she saw that he was unfastening his belt and she grew quiet. Soon he'd ease this tension building within her.

She sat up, intending to hurry him along, but froze as someone spoke. "Do you think anyone will see us?" a woman asked.

"Nah. There's nobody back here," assured a man.

Taylor grabbed Dylan's hand and stared at him, her heart racing. He helped her to sit up again and together they stared into the darkness behind them.

Shoes crunched on gravel. A woman giggled and the man rumbled an answer. Taylor thought she could make out two darker shadows moving toward them and then away. The voices faded and the air around them hummed with silence.

Dylan began buttoning his shirt again. "That was close," he murmured.

She smoothed her dress, avoiding looking at him. "There's one thing I forgot to mention. As a teacher, I have to be somewhat discreet." She slanted a glance at him. "Although, since I'm going away, I suppose it doesn't matter so much for me. But there's your reputation to consider. We'd have to be careful."

"How are you going to manage that if we're supposed

to be reenacting all those things we were accused of? I seem to recall some supposedly public spectacles.''

''Don't worry, I've got it all figured out.''

''Then you still want to go through with this?''

Was that doubt she heard in his voice? She turned to him, wishing she could see him more clearly in the darkness. ''Don't you?''

''Sure. But I don't want to get you in trouble.''

''You won't.'' She put her hand on his arm. ''Thanks for helping me.''

He smiled. ''It's not exactly charity work. I intend to enjoy myself, too.''

Her stomach fluttered and she resisted the urge to grin like an idiot. No sense reading more into this than there was. ''Yes, but I'm asking you to give up your normal social life and put yourself at my disposal for a few weeks.''

''Or months.'' He smoothed his hand down her arm. ''That doesn't sound like such a bad deal to me.''

''Good.'' She smiled and reached out to straighten his tie. ''Then why don't you meet me at my place in half an hour and we'll get started?''

3

WAS THIS THE CRAZIEST thing he'd ever done—or the smartest? Dylan couldn't decide as he followed the directions Taylor had given him to her house. He didn't know how smart it was to agree to a no-strings-attached affair with a woman he hadn't seen in ten years. Then again, he'd be crazy to turn down the chance to finally bed the woman he'd fantasized about for the past decade.

He found the restored bungalow Taylor rented in the middle of the block in an older section of town. He drove to the end of the street and parked in front of a shuttered minimart, then walked back up to the house. This time of night, the neighborhood was dark and silent. The still-warm evening air smelled of grass clippings and late-blooming roses. But when he brought his hand to his nose, he could smell Taylor, her spicy cologne and musky arousal, and he felt himself grow hard again.

He hurried along, his boot heels ringing on the sidewalk, echoing the rapid pounding of his heart. He felt the same edgy desire mingled with nervousness that he'd last experienced in high school, when he'd sometimes sneak into his girlfriend's house after her parents had gone to bed.

As he passed the house next to Taylor's, a dog began to bark. Great. All he needed was to have someone call and report him to police as a prowler. *It's all right, Officer. I can explain. You see I was on my way to meet a woman to do all the things everyone thought we did in high school. Why? Uh, because we can?*

For some reason revisiting the past like this was important to Taylor and he was willing to go along with it. Maybe that made him crazy. Or very, very lucky.

The porch light cast a golden glow over her front door. He walked up the steps and raised his hand to knock, but the door swung inward before his hand met wood. Taylor smiled up at him, relief in her eyes. "I thought maybe you wouldn't show up."

"I stopped off for a few things." He put his hand in his pocket and felt the packets of condoms.

"Come on in." She held the door open wider. She was still wearing the formfitting black dress, but she'd taken off her shoes. Barefoot, she looked more vulnerable. More like the girl he'd known in school.

He moved past her and she switched off the porch light. "Can I get you something to drink?"

"No thanks." He stood in the middle of the room, hands in his pockets, looking everywhere but at her. The furniture was elegant and feminine—dark wood tables and gold-brocade upholstery. Candles flickered on the coffee table and along the bar that separated the living room from the kitchen. The lamp by the sofa gave the only other light, reflecting on a Degas print of ballerinas.

"Why don't you sit down?" She took a seat on the sofa and patted the cushion next to her.

He sat, hands gripping his knees. Now that he was here, he was more nervous than ever. All his fantasies of making love with Taylor were mixed up with the conservative caution that was inbred in every boy who had been raised in the southernmost notch of the Bible belt. "So, um, how exactly do you want to do this?"

"My idea was to re-create, as much as possible, all the

wild stories people made up about us in high school. We can use this to refresh our memories.'' She picked up a small blue book from the coffee table.

''What's that?''

''It's the diary I kept my senior year.'' She opened it and began flipping through the pages. ''Everything's in here. Of course, it all started with that camping trip.''

''The senior camping trip.'' Taylor hadn't even wanted to be part of that trip, but he'd convinced her to go, telling her it was a tradition and a great way for her to get to know her classmates better. What he'd really hoped was that sometime during the weekend, he'd be able to work up the courage to kiss her. And that she'd kiss him in return.

Instead he'd never found the right opportunity to make his move. And then they'd ended up sharing a sleeping bag. True, they'd both had on so many clothes they'd have had a tough time doing much of anything, but still, he recalled it as one of the most miserable nights of his life. As soon as they'd thawed out, he'd had to lie there with Taylor asleep in his arms and a hard-on that wouldn't quit.

''It wouldn't really be practical to start there,'' Taylor said. ''So I thought we'd just pick a different rumor each time, sort of as the mood hits.'' She smiled. ''We can take our time.''

Oh, he planned to take his time, all right. He intended to devote himself to exploring every inch of her luscious body, but the sooner they got to it, the better. ''Do you have something picked out for tonight?''

She opened the diary and smoothed her hand down the page. ''Listen to this.'' She began to read. *''At my locker this morning, Alyson asked me if I had a good weekend. I knew she wasn't asking to be nice, because Alyson is never nice. But I'm determined to be a better person than she is, so I just told her I hadn't done anything special.*

"'That's not what I heard,' she said with that evil little smirk that makes her look like a roadkill possum. One of these days I'm going to get mad enough to tell her that, too!"

Dylan laughed. "Alyson does sort of resemble a possum."

Taylor smiled. "I still have to fight the urge to tell her so sometimes. Now hush and let me finish." She turned back to the diary. *"I didn't even want to know what she'd heard, so I turned away, but she followed me down the hall.*

"'I heard that Dylan Gates's parents went out of town this weekend to his uncle's funeral and that you spent Saturday night at Dylan's house doing the wild thing!'"

"I remember that weekend," he said. "I was pissed because I had to stay home all weekend and look after my kid sisters. The wildest thing we did was stay up late watching 'Star Trek' re-runs."

She closed the diary and set it aside. "Here's your chance to make up for that. What would you have done if we had been lovers and we'd had your parents' house to ourselves for the weekend?"

He waited before he answered, savoring the tension humming between them. He let his eyes linger on the tops of her breasts, the dip of her waist and flare of her hips, his gaze drifting down to her long, smooth legs. Would she wrap those legs around him as he entered her? Would she scream when she came? He had so much to look forward to learning about her.

"Come on, Dylan," she prompted. "What would you do?"

"I'd do this." He pulled her into his arms and kissed

her, a long, hungry kiss with none of the hesitation they'd experienced earlier. They kissed with open mouths, tongues exploring, lips seeking, nipping and sucking, speaking without words.

Long minutes passed as they savored the sensation of lips and tongues entwined, until their breath came in desperate pants and passion mingled with giddy dizziness. He held her tightly, the hard points of her breasts pressed against his chest, one hand at the small of her back, the other fumbling with the hook of her bra.

"Here, let me." She reached back with one hand and popped the clasp, then slipped the straps down her arms and out the sleeve of her dress. She grinned at him. "I'd have thought at your age, you'd have had more practice with that."

"It doesn't help that they're all made different." Freed of the bra, her breasts swayed gently as she leaned toward him again. He cupped her in his hands, savoring the weight and warmth of her. Her nipples brushed against his palms and he shifted to stroke them through the fabric of her dress, pinching them gently between his thumb and forefinger until she was panting, eyes half closed.

He was breathing hard, too, as he eased her dress down to her waist and sat back to admire her. Her skin looked golden in the candlelight, her breasts full and round, the nipples dusky. He cupped them in his hands once more and grinned.

"What are you smiling about?" she asked.

He shook his head. "I was just thinking—after five years in L.A., yours are probably the first *real* breasts I've seen in a while."

"I'm real, all right." She pushed her dress the rest of the way down to her ankles, leaving her covered only with black lace panties. "And right now, I'm real anxious to see you naked.'' She reached for his belt buckle and he sat back, letting her undress him. There was something to be said for slow torture, when you knew it would come to a glorious end.

TAYLOR FORCED HERSELF not to hurry, slipping his belt slowly from his pants, prolonging her anticipation. His erection strained at his fly, making it more difficult to unfasten the button and pull down the zipper. Was he a boxer or a brief man? she wondered, then smiled as the answer was revealed.

He wore black bikinis, stretched tight now across his erection. She trailed her fingers over him, feeling every ridge, stroking the head until he groaned. Then she bent and exhaled her hot breath on him, almost, but not quite touching him.

In one movement he pushed her away and ripped off the briefs, freeing himself. He stood over her, his arousal straining toward her. She swallowed hard. To think she'd missed all this in high school. ''Maybe we should go into the bedroom,'' she said.

He shook his head. ''No. When we were in high school, I don't think we'd have ever made it to the bedroom.'' He touched her shoulder, urging her back against the cushions.

She leaned back, stretching her legs along the length of the sofa and resting her head on a pillow. He helped her out of her panties, then sat beside her and stroked her stomach, sending ripples of arousal through her. She struggled to lie still, to savor the delicious tension coiling within her.

''I always knew you were gorgeous,'' he said.

Then why didn't you say anything? She thought, but then all thought fled as he begin to kiss her breasts. He moved slowly at first, making easy circles with his tongue around her nipples, first one and then the other, until she was moaning and writhing beneath him.

He chuckled softly and put his hand on her thigh. "Patience, patience."

"I never had any patience in high school. What makes you think I have any now?"

He laughed. "That's okay. I like a woman who's eager." He slid his hand up her thigh and slipped between her legs. "And you are eager, aren't you? You're soaking wet." He dipped two fingers into her, his thumb and fingers stroking, coaxing her closer to the edge.

She closed her eyes and arched against him, gasping. "Dylan!" Words failed her.

His hand stilled. "Look at me."

She opened her eyes. "Don't stop," she pleaded.

"I want to see you when you come."

She nodded and he began to fondle her again, lightly at first, then with more pressure, faster and faster until her vision faded. At the moment when she was sure she could stand no more, his hand left her. She thrust toward him and groaned in frustration. "No!"

He leaned over and kissed her on the lips. "I promise it'll be worth the wait." He picked up his jacket from the floor. "Here, you put this on." He tossed a condom to her.

She raised up on her elbows and tore open the packet, then leaned forward and reached for him. "I can't believe my hands are shaking."

"Yeah." He put his hand on her shoulder and she felt his own tremors run through her.

She rolled the condom onto him, then lay back and looked into his eyes. "Hurry."

He nudged her leg aside and knelt between her thighs.

She opened to him and he filled her completely with one deep thrust. One hand on her hip, he caressed her thigh, while the other hand moved again to her clit.

Desire claimed her like wildfire, consuming her. She kept her eyes locked to Dylan's face, seeing him caught in the same firestorm. Arousal transformed his face, sharpening the lines and planes, giving him a harsh beauty that stole her breath as surely as his thrusts.

She wrapped her legs around his waist, angling her body, silently urging him to bury himself more deeply within her. He thrust harder, increasing his pace, driving her to the brink, then following her over.

Their cries rang in the silence that followed. Dylan collapsed against her, his head resting between her breasts. She buried her fingers in his hair, savoring the feel of him filling her completely.

"That was incredible," he whispered.

She smiled. "It was pretty incredible, wasn't it?"

He levered up onto his elbows and withdrew from her. "The bathroom's down the hall, if you want to use it," she said.

While he was in the bathroom, she went into her bedroom and cleaned herself, then slipped into the blue silk robe she'd bought as an indulgence last fall. Tonight wasn't a night for her everyday pink terry cloth.

When she returned to the living room, Dylan was stepping into his pants. She paused in the doorway, admiring the fit of those black bikini briefs around his backside. "I'm going to have a glass of wine, would you like some?" she said when he turned to face her.

"Yeah, that sounds good."

She returned with the wine and found him seated on the sofa, shirtless and barefoot, the diary in his hand. She felt another tremor of desire at the sight of him, so masculine against all her feminine things.

He looked up at her approach. "I can't believe you kept this all this time," he said, hefting the open diary.

"Don't you have things you kept from high school?" She handed him a glass and sat beside him.

"A couple of football trophies, maybe. A jersey. But nothing like this."

"Nothing sentimental."

"Nothing this…immediate." He closed the book and laid it aside. "I hope you don't mind. I guess I should have asked before I read anything."

She smiled. "After what just happened, I wouldn't say we had many secrets anymore."

He took a long drink and shook his head. "It wouldn't have been that good when we were kids."

"No. I'm sure it wouldn't have."

He glanced at her. "Were you a virgin? I mean, back in school."

She shrugged. "Almost. I'd had one experience with a guy back in California, but it wasn't very satisfying."

"What happened?"

"Oh, you know. He was overeager. I was nervous. We were in his car and things got out of hand. Before I knew it, it was over and I hadn't enjoyed it very much."

He put his hand on her leg. "I would have treated you better than that."

She smiled. "I think you would have. You were always very considerate. What about you? When was your first time?"

He thought a moment. "Summer of my junior year. A girl I met on vacation in Corpus." He grinned. "An older woman. She was a senior." He took another drink of wine. "The first time was a little awkward, but we had a good time."

"Sex ought to be a good time," she said.

"It was good tonight."

"Yeah." She couldn't recall when it had been better for her. She couldn't recall anything right now. Dylan had wiped out the memory of every other man. Not that there'd been that many. None like Dylan, able to move her so deeply and to satisfy her so completely.

He set his empty wineglass on the coffee table. "So, how is this going to work? When should we see each other again?"

"Soon." She set her own glass beside his. "When are you free?"

"How about tomorrow?"

She smiled, pleased by his eagerness. "How about Monday?" She didn't want to take this too fast. The longer it took to work their way through all the old rumors, the more time they'd have to spend together.

"What rumor do you have planned?"

She laughed. "I'm not sure. I'll call you."

He nodded, but made no move to finish dressing. He sat with his elbows on his knees, staring at the flame of a candle on the coffee table. "Do you think this is going to work?" he asked after a moment.

"What do you mean?"

He glanced at her. "Us, getting together like this? Is it really going to make you feel better about what happened in high school?"

She nodded. "I think it will. For so many years, I've felt like I should have stayed and faced all their lies. It's too late to change anyone's mind now, but by doing this, we're turning their lies into truth." She looked at him. "Does that make sense?"

He nodded. "Sort of." He grinned. "I guess the way I look at it—they all thought we were having so much fun back then, we might as well enjoy ourselves now."

She grinned back at him. "We're going to have fun."

He turned and pulled her to him once more. "Yeah. I think we are."

He held her close and kissed her cheek, a sweet gesture that made her heart skip a beat. She buried her face against his shoulder and closed her eyes, breathing in the scents of soap and sex. It wouldn't be fun if she made a mistake and lost her heart to him. Their time together was supposed to be pure fantasy and everybody knew fantasies—like rumors—were usually very different from the way things really were.

4

WHEN TAYLOR PROPOSED re-creating all those old high school rumors, she hadn't expected doing so to make her *feel* as though she was in high school again. Yet here she was, all fluttery-hearted and foggy-brained, staring idly into space one moment and unable to sit still the next. She spent long minutes during her break Monday morning staring at her cell phone, willing herself not to call Dylan. "Next thing you know, I'll be scribbling his name in the margin of my notebook," she muttered as she forced her attention to a stack of papers that needed grading.

Of course, there were other feelings she'd definitely never experienced in high school. Heat simmered through her when she remembered the way he'd moved his hands across her body. Her nipples rose in hard points as she recalled his hands on her, tender yet so skillful. She closed her eyes and saw again the smoldering looks he'd given her, as if he had never wanted anyone more.

Is this how it would have been if she and Dylan had been more than friends in high school? Would he have had this power to arouse her even when he wasn't around? The ability to cloud her thoughts even when she wasn't with him?

She shook her head. The whole point now was to get over any lingering obsession she had with Dylan Gates. To get the man out of her system for good.

She couldn't hold back a grin. If she had a spectacular time doing so…

"Somebody had a good weekend, judging by that smile." Mindy slipped into Taylor's otherwise empty classroom and perched on the edge of the desk. "I gather the reunion was worth going to?"

Taylor attempted an indifferent shrug. "It was all right. I left early." Which wasn't exactly a lie.

"Did you see Dylan Gates? Was he as hot as ever? Did you talk to him?" Mindy's questions came in a breathless rush.

"Dylan was there. We talked…a little." She busied herself shuffling through the stack of student papers. She didn't want to lie to her best friend, but this whole "experiment" with Dylan felt too new and unreal to talk about just yet.

"Uh-huh. Well, what did he say?" Mindy leaned toward her. "I want to hear all the dirty details, girlfriend, and I intend to harass you until I have them."

Taylor glanced up at her friend. "Why are you so interested? I mean, you don't even know Dylan."

"I have no social life of my own, so I have to live vicariously through you."

"And whose fault is that? I know a certain handsome principal who'd probably be thrilled to go out with you if he knew how you felt."

Mindy sat up straighter. "This morning I volunteered to serve on a task force he's chairing. I'm going to show him I can be as dedicated and hardworking as he is. Plus, this should give us a chance to get to know each other better."

"Chicken!"

"You're one to talk. Don't think I don't know you're

trying to change the subject. Come on. Tell me about Dylan Gates.''

"The man is twice as gorgeous as he ever was, I'll tell you that." Alyson swept into the room, trailing a paper banner painted with the slogan Stuff The Bears! behind her. Dressed in the school colors of blue and gold, Alyson looked like an escapee from cheerleading camp. She smirked at them. "He and Taylor danced one dance together and then they left." She raised her eyebrows. *"Together."*

Taylor squirmed, fighting the urge to wrap Alyson in that spirit banner like a modern-day mummy. "Dylan and I went outside to talk. It was too hot in the gym."

"I'll say it was hot." Alyson's laugh made Taylor cringe. "It didn't take any time at all for that old flame to heat up, did it?"

Mindy clapped her hands together. "I knew it! So you two hit it off just like old times, huh?"

Taylor opened her lesson planner and pretended to study it. "It's not like you think. Dylan and I are just friends."

"Uh-huh. The way you were *just friends* back in school?" Alyson laughed. "The rest of us should be so lucky to have friends like that." She draped the banner around her shoulders like a paper shawl. "I do hope you'll manage to be a little more discreet than you were last time you two got together. After all, as a teacher you have a certain position in the community. You can't expect to get away with being a wild glamour girl anymore. You owe it to the reputation of the school to act with a little more dignity."

"Dignity. Of course." Somehow, Taylor managed to keep a straight face.

Alyson threw one trailing end of the banner over her left shoulder. "I'd better get busy hanging the rest of these banners before the pep rally this afternoon." She stalked from the room, the ends of the paper banner flapping behind her.

She was scarcely out the door before Mindy collapsed in a fit of laughter. Taylor joined her, both hands clapped over her mouth to try to keep the sound in. "Imagine— the p-perpetual cheerleader l-lecturing you on *dignity!*" Mindy gasped between giggles.

"While wrapped in that stupid banner!" Taylor coughed, trying to regain control of herself. The hilarious thing was, Alyson had no idea how ridiculous she looked.

"She does have a point, though."

Taylor looked up to find Mindy's gaze fixed on the classroom door, her expression sober. "Who? Alyson?"

Mindy nodded. "Teachers do have a public image to uphold. You blow your nose in this town and the next day everyone is talking about your bad cold. If you want to fool around with someone, you practically have to drive to the next town."

Taylor shrugged, ignoring the mixture of guilt and apprehension that knotted her stomach. She and Dylan had already talked about this. They were going to be careful. And what did it matter if people thought she was up to something scandalous? She was going away in a few months, anyway.

"So what did you and Dylan talk about?" Mindy asked.

"Nothing important." She manufactured a smile for her friend. "Honest."

Mindy shook her head. "I don't believe you, but I guess when you're ready to tell me, you will."

"I will."

"Then I'd better get back to my classroom and try to convince twenty-five freshmen that algebra really is more important than the opposite sex." She slid off the desk. "Though I tell you, some days I have my doubts."

When Taylor was alone again, she picked up her cell phone. Time to see if Dylan was still willing to go through with this, now that he'd had a couple of days to reconsider.

DYLAN SPENT MONDAY morning moving the last of his books and supplies into his new office, debating whether or not he should call Taylor. She'd said she'd be in touch with him, but he wasn't a man who liked to wait on other people.

Still, this whole thing had been her idea, so that meant she was calling the shots—at least for the time being. He'd volunteered to tag along and follow her lead.

A smile stole across his lips. As if that were any great hardship. Saturday night had been incredible. Better than any of the tortured fantasies that had plagued him as a teenager. He'd spent years kicking himself for never making a move on Taylor, but now he had to concede she'd been worth the wait.

Which rumor would they turn into reality next time? He opened a carton of law books and began arranging them on the shelves. Outside of the camping trip, he couldn't remember much of the gossip that had circulated about them ten years ago. Maybe because he was already established in the community or because he was male, it hadn't affected him as much. He seemed to recall something about a scene in the boys' locker room shower…and wasn't something supposed to have happened at the drive-in…?

"You look awfully serious for a man moving into a new place. Or is that your lawyer face?" Troy Sommers leaned around the doorway. "Thought I'd stop by and make sure everything was going okay."

"Great." Dylan shook Troy's hand. "I'm almost ready to open for business."

Troy looked around the room and nodded. "You'll have more work than you can handle. Lots of folks around here still remember you from high school."

"I don't know whether to be flattered or worried about that."

Troy laughed. "Maybe a little of both." He winked. "I saw you Saturday night renewing one particular acquaintance from our high school days. Taylor Reed?"

Dylan cleared his throat and folded in the flaps of the empty box. "It was good to see Taylor again."

"Made me want to be a high school student again, just so I could be in her class." Troy laughed. "Teachers weren't that hot-looking when we were students, were they?"

Dylan frowned. "I'm sure Taylor's an excellent teacher."

"Oh, sure. An excellent teacher who's also a real babe." Troy clapped him on the back. "I've got to hand it to you—you didn't waste any time picking up where you left off with her."

"Taylor and I are just good friends."

Apparently, Troy didn't believe this any more than he had when they'd been in school. "Sure, buddy. And from the looks of things, you're going to be even better friends very soon." He chuckled. "Or did you get lucky Saturday night?"

Had Troy always been this annoying? Dylan glared at him. "Did you stop by for something in particular? I'm pretty busy here."

Troy took a step back. "Hey, no need to cop a big-city attitude around here. What you do is your business. I was just being friendly."

Dylan forced himself to relax. He leaned back against the desk. "Sorry. I guess I'm tired from the move and all."

"Sure. I understand. I stopped by to see if you wanted to have lunch at the Rotary meeting. I can introduce you to some of the members. You said you wanted to be involved and this group will give you a good picture of everything that's going on."

He nodded. "Sure. That sounds good."

"All right. I'll stop by here about eleven-thirty and we'll walk over together. It's upstairs at the café." He nodded in the direction of Courthouse Café.

"Great. I'll look forward to it."

"So about Taylor Reed—"

He was saved by the ringing of the telephone. He gave Troy an apologetic look and picked up the receiver. "Dylan Gates speaking."

"Oh, hello, Dylan." Taylor's voice was breathy. At her first words, his heart beat faster. "I thought maybe your secretary would answer."

"I don't have one yet. Do you know any good candidates?" He waved and mouthed a silent "goodbye" to Troy as the agent backed out of the room.

"I don't know. I'll have to ask around."

"How did you get my number?" he asked. "I just had the phone connected this morning."

"Sylvia Piper—she used to be Sylvia Ramos—works in new accounts at the phone company. She gave it to me." She laughed. "One of the advantages of small-town living."

Her laughter sent heat curling through his middle. How was it even a woman's laughter could be erotic? "I'm glad you called."

"You are?" She sounded surprised.

"Why shouldn't I be?" He leaned over and shut the door to his office, then lowered his voice. "I had a great time Saturday night."

"M-me, too."

"So are you ready to do it again?"

"Are you?"

"Oh, yeah. I'm ready." Ready to see every gorgeous curve of her body, to smell the sex-and-spice scent of her skin, to hear her moan with passion, to taste her sweetness—to discover what made Taylor Reed want to relive things that had never happened ten years ago. To sort out his own mixed-up feelings for her that he'd carried around all these years. "Do you have a rumor picked out for us to tackle next?"

"I was thinking…Inspiration Point."

The words sent a rush of nostalgia through him. "Is that place still around?"

She laughed. "It's still there. Do you want to go there…this evening?"

Making out in the car at Inspiration Point. He hadn't done anything like that since…since high school. He grinned. That was the point, wasn't it? To relive those times and discover what *inspiration* they offered for the present. "I'll pick you up at six."

"I'll be waiting."

Her voice was a soft purr, sparking desire. Who said high schoolers were the only ones at the mercy of raging hormones? Dylan felt almost as if he'd been transported back ten years, to the days when he'd been an awkward, perpetually horny boy mooning after the girl of his dreams.

The difference was, this time the girl was right where he wanted her. And he knew exactly what to do with her.

FOR THE FIFTH TIME in as many minutes, Taylor checked her reflection in the bathroom mirror. Was her lipstick straight? Did she look all right? She was still wearing the skirt and blouse she'd worn to school this morning. Should she change into something dressier? Or maybe she should go for a more casual look....

She shook her head and turned away from the mirror. It didn't matter what she wore tonight. Dylan had seen her naked and liked what he'd seen. Apparently very much...

The thought sent a shiver of anticipation through her. Knowing she'd see him again tonight had lent a delicious edge to the day. While she lectured her students on the symbolism in *Beowulf,* she'd pictured Dylan as the monster-slaying hero and herself as the woman waiting to welcome him home. Tonight they'd attempt to create a different kind of fantasy....

She picked up the blue leather diary from the bar and flipped it open to the spot she'd marked.

November 26, 1993. All morning, I couldn't go any-where without hearing people giggling and whisper-

*ing behind my back. Finally, after second period so-
cial studies, I'd had enough. I slammed my locker
shut and asked Ashly Crumley, who was standing two
doors down, what was so damn funny. She just
blinked at me and got all huffy. "There's no need to
use profanity," she sniffed, and prissed away.*

*If she'd heard what I was thinking about her just
then, her ears would have been burning, I tell you!*

*Of course, right then, Alyson walked by and
smirked. "I heard you and Dylan had a really good
time up on Inspiration Point Saturday night," she
said.*

*I rolled my eyes. I didn't want to ask, but I had to,
you know? "What did we do up on Inspiration
Point?" I asked.*

*She laughed. "Don't pretend you don't know. It's
all over town how Old Mullet Face Mullins caught
you both stark-naked in the back seat of Dylan's
mom and dad's Crown Victoria."*

*Honestly, where do people come up with these sto-
ries? I was home alone—as usual—on Saturday
night.*

*Just then, the man himself walked by. Dylan, I
mean. He sort of glanced at me and mumbled "Hi,"
then hurried away. I stared after him, feeling all sick
to my stomach. Couldn't he even come over and talk
to me? Would that have killed him?*

*Even after all that, I guess it's pretty pathetic that
I* would *have gone out with him last Saturday if he'd
asked me. I must be insane!*

She shut the book. She'd been crazy, all right. As crazy
as any other lovesick teenager. And as Mindy had made

her realize, she'd carried a little of that craziness over into her adult life. Why hadn't she seen before how silly it was to be still mooning over Dylan after all these years? Good thing this opportunity had come up to get over him once and for all.

The doorbell rang and she jumped, her heart speeding up. She smoothed a hand over her hair and straightened her skirt, then went to open the door.

For a moment she felt an eerie sense of déjà vu, as she stared at the man who stood on her doorstep dressed in jeans and a T-shirt—the uniform of their high school days. Only the shoulders filling out the shirt were broader now, the thighs beneath the jeans more muscular, the man himself more confident and comfortable in his own skin than that teenager had ever been. He smiled, a look of warmth and welcome. "Hi. You ready?"

Oh, yeah. She was ready, all right. She collected her purse and followed him outside to a red crew-cab pickup truck. "What do you think about grabbing a bite to eat first?" he asked as he opened the passenger door for her.

"That sounds good." She slid across the seat and fastened her seat belt.

"You're more familiar with the town now than I am." He started the engine. "Where should we go?"

"Where would we have gone in high school?"

He laughed. "Danny's Drive-in, I guess. That was the big hangout."

She nodded. "Then let's go there."

"You mean, it's still around?"

"And it's still the hangout. Some things never change."

They drove the few short blocks to Danny's. The

orange-and-blue neon sign had faded over the years, but the same metal awning stretched out from the squat white building. Modern speakers and lighted menus had replaced the hand-painted signs and drive-in movie relics of their senior year. Dylan steered the truck into an empty bay and rolled down the driver's-side window to study the menu. "They didn't have veggie burgers or chicken wraps when I was here last."

She laughed. "Even Danny has had to make a few changes to keep up with the times."

He leaned out to press the speaker button. "What will you have?"

"I think I'll try that veggie burger. And a cherry lime-ade."

He placed their order, then leaned back in the seat and sighed. "I never would have thought this place would have survived the fast-food invasion." He glanced at her. "I had a lot of good times here when I was a kid. I must have eaten hundreds of Danny burgers."

"When I moved here, I couldn't believe a place like this still existed." She unfastened her seat belt and turned toward him. "It was one of the few things I actually liked about my new home."

He made a face. "I guess there wasn't much to like for you, was there?"

"Oh, I was a snob, I'll admit it." She shook her head. "As far as I was concerned, this hick place couldn't compete with the glamour of L.A."

"But you see it differently now?"

She nodded. "I do. Maybe it's growing older or just growing up." She smoothed her hand along the seat. "I guess I've come to appreciate that sense of...I don't know…*belonging*…that a small town can give to some people.''

''Some people…but not you.''

She shifted. How could she explain to this man, who wanted nothing more than to settle down forever in his old hometown, that she hadn't found what she was looking for yet? ''I guess maybe I'm not really cut out for small-town life. And this opportunity at Oxford was too good to pass up. I mean, it's not like I have any real ties here to hold me back.''

''Sure.'' He nodded, his expression guarded. ''I'm sure you'll love it over there. Little Cedar Creek, Texas, will seem pretty pale next to ancient Oxford.''

She hadn't mean to insult him, or the town, but that was apparently the way he was taking it. She started to protest, but they were interrupted by the arrival of the car hop with their order.

Patrice Miller, dressed in cropped jeans and a red Danny's T-shirt, hooked the tray onto the edge of the window. ''Hey, Ms. Reed.'' She smiled shyly, showing a row of braces. ''How are you?'' She glanced at Dylan, a question in her eyes.

''Patrice, this is Dylan Gates. Dylan, this is Patrice Miller, one of my students.''

''Nice to meet you, Patrice.'' He accepted the bill from her. ''So is Ms. Reed a mean teacher?''

''She's not too bad.'' She looked at Taylor, then back at Dylan. Taylor could almost see the questions bouncing around in her brain. She took the bills Dylan handed her. ''I'll be right back with your change.''

''That's okay.'' He waved her on. ''You keep it.''

''Thanks.'' She turned and darted away.

Dylan handed Taylor her burger. "I guess it'll be all over town by tonight that we were out together."

She nodded. "Considering how many people saw us leave the reunion together on Saturday, I wouldn't be surprised."

"Does that bother you?"

She considered the question. On one hand, it would be nice to keep her trysts with Dylan secret—something they did just for themselves. They might have done so in an anonymous big city, but never in Cedar Creek, Texas. She shrugged. "We've already agreed it's useless to try to keep a secret in this town." She remembered Alyson's warning about discretion. "Besides, that doesn't mean they have to know everything we do."

"No." He swirled a French fry through a puddle of ketchup. "They'd rather make up their own story anyway."

"Let them. It doesn't matter anymore, does it?" She spoke with a nonchalance she didn't quite feel. Words *did* matter. Didn't the fact that she felt compelled to lay to rest old rumors prove it?

They fell silent, eating, the reminder of what would come later hanging in the air between them, a promise and a temptation. She finished her burger and crumpled the wrapper. "I'm curious. How did you end up in L.A.?"

"My original plan was to move back here after I'd finished college and law school. But after my parents died, things felt too uncomfortable to come back." He glanced at her. "I guess you heard there were some hard feelings between my dad and some of the townspeople."

"I heard some people were upset about a book he wrote—about the Civil Rights movement?"

He nodded. "*A Ranger Remembers.* It won a Texas

PEN award for nonfiction, but instead of being proud of him, folks whined about how he'd made the town look bad.''

She saw the impact of that old hurt in his hunched shoulders and tight jaw, and her stomach clenched in sympathy. ''Surely not everyone felt that way.''

''No. But the ones who did object made a lot of noise.'' He stared out the side window, so she could no longer read his expression. ''I know it hurt Dad, though he never would have said so.''

''I can see why you didn't want to stay in town after that.''

He took a long sip of soda and set the cup aside. ''I got an offer from one of the big law firms out in L.A. I'd always wanted to see the West Coast, so I thought it was a great opportunity.''

''And was it?''

''It was interesting work. Lucrative work. But I never really fit in to that Hollywood lifestyle.'' He shrugged. ''I guess I'm a small-town boy at heart.''

''So what are your plans now?''

''Get my practice going here. Fix up my parents' old place, get involved in the community again. After living so many years among strangers, it feels good to walk around town and see so many familiar faces.''

He angled toward her, his back against the truck door. ''And you're off to Oxford. When?''

''January. It's a special year-long program focusing on Shakespearean sonnets.''

'''When to the sessions of sweet silent thought I summon up remembrance of things past, I sigh the lack of many a thing I sought, And with old woes new wail my dear times' waste.'''

His voice was low, husky, lending an unexpected eroticism to the words. Heat pooled between her thighs and she shifted in her seat away from him.

"Did I get the lines wrong? It's been a long time."

She shook her head, unable to meet his eyes. "No, you got them right. I'd forgotten you liked poetry." Had he chosen that particular sonnet for a reason? Did he, too, have regrets about the past? Their past?

She was aware of his eyes lingering on her, his glance like a caress across her skin. She set her empty cup on the dash and brushed crumbs from her lap, anxious to change the subject. "Anyway, I'm excited about this opportunity. It will be fun to see a little more of the world before I settle down in one place." She flashed him a sly smile. "I have a few things I want to do first."

"Oh, yeah?" He leaned toward her. "Such as?"

"Such as drive up to Inspiration Point with you."

"Best idea I've heard all day." He disposed of their trash, then started the truck and headed to the west side of town, to the bluff overlooking the lake that had been the preferred make-out spot for several generations of Cedar Creek youth.

He guided the truck up the rutted dirt road and parked against the line of boulders that marked the edge of the bluff. When he switched off the engine, the night silence closed around them like a curtain. Taylor looked out the windshield, at the beads of light marking the houses on the lake's far shore.

Dylan rolled down the window, filling the truck with the scent of honeysuckle. He patted the seat beside him. "We have to do this right. Slide on over here."

She unfastened her seat belt and moved closer to him. He draped his arm around her, gathering her closer still.

"I seem to recall everyone always said they were coming up here to watch the sunset, didn't they?" he said.

"Or the fireflies." She snuggled closer. It felt good to sit here with his arm around her. Her earlier nervousness had vanished, replaced by a deep contentment.

"Does old Officer Mullins still patrol up here?"

"Old Mullet Face? He died two years ago. A heart attack. There are some younger officers on the force now. Even a couple of women. From what I hear, they still keep an eye on this place."

He glanced around them. "We seem to have it to ourselves tonight."

"It's a weeknight." She shifted to look at him. "Did you ever come up here when you were in school?"

"A few times." He met her gaze. "Did you?"

She shook her head. "Despite my reputation, I never dated after I moved here." How could she, after the rumors started? Besides, the only boy she'd ever been interested in had only thought of her as a friend.

"You missed out on one of the rights of passage of growing up in Cedar Creek. We'll have to fix that."

He leaned forward and switched on the radio. Soft music filled the air. She recognized a song that was popular ten years ago.

He angled his body toward her and she tilted her face up to his. She was a young girl again, breathless with anticipation, waiting for a great mystery to be revealed.

Despite what had happened between them last night, it was still a mystery. Each moment they spent together revealed new facets of their personalities, new revelations about their bodies.

She closed her eyes and filled her senses with the gentle pressure of his lips, the warm caress of his tongue, the brush of his hair across her cheek. She slid her arms around him, deepening the kiss, memorizing the sweet-salty taste of his mouth and the masculine roughness of his cheek. He slid his hand up to caress the back of her neck, then moved with teasing slowness to the side of her breast, the warmth of his palm burning into her.

She tried to move closer, her thigh pressed against his thigh, her body arched toward him. Her eagerness startled her. She'd intended to take things more slowly this time. But the close confines of the truck lent a different kind of intimacy to the moment—a delicious thrill of the forbidden.

As if sensing her impatience, he moved his hand at last, shaping his palm to her breast, stroking the aching tip with his thumb. He bent to trail slow kisses down her neck, his tongue flicking across her fevered skin, mimicking the movement of his thumb. Her body hummed with a music he was making, a melody of unvoiced longing for something she couldn't quite name.

She pulled back enough to allow her to slide her hand beneath his T-shirt, her fingernails grazing his muscled stomach, pulling the fabric of the shirt up to his shoulders. Pushing back farther still, she bent and kissed her way across his chest, until she found the pebbled nub of his nipple and took it into her mouth.

He smelled of expensive cologne, laundry starch and the faint hint of male sweat. As she flicked her tongue across him, he squirmed and sucked in his breath, his fingers fumbling with the buttons of her blouse. She smiled, elated that she could arouse him this way.

Gently but firmly, he pushed her back until she was half lying across the seat. He made quick work of her buttons, and parted her blouse to reveal her lacy white bra. With one finger, he traced the swell of her breast above the lace, then dipped one finger beneath the fabric to curl around her nipple. She gasped and arched against him.

Moonlight through the windshield cast much of his face in shadow, but she saw his smile and heard the snap of his jeans as he unfastened them, then felt his hand sliding the hem of her skirt above her hips.

She closed her eyes and pressed her body to his, silently encouraging him.

Bright light razored into the cab like a bucket of ice water freezing their desire. A voice boomed somewhere just beyond the light, shattering the night's peace. "What do you two think you're doing in there?"

5

DYLAN STRAIGHTENED, hitting his elbow on the steering wheel. Muttering curses, he shielded his eyes against the light's glare and squinted toward the voice. "Who's there?" he demanded.

"The police. You'd better get out here right now."

Taylor made a whimpering sound and scrambled to button her blouse. *Oh, hell,* Dylan thought. *The gossips will have a field day with this one.* "Get in the back," he told her. "I'll take care of this."

She dove toward the back seat and he opened the door and climbed out, pulling his T-shirt down as he did so. The light lowered and a tall lanky man in the blue uniform of the Cedar Creek P.D. confronted him. "What the— Dylan Gates, is that you?"

Dylan peered closer at the cop. Something about that crooked nose and dimpled chin looked familiar. "Pete Alavero?" Laughter burst out of him at the idea of the chief troublemaker of his high school crowd now upholding the law he'd once been so determined to break.

Pete relaxed, hands on his hips. "I heard you were back in town, but I didn't expect to find you here, of all places." He nodded toward the truck cab. "Reliving old times?"

"Something like that." Old times he'd wished had been, anyway.

Pete laughed. "The girls always did go for you, didn't

they? The rest of us were happy to tag along and pick up the leftovers.'' He glanced at the truck again. ''I don't suppose you're going to tell me who you're with?''

''Now, Pete, you wouldn't expect me to kiss and tell, would you?''

Pete stepped forward to slap him on the shoulder. ''It's good to see you again. I hear you're a big-city lawyer now and everything.''

''Make that a small-town lawyer. I'm opening up a practice down by the courthouse.'' He folded his arms over his chest and leaned back against the truck. ''And you're a police officer. Who would have thought?''

Pete shrugged. ''Surprised myself, but it's a good job.'' He looked around them, at the lights below. ''I guess you could say Old Mullet Face himself is responsible for me being here. He hauled me in one night for drag racing over on Dump Road and told me if I didn't straighten up soon I'd know the meaning of real trouble. I spent the night at the jail and he stayed up talking to me. By morning, I'd decided to enroll in the police academy.''

Dylan nodded, warmed by the idea that people here still cared enough to look after their own. He'd come back home looking for that kind of caring. ''I'll bet you make a good cop,'' he said.

''I guess I stay on the kids around here about as much as Mullet Face stayed on us. We hated it at the time, but looking back, I can see he was really just watching out for us.'' He shifted his weight to the other hip. ''Sorry I missed the reunion. I was working.''

''I missed seeing you, too. What else have you been up to? Do you have a family?''

Pete's grin stretched from ear to ear. ''I married Becky Sue Waltham a few years back. We've got us two little boys. What about you?'' He cast another speculative look at the truck.

Dylan shook his head. ''No, I haven't settled down yet.''

''Still sowing a few wild oats, is it?'' Pete cocked one eyebrow.

''I guess you could say that.'' He shifted, suddenly aware of his untucked shirt and undone belt and the almost-naked woman waiting for him. He felt seventeen again, caught out in something daring and even dangerous. ''So, uh, what happens now?''

Pete glanced around them. ''It's not like anybody else is up here. And I reckon you're old enough to look out for yourself.'' He chuckled. ''I know how it is sometimes. To tell you the truth, Becky Sue and I have been up here a time or two ourselves. When you've got two little ones running around, sometimes you have to get a little, you know, creative, to keep the fire going.''

Dylan stifled his own laugh, trying to block out any image of skinny Pete and the well-endowed Becky Sue getting it on in the police cruiser. Some images were best kept private.

Pete took another step back. ''It was good seeing you again, Dyl. Let's get together for lunch sometime.'' He waggled the flashlight toward the truck. ''And tell your lady friend hello for me. Hope I didn't spoil things for you.''

Dylan shook his head. The only thing Pete had spoiled was this insane plan to act like teenagers again when he and Taylor were both adults with adult responsibilities. He was all for helping Taylor work out her past, but they'd have to find a more discrete way to do it. The last thing he wanted was her reputation dragged through the mud the way it had been years ago. He owed her that much at least.

TAYLOR CROUCHED in the ridiculously small back seat of the pickup, her calves cramping and her bra strap rubbing a groove into her arm. Her hair was in her eyes, her nose itched and she could feel a scream of frustration gathering in her throat. She could hear the indistinct murmur of Dylan's conversation with the cop, low and easy, like two friends catching up on old times. While she hid out back here like some high school girl afraid of being caught by her angry father.

She leaned forward on her elbows, trying to get comfortable, but only ended up with the seat-belt buckle jabbing her in the hip. *Go away!* she silently urged the cop.

Her plan to re-create those old rumors had been going so well before they were interrupted. As she'd done the things she'd only imagined as a teenager, she'd felt a little of her old bravado creeping back. She was ready to enjoy this moment, with this man—to savor everything he made her think and feel.

When had she lost that daring side of herself? When her classmates' rumors and jeers had taunted her? Or was it when Dylan had turned away from her and she'd been left to face the lies alone? Despite her best efforts, she'd never quite made it back to that fearless girl again. And then she'd found her diary and Dylan and had seen a chance to recapture that part of herself.

So what was she doing now, hiding in a back seat? To protect her reputation? Why should she care about that when she was going to be leaving? What was wrong with letting people see this other, secret side of her before she vanished out of their lives forever? If nothing else, it would give them something entertaining to talk about.

And it would give her wonderful memories to savor on future evenings alone.

With a grunt, she shoved up onto her hands and threw her leg over the front seat. She pushed open the door and half fell against Dylan. By the time he helped her stand, she'd managed to straighten her skirt and paste a big smile on her face. "Hello, Pete," she said, recognizing her former classmate. "Imagine meeting you here."

Pete's goggle-eyed glare was worth every minute of discomfort she'd felt. His mouth fell open and he juggled to keep from dropping the foot-long flashlight he held in his right hand. "T-Taylor?" He glanced at Dylan, then back to her. "I, uh, I didn't know you two were seeing each other."

"We met up at the reunion and it's been like old times ever since." She clung to Dylan's arm. "And now you've caught us being naughty."

Pete flushed a shade darker as his gaze flickered to the neckline of her blouse, which was still unbuttoned at the top. "Yeah, uh, well." He took a step toward his patrol car. "Like I was telling Dylan, no harm done. Y'all just…be careful. Okay?" He saluted them with the flashlight, then hurried toward the cruiser and climbed in.

Taylor clung to Dylan, shaking with silent giggles. When the lights of the police car had faded into the distance, he turned to her. "What was that all about?" he asked.

She shook her head and climbed back into the truck. "Did you see the look on his face when he saw it was me? I wish I'd had a camera."

He slid into the driver's seat and shut the door, frowning. "By morning, it will be all over town that we were up here together."

"I imagine so." She smoothed her skirt over her knees. "Like old times."

He angled toward her. "Is that what you want? For all the talk to start again?"

She leaned over and put her hand on his. "I'm leaving town in a few months. It doesn't matter to me. But what about you? Does it matter to you?"

He shook his head. "Only that it might hurt you." He turned his hand over to cup her fingers in his palm. "I know it hurt you before."

"Only because I let it." She leaned closer, her face inches from his so that she could see the glint of moonlight on his cheeks and the faint shadow of beard on his jaw. "What I want is the chance to do things over and to do them right this time." She slid toward him, until her thigh touched his. "Before, I worried so much about what everyone thought of me, I forgot about what I really wanted anymore. I don't want to make that mistake again."

He stared at her, eyes heavy-lidded, lips parted, his voice a whisper. "What do you want?"

"Right now, I want you." She leaned in to kiss him, her lips demanding, claiming him. She slid her arms around his neck and he gathered her close, their bodies shaped to each other from shoulder to hip. He smoothed his hand up her thigh, his touch strong and sure, and hooked a thumb beneath the waistband of her panties. The movement sent a tremor through her, like the first warning before an earthquake.

She arched toward him, a delicious edge of desire sharpening every nerve. She felt bold and daring, willing to do anything, risk everything. All the fears and insecurities she'd battled had melted away, replaced by a joy that bubbled up inside of her like laughter.

Dylan buried his nose in her neck and she felt the curve of his smile pressed against her collarbone. "Now, where were we, before we were so rudely interrupted?"

She wriggled against him, and slipped her hand beneath the placket of his shirt. "I seem to recall buttons being unbuttoned and zippers unzipped."

"Like this?" He undid the first button of her shirt, and then the second, following after his fingers with his tongue.

"Y-yes." She let her head fall back and closed her eyes, savoring the rush of sensation as he planted tender kisses on each inch of newly exposed skin.

"Do you think Pete's still out there, watching?"

The question reverberated against her chest, setting up an answering quiver in her stomach. She clung to him more tightly, riding the sensation. "Wh-what if he is?"

He pulled back far enough to look into her eyes, his gaze searching, demanding to know her inmost secrets. "Have you ever fantasized about someone watching?"

She wanted to look away, to hide from his probing gaze, but she had promised herself the truth this time. "Sometimes. No one in particular, but..." She slid her hand up under his shirt, the tips of her fingernails scratching lightly at his chest, then moving over to draw lazy circles around his nipples. "Doesn't it excite you, to think someone could get turned on just watching you?"

A heated smile tugged at the corners of his mouth. "Maybe they're jealous."

She wet her lips. "They should be. I would be, I think. Aren't you glad we're us? Getting to enjoy this now?"

"Then let them watch." He pushed her blouse back over her shoulder and undid the clasp of her bra, pushing it out of the way to reveal her breasts.

Dylan would readily admit he was a breast man. Let

others admire long legs or tight asses—he always zeroed in on a woman's chest. No matter the size or shape, the cream and rose perfection of a woman's soft curves never failed to move him.

As the sight of Taylor's naked breasts moved him now. Moonlight made her skin shine like old ivory and cast her nipples into dusky shadow. He cradled her in his hands, feeling the pebbled tips rise up against his palms. She arched against him, silently pleading for more. And he wanted more. So much more. But not yet. They had time now to make the pleasure last.

He traced his tongue over each aroused tip, making lazy circles that flicked around and across that sensitive center, slow strokes building until her breath came in hard pants. His hands shook as he smoothed her stomach and her thighs, moved by how much she wanted him. By how much he wanted her.

He raised up on his elbows and started to push her skirt above her waist, but her hands stopped him. "Let me take this off," she said.

"You're not worried someone might come along and see?"

She smiled, a teasing curve of her lips. "What if they do? Don't you want to see?"

The words sent lust shuddering through him and it was all he could do not to rip the clothes from her as he helped her find her way out of skirt, blouse and underwear. Then she helped him do the same. It was awkward and a little ridiculous with much knocking of elbows, tangling of arms and a few muttered curses. But it was also surprisingly intimate—undressing with and for one another, working together toward their anticipated pleasure.

When they were finally naked, he pulled her to him again, covering her with his body as she lay the length of the truck's bench seat. Her skin was heated, smelling of spices and musk, exotic and yet so familiar, a scent he had carried in his mind for years without even knowing what it represented.

He stroked his hands down her body, looking into her eyes as he did so, watching her desire for him build. She met and held his gaze, baring all of herself to his scrutiny. His heart pounded, captivated. This was the Taylor he first knew—the brash, exotic girl who breezed into town like a tropical storm and turned his life upside down.

Only this version had matured from girl to woman. A woman who knew what she wanted and wasn't afraid to go after it. A woman willing to experiment, to take risks. And he was the man she wanted to risk with.

"I don't want to wait any longer," she whispered.

He nodded and reached past her head to the glove compartment where he'd stashed the packet of condoms. She smiled in amusement. "Did you carry those around when you were in school?"

He laughed. "Not hardly. One of my little sisters was likely to pop open the glove box and find them. I'd have been mortified." He tore open the packet and raised up to sheath himself.

"I guess you don't have to worry about that now."

"Right now, I'm not worrying about anything." Except making this the best for them both that he could. Somehow, with Taylor, that seemed the easiest thing in the world to do.

He stretched himself alongside her once more and slid a finger inside her, her wet heat closing around him, tight and beckoning. He moved slowly, deliberately, fighting the urge to hurry. Her eyes glazed and her face went lax. He felt himself twitch, anxious to be in her, surrounded by her, but he forced himself to wait.

He suckled her breast again, her skin satin against his cheek. The tension in them both was building, muscles tightening, hearts pounding, breath coming in gasps. He cradled her head against his shoulder, silently urging her on, shaking with the force of his own desire.

She convulsed around him, the tremor of her climax rocking him. With a groan, he pressed her back against the seat and leveled himself over her. He plunged into her with the impatience of a boy, abandoning himself to desire, his climax building with each thrust. She arched against him, matching his rhythm, the slick warmth of her tightening around him, holding him, until he exploded in a white heat that left him breathless and blind, clinging to her.

They lay together for a long while, his head against her breast, the only sounds their slowing breathing and the ping of the truck engine cooling in the night air. Taylor brought her hand up to stroke his hair, the gesture strangely comforting. "We'd better get dressed," she said after a while. "We both have to work tomorrow."

He closed his eyes against the words. He didn't like being reminded that they had to return to the real world now, a world where making out in pickup trucks was considered irresponsible behavior and where gossips entertained each other with the latest scandals.

He sat up and reached for the pile of clothes they'd discarded on the floorboard, sorting through it to find his pants and her shirt. As he worked, he watched her out of the corner of his eye. Her face was calm, her expression unreadable. What was she thinking?

She'd said she didn't mind what people said about her, but dammit, he minded. He tugged on his underwear, scraping his knee against the dash as he did so and biting back a grunt of pain. If he heard one word against her this next week, he was liable to punch the guilty party in the mouth and walk away.

Neither spoke as they dressed, their movements even more awkward now. He lent her his handkerchief to clean herself and avoided watching her. She kept her gaze averted, as well. Because she was embarrassed?

He wasn't ashamed of what they'd done, but the power of the moment had left him shaken, unsure of himself and what he ought to say or do, how he ought to act. What did it mean that a casual encounter—an attempt to re-create a high school make-out session—had left him with this feeling of both completeness and loss?

For a moment he thought he'd felt something special with Taylor, something meaningful. And then the feeling had fled. These moments they had together were pure fantasy, meant to stay that way. Taylor was going away at the end of the year and he had a life to rebuild here. They could have fun while they were together, but that was all that could ever be between them.

Part of him had known that even when they were in school. Maybe that was the reason he'd never acted on his feelings for her. He was a common country boy, with roots deep in the hardscrabble earth, while Taylor was an elusive butterfly, meant for bigger and better things. Any fool could see that combination would never work.

Better to enjoy her while he could and then let her go when he had to. At least one day he'd have these moments to look back on and smile about. Not many people could say they'd been that lucky, could they?

6

_____

IF TAYLOR HAD ANY DOUBTS about whether or not word had gotten around about her and Dylan's encounter with Pete Alavero up on Inspiration Point, they were dispelled as soon as she walked into the teachers' work room the next morning.

"Seen any inspiring sights lately, Taylor?" Grady asked as she passed him on the way to the coffeepot.

Mindy greeted her and tore the end off a packet of artificial sweetener. "Don't mind Grady. He never makes sense before his third cup—if then."

"I learned not to pay any attention to Grady a long time ago." Taylor took her mug from its hook on the wall and reached for the carafe of coffee. After her incredible evening with Dylan, she'd awakened feeling much too good for anything anyone said to bother her—least of all Grady Murphy.

He smirked at her over the edge of his cup. "Somebody told me you and Dylan Gates were doing a little sight-seeing up on Inspiration Point last night. Just like old times."

Mindy choked on a mouthful of coffee. Coughing, she grabbed a napkin and blotted a spreading coffee spill. "Inspiration Point?" She gaped at Taylor. "That old make-out place? You went there—with Dylan?"

Taylor leaned back against the counter, cradling her cup. "That's what they say." She smiled, a warmth spreading through her that had nothing to do with coffee and everything to do with the memory of those magical moments in the front seat of Dylan's truck. "Of course, I'll never tell."

Grady looked smug. "Pete Alavero works out at my gym and he told me himself that he caught you and Dylan up there last night."

"Pete told you that?" She shook her head. "It's amazing to me, the things people think are newsworthy." She winked at Mindy.

Mindy grinned. "It's amazing to me how you'll believe anything you hear, Grady. Why would Taylor and Dylan be up at Inspiration Point when they've both got perfectly comfortable houses?"

Grady's coffee cup rattled against the table as he set it down. "You'd better ask Taylor that question, not me. All I know is Pete said he caught them up there, making out like a couple of kids." He waved at Taylor. "You're not even denying it, are you?"

She took the seat across from him and pretended to riffle through a folder of student papers, watching him out of the corner of her eye. "I guess I don't see what difference it makes one way or another whether I was up there or not."

Her seeming disinterest obviously took Grady by surprise. His mouth dropped open, then he closed it. His eyebrows rose, and his shoulders followed as if hoisted by invisible ropes. He stuck his nose in the air. "Some people might consider it shameful for a teacher to be conducting herself that way in public."

"Conducting myself what way?" She leaned toward him, struggling to keep her expression earnest, enjoying watching a bully who couldn't convince his victim she was being bullied. "And what exactly is so public about Inspiration Point?"

Grady frowned. "You're not a teenager anymore, Taylor. You'd do well not to act like one."

When I was a teenager I never acted the way I did last night, she thought. *I wouldn't have known how.* She shook her head and took another sip of coffee. "Don't lose any sleep over my reputation, Grady. I certainly won't."

Mindy joined them at the table and gave their tormentor a pitying look. "I think Grady's jealous. He can't get anybody to go up to Inspiration Point with him."

He made a huffing sound. "The women I date wouldn't be interested in something like that."

Mindy nodded at Taylor. "What did I tell you? He's jealous."

Taylor sipped her coffee and ignored their bickering. Maybe she ought to be more embarrassed about her and Dylan's affair being played out in the public eye, so to speak. But how could she be sorry about something so magical? The night had turned out like nothing she had imagined—and everything she had hoped for. With her skin still warmed by the memory of Dylan's touch and the shape of his body still imprinted on her limbs, she had no room in her mind for others' concerns.

The door opened and the room fell silent as Clay Walsh walked in. "Good morning, everyone."

"Good morning, Clay," they chorused. Taylor and Mindy exchanged glances. Taylor gave her friend what she hoped was an encouraging look. Honestly, if Mindy would only let Clay know how she felt—

"Taylor, I need to talk to you when you have a chance."

Clay's words sent her heart rushing straight to her throat. Had he heard the gossip about her and Dylan? It was one thing to ignore what people said or thought about her, but if it affected her job— She swallowed hard and stared at him. "Y-you do?"

"When you have a chance." He topped off his cup and selected a doughnut from a box on the counter. "Did you have a nice evening?"

She was saved from having to answer by an outburst of coughing from Grady. While he groped for a napkin and Mindy pounded his back, Taylor studied Clay. His expression was innocent, showing only polite interest. Either he didn't know about the latest gossip or he was deliberately ignoring it. Clay had always been a fair man, treating every student and teacher with respect and consideration. If he was a little reserved sometimes, maybe it was because he felt he had to be.

"I had a nice evening." *A very nice evening.* She closed her file folder and sat up straighter. "What did you want to talk to me about?"

"We need to get together and discuss possible candidates to take over your classes when you leave us at the end of the semester." He gestured toward her with his cup. "I hope you know, you're going to be hard to replace."

She flushed at this praise and looked away. Strange how she'd forgotten all about Oxford for a little while. Or about anything else that had to do with real life. Living a fantasy could do that to a person, she guessed.

"I've been trying to talk her into staying," Mindy said. "But she won't listen to me."

Clay moved to stand beside Mindy. "Maybe that's a joint project you and I should work on."

Taylor left the two of them making goo-goo eyes at each other and headed for her classroom. Honestly, how could two supposedly smart adults not see what was right in front of their noses? Mindy and Clay were perfect for each other. So what if they were a few years apart in age and a few thousand dollars apart in salary? Didn't differences spice things up a little?

At her classroom door, she almost collided with Patrice Miller. "Hello, Ms. Reed. Did you have a nice night?" Patrice asked.

Why was everyone so concerned about her night? What did her nights matter to anyone but her?

But Patrice's bland expression told her the girl was only being polite. She relaxed and smiled. "I had a nice time. Thank you."

"It was funny seeing you at Danny's." Patrice blushed. "I mean, not funny really, just…well, I'm not used to seeing my teachers out on dates."

"What teacher was on a date?" Jessica joined them at the door.

"Ms. Reed was out last night with a really hot guy." Patrice glanced at Taylor and her face reddened farther. "I mean, he was nice-looking and everything. For a guy that age."

Taylor covered her laughter with a cough. Wait until she passed that assessment on to Dylan.

"Is he your boyfriend?" Jessica's eyes looked as big as dollar coins. "What's his name? Is he from here? How did you meet him?"

The first bell rang, providing Taylor with a convenient escape. "You'd better get to your seats, girls. It's almost time to get started."

"We're not being nosy, Ms. Reed," Patrice said. "We're just really interested." She glanced around her, then leaned in and lowered her voice. "And he really is cute."

Taylor followed the girls into the room. "I'm sure the

details of my personal life would bore you all into a coma within five minutes.''

''It couldn't be any worse than studying English,'' Jessica said.

By the time the laughter faded, Taylor had pulled a single sheet of paper from the stack on her desk and stood by the blackboard. ''Today, we need to decide on a book to study for the rest of the semester. Until Christmas break, the majority of our class activities will revolve around this book. I have a list of suggestions from the State Board of Education, but you're welcome to give me your own ideas, as well.''

''Something short,'' a boy named Dale said.

''Something with lots of pictures for Dale,'' his friend Eli countered.

''Let's skip the book and go straight to the movie version,'' Jessica said. ''We can make a field trip to the video store to decide.''

Taylor smiled, listening to the friendly bickering as she wrote the rest of the state-approved titles on the board. Then she stepped back so the class could read the list.

''None of them sound very interesting.'' Jessica worried her lower lip between her teeth.

''I've already read most of them.'' Patrice's words were met with groans. She turned and gave her classmates a withering look. ''Well I have.''

''I think we should study *A Ranger Remembers*.''

Taylor turned to see who had spoken and was surprised to find that Berk had come up with this suggestion. Odd that he should mention that particular book now, when she and Dylan had talked about it only last night. ''What can you tell us about the book?''

He squirmed. ''It's by a local guy, isn't it? He was a Texas Ranger during the Civil Rights movement and he wrote about what happened." He shrugged. "It sounded interesting."

"It is interesting." She leaned against the front of the desk and studied the students. "The book is by Samuel Gates, whose family lived here for many years. He was a member of the Texas Rangers during one of the most turbulent periods in the state's history and wrote about his experiences. The book won a number of awards, but it's also quite controversial."

"Then it must have sex in it." Dale's comment was met with laughter. He rolled his eyes. "I'm serious. Adults don't want to think we know it exists."

"At one time, *A Ranger Remembers* was on our reading list," Taylor said. "It was removed at the request of a school-board member, but whether or not we study it is at the discretion of the English department head here at the school."

"Who is the department head?" Jessica asked.

"This year it's Mr. Murphy."

A groan rose over the classroom and Taylor ducked her head to hide her smile. "Berk, why did you suggest we study that particular book?" she asked.

A sunburn shade of red washed up his neck and face and he cracked his knuckles with a loud pop. "I found a copy in the library and thought it sounded interesting."

"Can we do it, Ms. Reed?" Patrice asked. "Will you ask Mr. Murphy if we can study it?"

Even a week ago, she would have said no. Why ask for trouble? But last night with Dylan had changed her mind about a lot. Some things, such as honoring your true feelings and doing what's right, were more important than worrying about what others think of you. Her job was to give these young people the best education she could.

That meant helping them make difficult choices and teaching them to think for themselves.

She nodded. "All right. I'll see what I can do." She turned and added the title to the list on the board, then faced them again. "But if I'm going to go out on a limb for you this way, you have to do me a favor, as well. You have to study and make this semester project something we can all be proud of."

"We can do it."

"Thanks, Ms. R. You're the best."

Taylor smiled and made a note in her planner to talk to Grady. Seeing the students eager about learning reminded her why this job was such a rush sometimes.

And in a way, this would be her gift to Dylan, too, revisiting his father's work and reminding the townspeople why Sam Gates had been important and worth remembering.

THE REST OF THE WEEK, every time Dylan sat down to work, thoughts of Taylor intruded on his efforts. On Thursday, he started to compose a Help Wanted ad for a secretary, only to discover he'd written "experienced legal secretary, excellent computer skills and amazing brown eyes."

He shook his head and turned away from the laptop screen. Her eyes weren't the only thing amazing about Taylor. Over the years he'd carried this image of her around in his head, only to discover upon meeting her again that everything he'd thought about her was true, only more so. He'd remembered her as an independent girl with her own sense of style and she'd reintroduced herself into his life as a free-spirited woman who would strip naked in the front seat of his truck and hide nothing from him.

The women he knew in L.A. weren't like that. Even the sweetest of them worried about image, about what they looked like, about what people thought of them. He'd written it off as part of being a woman, until Taylor made him think that wasn't necessarily so.

In high school, Taylor had snubbed her critics and he'd thought it was because they'd hurt her. Now he wondered if it was because she knew something they didn't—something about which feelings were really important.

Being with her Monday night made him want to know what she knew—to learn her secrets. He wanted to borrow her confidence, to latch onto her faith in the future and to use those things to make peace with his past. He'd come back to Cedar Creek knowing this was his home. He belonged here, but that didn't mean he knew yet exactly where he fit in. His father had been branded the town rebel, a man who'd spent his life both upholding the traditions of the community and reminding them of the mistakes of the past. What role would his son play now?

A knock on the door pulled him from his reverie. "Come in," he called, standing in time to welcome the three men who filed in. Troy was first, followed by two older men Dylan remembered from the Rotary luncheon. "Dylan, you remember Bob Packer and Lucas Talifero, don't you?" Troy said.

"Of course. How are y'all doing today?" The men shook hands all around and Dylan invited them to sit. He pulled his desk chair around and offered it to Packer, then perched on the edge of the desk. "What can I do for y'all?"

"Lucas, Bob and I have a rather interesting proposition for you." Troy grinned.

Dylan ignored a nervous tremor in his stomach. Whatever Troy was up to, it couldn't be that bad. "What kind of proposition?"

"Troy tells us you're really interested in getting involved in the community again," Talifero said.

He nodded. "That's right."

Packer stroked his neatly groomed goatee. "Would that include, perhaps, running for local office?"

Dylan shifted. "Maybe. I've thought about it for a while. It seems like a way to have a real impact on the community." His father had run for city council back in the eighties, but he'd been defeated in the primary. After that, he'd said politics was better left to others.

Troy leaned forward in his chair, elbows on his knees. "There's a recent opening on the school board and we think you'd be perfect for the position."

"School board?" Troy frowned. "I don't even have children in school."

"Doesn't matter." Talifero dismissed this concern with a wave of his hand. "School board is merely a jumping off point anyway. Serve out a two-year term there, get your name known, then move on to the county level, then on to the state legislature. It's a formula that's worked for many an up-and-coming young man over the years."

Dylan's skin prickled as he listened to the older man lay out this picture of his future. "I'm flattered you have such confidence in my abilities," he said.

Talifero smiled. "I remember when you played quarterback for the Cyclones back in the early nineties. I told myself then, a smart, talented kid like that could be a real asset to this community."

"Will you do it?" Troy asked. "Will you run for school board?"

He hesitated. "I'm not sure. I need a little time to think about it."

"Don't think too long," Packer said. "The election is only six weeks away. We're proposing you run as a write-in candidate for the position left vacated when Rennie Sellers came down with colon cancer. We're willing to put money behind you to get the word out."

Dylan frowned. "Who else is running?"

"Maidy Sellers, but she's only doing it because Rennie wants to keep his hand in. And a new guy, Jes Ramirez. Nobody knows much about him, so we figure an established name like yours would be a good draw."

Dylan was beginning to get the picture. These men, and whoever else had hatched up this plot with them, wanted to back a safe, sure thing. "I've been gone almost ten years," he said. "What makes you think anybody would remember me?"

"If they don't remember you, they remember your daddy," Talifero said. "He was a big man around here in his day."

Sam Gates had been a big man, period, one who seemed even bigger with his ramrod-straight back and Texas Ranger swagger. Dylan looked Talifero in the eye. "I seem to recall my dad wasn't all that popular with a lot of people in town. Especially after his book was published."

"Yeah, the book did stir things up for a while, but who remembers that now?" Talifero straightened and clapped his hands on his thighs. "Beating our chests about the past has kind of gone out of fashion now. What we're looking for is a smart, young candidate with local ties who'll appeal to a broad cross-section of the voters."

Dylan fought back a smile. Talifero made him sound like a new fast food offering. "And you think that's me?"

"It's you." Troy stood. "Come on, Dyl. Say you'll do

it. If you really want to be involved, this is the way to do it.''

Dylan studied them. The eagerness on their faces didn't fool him. They'd probably try to use him for some kind of agenda; but he'd use them, too, to help him win the election. Then he'd take a page from Taylor's book and do things his own way.

"How about if I let you know tomorrow? I think I really need to sleep on this."

"Tomorrow, then." Packer stood and the others rose, also. They shook hands again. As they all walked to the door, Packer stopped and turned to Dylan. "Say, I heard an interesting bit of gossip this morning about you and one of the teachers over at the high school."

Dylan froze, every sense on alert. "Oh?"

"It's understandable there's going to be a certain amount of talk. You're young and single and I suppose good-looking. I'm not telling you to become a hermit or anything, but you need to be aware of the kinds of things that might be said."

He had a disorienting sensation of déjà vu. Hadn't he been through this all before? "I wouldn't pay any attention to gossip if I were you," he said.

"You can learn very interesting things from gossip. Especially in a small town." Talifero nodded. "Just keep in mind that a man living in the public eye has to be careful. Today we're talking about the school board, but next year and the next, we could be discussing much more important offices."

When they were gone, Dylan went back into his office and sank into the desk chair. So the powers that be had decided to place a bet on his future. They thought he could make something of himself here. He tapped a pencil on the desk. Was he ready to take this step? So soon?

He reached for the phone. He needed to talk to someone else about this. Someone who'd have a better idea than he did of what the town was like these days. Taylor answered on the third ring. "Have dinner with me," he said as soon as she answered the phone. "There's something I want to talk to you about."

"What is it?" She sounded wary.

"I've been asked to run for school board."

She laughed. "You're kidding!"

"I'm not kidding. A delegation of leading citizens came to my office this afternoon, wanting to back me as a candidate."

"They obviously have excellent tastes. Congratulations."

"I haven't agreed to run yet." He leaned back, phone cradled on his shoulder. "So you think I'd make a good school-board member?"

"You'd be good at anything you decided to do."

"What about dinner?" And maybe afterward, dessert, with a certain enticing English teacher....

"I can't. I have a senior study group that meets after school. Tonight's our pizza party."

"Did they do that when we were in school?"

"As a matter of fact, I started it. Why don't you join us?"

"A study group?" He lowered his voice to a sexy growl. "The only thing I'm interested in studying is you."

"There'll be time for that, I promise. Seriously, you should come over and have pizza with us."

"All right. I like pizza." Seeing Taylor in her own element, interacting with the kids, might be a blast.

"Five o'clock in the language lab. Oh, and we have a surprise for you."

"Darlin', you've had nothing but surprises for me." He

dragged the words out in an exaggerated, blatantly sexy drawl. "Does this involve lace lingerie and handcuffs?"

Her throaty laugh made him warm all over. "No, but you'll like it just the same. See you then."

"You bet." He hung up the phone, then grabbed a legal pad to make a list of things he'd need to do if he did decide to launch a campaign. While he was at it, he'd better make a note to pick up another box of condoms. He was going to need them to keep up with Taylor.

7

BY LATE AFTERNOON Taylor was wondering about the wisdom of inviting Dylan to the school. Wouldn't it be smarter to keep her relationship with him separate from her real life? She'd planned her time with him as an interlude of pure fantasy, something to be enjoyed for its own sake. Having him step into her everyday routine made things too confusing.

Then there was the whole gossip question to deal with. It was one thing to have people speculating on what they were up to—quite another to appear together openly as a "couple." He was thinking of entering local politics and she was headed off to England. When she left, people would assume they'd had some kind of falling out. No one would ever believe they'd never planned to stay together in the first place.

"Do you think Mr. Gates will be pleased we've decided to study his dad's book?" Patrice set a stack of paper plates on the table at the front of the classroom and walked over to where Taylor was laying out pads of paper and pens. The purpose of this meeting was to brainstorm ideas for an end-of-semester project her class would present at a public assembly. It was a chance for the students to show off for the community and for the community to see what their tax dollars were paying for.

"The book hasn't been approved yet," Taylor said. "I still have to talk to Mr. Murphy."

"He'll approve it, I know." She grinned.

Taylor glanced at the girl. Today Patrice wore a navel-baring T-shirt and low-slung jeans. The kind of thing Taylor would have worn at that age, if that had been the fashion. "What makes you so sure of that?"

"He wouldn't say no to you. He's in awe of you. All the male teachers are." She giggled. "You ought to see them gawking at you when you walk down the hall. They think they're so cool, but they're really pathetic." She rolled her eyes. "You're the one who's cool, totally ignoring them all. It's like the magazines all say—that makes them want you all the more."

Taylor looked away, not entirely comfortable with having her personal relationships analyzed this way. But then, that was high school for you. Everyone watched everyone else, like a giant study lab of human behavior.

"So, do you think Mr. Gates will be pleased we're studying his father's book?" Patrice asked again.

She nodded. "I'm sure he will be." At least she hoped so. The other night it had been obvious Dylan was still hurt by the town's ill treatment of his father. Would it make him feel better to know a new generation was interested in Sam's work?

The door opened and a group of students burst into the room, instantly filling the space with their energy. Berk was at the head of the pack and he headed straight for Taylor's desk. "You're really stylin' this afternoon, Ms. Reed. Teachers should wear jeans more often."

Taylor smoothed her hands down her hips, conscious of the formfitting denim. She didn't usually bother to change clothes for these meetings, but knowing Dylan would be here, she'd gone home and selected a more casual outfit. Something more flattering than the denim jumper she'd worn earlier. She'd even slipped into sexier underwear, just in case. The black lace thong was a constant reminder of the possibilities for this evening, once she and Dylan were alone....

Her heart sped up at the thought. Planning like this lent a sharper edge to desire, made her feel truly wild and wanton—definitely not something she experienced in her everyday life as a mild-mannered English teacher. Was it the fantasies they were re-creating, or the man himself, who made her feel this way? She grabbed up her planner and began reading down the columns. That was a question she wasn't prepared to answer.

"Did I find the right place?"

All conversation stopped as Dylan stepped into the room. Dressed in tight jeans and T-shirt, his hair falling across his forehead, he might have been walking into a classroom from his high school days, the most popular guy on campus commanding everyone's attention.

The girls in Taylor's class reacted the same way girls always had to Dylan's raw sex appeal, huddling together on one side of the room, staring at him and nudging one another. The boys assumed poses of unconscious imitation, straightening their shoulders and puffing out their chests.

One difference from their high school days struck Taylor: before she'd stood in the background, wanting what she couldn't have. Today, she knew Dylan was hers. At least for the next few weeks or months. At least in the bounds of this fantasy they were playing out together. She didn't dare think beyond that.

She struggled to keep her expression neutral, while her heart beat faster and her nerves hummed. She tucked her hair behind one ear and moved toward him, feeling his gaze on her like a caress. "You're just in time," she said. "The pizza should be here any minute."

"Pistol Pete's Pizza?" He named their favorite class hangout.

She laughed. "Of course."

"They had Pistol Pete's when you went to school here?" Jessica asked.

"They've had Pistol Pete's forever," Dale said. "My dad talks about going there when he was a kid."

"They'll probably have Pistol Pete's when your kids go to school here," Dylan said.

Patrice made a face. "Little Dales? There's a scary thought."

"Everyone, this is Dylan Gates," Taylor interrupted. "Dylan, these are some of my senior English students. I'll let you all introduce yourselves while we eat."

As if on cue, the delivery man from Pistol Pete's arrived, five insulated pizza bags stacked in his arms.

"You can bring the pizza over here," Taylor directed.

"Let me help." Dylan started distributing pizzas while Taylor handed out napkins. He helped serve the food and drinks. Once he looked across the table and winked at her. Mortified, Taylor blushed, while Jessica and the other girls giggled.

She started to sit at the end of the table, but Dylan motioned to his side. "I saved you a seat next to me," he said.

"I suppose I ought to sit where I can keep an eye on you." She slid into the chair at his side, aware of his thigh almost touching hers.

"Did the two of you know each other in high school?" Patrice asked.

Taylor looked at the girl, surprised. Had the rumors followed her all the way to the classroom? "How did you know that?"

Patrice shrugged. "I know you both went to school here and you're about the same age, aren't you?"

"Taylor and I were in the same class." Dylan helped himself to a second slice of pepperoni pizza.

"Dylan recently moved back to town after living in Los Angeles." Taylor wiped her hands on a paper napkin. "His family has lived in Cedar Creek for, what is it—three generations?"

"I'm sure these kids aren't interested in me or my family," he said.

"But we are," Patrice said. "Because of our class project."

"Class project?" Dylan sent Taylor a questioning look.

Her stomach fluttered as if she'd swallowed a half dozen moths. "Berk, why don't you tell Dylan a little bit about what we want to do."

Berk wiped his hands on his jeans, then reached under his chair and pulled a book from his backpack. "We wanted to study this and do some kind of project related to it."

Dylan took the book and stared down at the pale blue dust jacket with its pencil drawing of the Bee County Courthouse and the simple lettering, *A Ranger Remembers,* by Samuel D. Gates.

"That's a signed, first edition," Berk said. "I don't think our library realizes how valuable it is."

Taylor studied Dylan's face, searching for some clue as to how he felt about all this. His downcast eyes hid his expression from her as he ran his fingers across the dust jacket like a blind man reading Braille. Only the tight line of his mouth betrayed any agitation.

Should she have asked him first before agreeing to her students' idea? Did he see this as some attempt to manipulate him? To use him? She clenched her hands into fists and scrambled for some explanation to placate him. She was still searching for words when he raised his eyes to meet hers. "This was your idea?"

"It was our idea," Jessica said. She glanced at the others and they all nodded. "All of us."

"I suggested it," Berk said. "I found the book at the library and thought it looked interesting."

Dylan laid the book down in the middle of the table. It looked oddly formal, nestled among the pizza boxes. "I thought the book was removed from the school library in 1995." He frowned. "I was in college and my dad sent me the article from the local paper."

"Somebody must have put it back in," Berk said. "Or maybe they overlooked this copy."

"Why would they remove it?" Patrice asked. She touched the cover. "It says inside here that it won a bunch of awards and stuff."

"Some people thought it made the town look bad by bringing up things that had happened in the past."

Patrice frowned. "But if those things really happened, isn't it important to remember them?"

He nodded. "My father would have agreed with you."

"There isn't only bad stuff in the book, though," Berk said. "I looked through it and it talks about good stuff, too, like the first black students here at Cedar Creek High and the first Juneteenth Parade."

"That's right," Taylor said. "One of the things critics talked about was the balanced approach Mr. Gates took to the issue."

"Not everyone saw it that way." Dylan's gaze was on the book, but his eyes seemed to look beyond it, to another time.

Taylor touched his arm, the way one would touch a sleepwalker, to avoid startling him. "The students and I think it's important for people to remember your father's work," she said. "Is that all right with you?"

He straightened and glanced around the table. "Why wouldn't it be all right? My father would be flattered."

"I know you're thinking of running for school board," she said. "Perhaps now isn't the best time to bring up the past."

He shook his head. "No, it's the perfect time. Who knows? Reminding people of who my father was and what he stood for could be a real asset. Besides, we can't let the past influence the future, can we?"

The knowing look he sent her made her breath catch in her throat. She glanced away, smoothing her hands across her thighs. "We still have to get approval for this from the English department," she said. "But after that, I wonder if you might come back to class and speak to us about your father. Maybe you could bring pictures and other mementos."

"I'd like that." He shoved back from the table. "My father was an interesting man. He'd get a kick out of you all choosing his book for your project."

"What should the project be?" Patrice asked. She glanced at Dylan. "We can't just study the book—we have to make some kind of presentation to the community."

"Like a play," Jessica said.

"Last year's senior class wrote a rock opera based on Dracula," Dale said. "It was totally cool."

"Maybe we could do a photography exhibit," Berk said.

"Or a play," Jessica offered.

"Not a play—a movie!" Dale grinned. "We could film some of the places mentioned in the book and then film pictures of how they were back then."

Patrice jumped up. "And we could interview people who were alive back then who are still here now."

"And maybe we could interview you about your dad," Berk said.

Dylan nodded. "I'd be honored."

Taylor stood and began gathering up plates. "These are all great ideas. We'll meet again after I talk to Mr. Murphy. In the meantime, I want each of you to write a five-paragraph essay on what you hope to show with this project."

A chorus of groans greeted this assignment, along with some good-natured grumbling. Jessica swept a stack of paper plates into the trash and glanced at her watch. "Oh, my gosh, I have to go," she said. "It's almost time for my TV show!"

This prompted a rush of gathering up backpacks and exchanging goodbyes. "See you tomorrow, Ms. Reed."

"Nice to meet you, Mr. Gates."

"Later, everybody."

Dylan helped clean up the rest of the plates and boxes and straighten the chairs. Now that they were alone, the room seemed smaller, the atmosphere charged with an awareness that had been absent before. She reached for an empty cup and his hand brushed against hers, sending a shiver of sensation up her arm. He bent toward her and the scent of his cologne tickled her nose, instantly kindling memories of their bodies coming together in the cab of his truck.

He cleared his throat. "Thanks for inviting me here tonight," he said. "It was great meeting your students."

"They were excited to meet you. It's not every day they get to meet a living connection to something we're studying." She crumpled a napkin and tossed it in the trash. "Do you really think your dad would have been pleased?"

He nodded. "He always said someday people would understand what he'd tried to accomplish."

The regret she heard in his voice made her heart ache. "Was it very bad, when they shunned him?" she asked.

"It was pretty bad." He shoved a chair underneath the table. "It's the reason I had to get away right after the funeral. I couldn't deal with all these people pretending to mourn my father when they'd turned a cold shoulder to him only the year before."

"But you came back."

He sat on the edge of the table. "I came back." He shrugged. "This is my home."

She sat next to him. She wanted to reach for his hand, but held back. He would have to make the first move here. "They hurt you and you came back."

He turned to look at her. "Maybe I thought I had something to prove."

"I guess I can understand that."

She leaned toward him, lips parted in silent invitation. He brought his hand up to cradle the side of her face, and pulled her closer, their lips meeting in a tentative kiss.

Is this what you want? The kiss asked. *Is this the right time?*

"Yes," she whispered, and slid closer to him. This was all she wanted, all she had wanted since the moment he'd walked into the room.

His arms encircled her, warm and strong, supporting her and claiming her. He trailed kisses along her jaw, the heat of his mouth burning a path down her neck. "Did you have anything in mind for tonight?" His voice vibrated through her, echoing the humming of her blood in her veins.

"Something…in particular?" He trailed his tongue along her collarbone, making it difficult to form coherent thought.

"A rumor." He tugged down the neckline of her shirt and planted kisses along the tops of her breasts. "From your diary?"

"I—I can't remember." Her head fell back and a long sigh rose up from deep within her. Who could think when he was doing such incredible things to her body?

"Wasn't there something about us making out beneath the bleachers?" He tugged the shirt down lower and ran his tongue under the edge of her bra. "At the football game."

"Uh-uh." She arched into him, pressing her breasts against his chest.

"Why not?" He slid his hand up her stomach, cradling her breast.

"Spiders." She shifted to allow him easier access. "Creepy."

"I guess you're right." He rolled her nipple between his thumb and forefinger, sending shock waves of arousal through her. "I never could figure out how that was supposed to have happened anyway, since I would have been on the field during any game."

"Uh-huh." She nipped at the back of his neck. As soon as she could find the strength to move, maybe they could go somewhere more private.…

"Wasn't there something about a shower?"

He raised his head to look at her, allowing her senses to clear. She tried to think. "A shower? Oh, yeah. The story was, we took a shower together in the boys' dressing room. As if anyone could really get away with something like that."

"I don't know.…" He glanced at the clock on the wall

behind them. "It's almost seven. Practice is over. The coaches will have gone home to supper. The janitors don't show up until what—after nine?"

She stared at him. "You can't be serious!"

He grinned. "Why not?" He slid off the table and tugged her toward the door.

She held back. "Dylan, that's crazy!"

"Who said sanity was any fun?" He wrapped his arm around her and pulled her toward the door. "You said you wanted to make those old rumors come true. Here's your chance to add this one to the list."

"It's too risky."

"That's what makes it exciting, isn't it? The risk?" He traced his finger along her jaw, his eyes staring into hers. She got lost in that gaze, mesmerized by his voice. "The idea that at any moment, you might be caught. You might be right on the edge, about to come, and someone would walk in." He pulled her tight against him, his thigh thrust between her legs, rubbing her sensitive center. "But by then, it would be too late. All you could do would be to stand there and let your climax take you, while they watched."

Her eyes fluttered closed, surrendering to this image of herself, powerless against the force of her desire. "Didn't you say you always regretted not doing things?" His voice was a whisper, a cooling breeze across her fevered senses. "Don't regret not doing this."

She nodded. "Yes," and allowed him to lead her out of the room and down the deserted hallway.

Their footsteps squeaked against the gym floor, the sound quickly swallowed up in the high-ceilinged room. They kept to the shadows along the wall, skirting the bleachers, moving around stacks of mats and a bin of basketballs, toward the door on the far side marked Boys.

The door creaked loudly as Dylan pulled it open and she stifled a squeal. As he reached for the light, she grabbed his hand away. "No! Someone might see," she hissed.

He nodded, and led her into the room.

The parking lot security lights cast a yellow glow through a row of narrow windows near the ceiling, illuminating the tiers of basket lockers and double ranks of benches. Taylor stepped over a discarded pair of basketball shoes and looked around. "It's not as bad as I thought," she whispered.

He laughed. "What did you think?"

She shrugged. "You know—gross." She wrinkled her nose. "I thought it would smell more."

He coughed. "It probably does when it's occupied."

As it was, it smelled of bleach and liniment. Not wonderful, but not unpleasant. She made a mental note to thank the janitor next time she saw him.

"Is it that much different from the girls' lockers?" he asked, following her farther into the room.

"It's messier." She kicked aside a single dirty sock someone had left behind. "The girls tend to have more beauty products sitting around." She stopped to examine a jar of hair gel someone had left by the sink.

He opened a closet and pulled out a stack of the thin white towels familiar from years of gym classes. "Not up to Ritz-Carlton standards, but they'll have to do."

Her stomach quivered. Were they really going to do this? She'd told herself she wanted to risk more, but was this going too far? She looked toward the showers. "You don't think there are any spiders, do you?"

He came to stand behind her and put his arms around her. "No spiders. Nothing to be afraid of." He pulled her close, leaving no doubt as to his own state of arousal. "Unless you're afraid of me."

She swiveled her hips, grinding against him, forcing a bravado she didn't quite feel. "Maybe you should be afraid of me."

He tugged at her shirt, but she slipped out of his grasp, ducking behind a laundry bin. "I'll undress over here."

"Oh no you don't." He grabbed her hand and pulled her out into the middle of the room. "No. I want to see you." He grasped the hem of her shirt and pulled it up over her bra. Reluctantly, she raised her arms and allowed him to pull the shirt off.

"Stand there like that," he said, holding her arms up. He reached around and unsnapped her bra, freeing her breasts. Cool air rushed over her, puckering her nipples, a corresponding tightness building between her thighs. He shaped his hands to her breasts, supporting her, abrading the nipples with a tantalizing friction against his palms. She squeezed her thighs together and swayed, every nerve throbbing with need.

One hand continuing to tease her breast, he reached down and unfastened her belt. She arched against him. "Hurry."

"Oh, I'm enjoying this too much to hurry." He slid the belt slowly from her waist, then flicked open the top button of her jeans. He looked at her a moment, as if contemplating his next move. She wanted to wrap her arms around him and to pull him to her, but she forced herself to hold still, arms in the air, waiting.

He bent to suckle first one nipple, then the other, his mouth hot against her skin, his tongue caressing, teasing, dragging out her desire in a delicious agony. She felt suspended here in the shadows, poised against his mouth, held up by his hand at her waist.

He pulled down her zipper and parted the fabric, his hand sliding down to cover her mound, squeezing her through the thin layer of silk.

She bit back a moan. ''Why am I the only one getting undressed?'' she whispered.

''My turn is coming.'' He grabbed the waistband of her jeans and shoved them down over her hips, dragging her panties down as well. Then he helped her kick off her shoes and step out of her jeans.

As soon as they straightened, her hands were on him, tugging at his shirt, loosening his belt. He pulled his shirt over his head and sent it sailing, followed quickly by the rest of his clothes. They embraced, heated skin to heated skin, hard muscle to soft curve, smooth complimenting rough in a design that would never be improved upon.

He smiled down on her, his face softened by shadow. ''Let's take a shower,'' he said, and led her into the stall.

8

TAYLOR HAD NEVER BEFORE thought of sex as being a particularly graceful act, but as she and Dylan moved into the shower, she was reminded of dancing. Hands on her hips, he guided her under the shower head, holding her steady on the slippery tile floor, communicating without words. Warm water cascaded over them in a soft spray, the droplets glittering like jewels on their bodies in the silvery light.

He turned her until her back was to him and pulled her close, one arm clasped around her waist, the other reaching for the soap. Working up a lather in his hands, he soaped her breasts, moving from one to the other, stroking her nipples, sliding her hands along the undersides, cupping her in his palms. The velvety soapsuds and warm water caressed every nerve, soothing the ache building within her, even as his constantly moving fingers coaxed her to a fever pitch.

He pulled her tightly to him, until she could feel his erection hot against her back. She ground into him, shimmying, their soapy skin sliding together. He smoothed his palm down her torso to her stomach and then to her thighs, lathering her skin, squeezing, forcing her legs farther apart. A stream of warm water ran over her clit, heightening her arousal, until she was biting back a moan.

She whirled to face him then, plastering her body to his, her mouth claiming his in a devouring kiss. The water pounded over them, steam rising around them. She'd never been more aware of her body—of the shape of her muscles and the sheen of her skin, of the way her hips flared and her buttocks jiggled when she moved, of the flexing of her calves when she brought one foot up to rub along his leg.

He slid his hands down her back to cup her bottom. "You're beautiful," he said, the reverence in his voice raising a sudden lump in her throat. Had anyone ever said that to her with so much meaning?

She leaned in to kiss him again and bumped his arm. The soap squirted out of his fingers, landing with a wet *plop!* on the tile and skidding away. "I'd better get that before one of us steps on it," he said.

He bent to retrieve the runaway bar, presenting a tantalizing view of his tight rear end. Unable to resist, she grabbed a towel from a hook on the wall and snapped it at him.

"Oh no you don't!" He lunged for her and she darted away, squealing. She managed to evade him for several seconds before he caught her and hauled her, breathless, up against the far shower wall.

Laughing, she looked into his eyes and the heat she saw there—the naked *wanting*—made her knees weaken and her arms go limp. His mouth claimed hers, the kiss powerful, bruising, blocking out thought and reason and anything but the feel of his lips on hers, the heat of his tongue in her mouth, a connection forged between them that went beyond the physical. Mouth to mouth like this, their bodies melded together to almost one being, who was to say they didn't glimpse one another's souls?

She clung to him, drinking in that kiss, his hands moving down her body, parting her legs, his fingers delving into her, caressing, desire building past bearing.

She thrust against him, trying to climb to that height she knew he would help her reach. Immediately, his hand stilled, leaving her poised on the brink, gasping for breath, eyes squeezed shut. Water beat around them and, underneath the drum of the shower on tile, she heard his ragged breathing. "Hold on," he whispered. "Just a minute."

He reached above his head, groping for and finding the condom he'd balanced on the edge of the stall. He ripped the packet open with his teeth and sheathed himself, grunting with the effort of maintaining control.

She closed her eyes again and leaned her head back, waiting. He kissed her neck, her throat, his mouth burning a path down, to her breasts, while his hands kneaded her hips. She felt him, poised at her entrance and arched toward him.

Some sound disturbed her, something out of place. She caught her breath. Was someone out there? Had they been discovered?

Then it was too late. He plunged into her, the feel of him taking her breath away. She wrapped one leg around him, both steadying herself and coaxing him deeper. His movements were strong and sure, each withdrawal sending tremors through her, each return making her coil around him, tensed and ready.

On the edge of consciousness, she thought she heard the noise again. An image flashed through her mind of someone watching them, mesmerized by the force of their passion. The idea sent her over the edge in a blinding, quaking climax. She bit his shoulder to keep from screaming her pleasure, shock waves still rocking her as he followed her to his release.

She didn't know how long she clung to him, but eventually she became aware of her surroundings once more: the slick tile at her back, the cooling water flowing over her, his chest crushing her against the wall. She shifted and he pulled away, turning to shut off the water.

Neither of them spoke as he lifted a towel from a hook and began drying her. His movements were gentle. Tender. He blotted the water from her shoulders, her breasts, her stomach and back, focused on his work. She closed her eyes and sighed. When had she ever felt so cared for? So *cherished?*

So vulnerable, whispered a voice inside her head, but she pushed the thought away. She had nothing to fear from Dylan. "Do you think I could get you to come over every morning and give me a shower?" she asked softly.

He grinned. "If I did that, neither one of us would ever get to work."

The sound of a toilet flushing in the next room made them both jump. She choked back a scream and stared at him. "Somebody's here!" she hissed.

He nodded and handed her the towel, then snatched up one for himself. "We'd better get dressed and get out of here."

They hurried into their clothes, frantically groping for buttonholes, hopping on one foot and then the other as they pulled socks on over still-damp skin. Taylor's hands shook as she zipped up her jeans. What would happen if they were caught? Would she be fired? Would Dylan's political career be over before it even started? She caught a glimpse of herself in the mirror and moaned. All her makeup had washed off and her hair was plastered against her scalp in a tangled mess. She searched in her purse and found a comb, but she'd barely dragged it through her hair before Dylan grabbed her hand and pulled her behind a laundry cart just as the door opened and lights blazed on.

Kneeling on the hard tile floor, she peered around the

edge of the laundry cart and saw the janitor wheeling a mop bucket into the room. Head bobbing and hips sway-ing, he hummed snatches of a song. She realized he was listening to the stereo hooked to his belt.

He moved over to the sinks and began to spray cleaner from an industrial-size plastic bottle. Dylan squeezed her hand and indicated they should keep low to the ground— out of view of the mirrors—and slip out the door.

Heart pounding, she swallowed hard. She checked the janitor again. He was scrubbing the sinks now, still hum-ming to himself. Dylan nodded and jerked her toward the door.

They ran, feet slapping against the floor, out the shower room door, across the gym and down the hall. They didn't stop running until they were in the parking lot, where they collapsed against the side of Dylan's truck, gasping.

"D-do you th-think he saw us?" she asked, clinging to the truck door handle. She had a stitch in her side from running so hard.

He shook his head. "I don't think so." He glanced back toward the door leading into the school. "He didn't come after us, so I'm sure he didn't see anything."

"Then I guess…we'd better go."

He looked around them again. "Where are you parked?"

"In the teacher's lot—up front."

"I'll walk you."

MINDY SAT IN THE conference room off the principal's office and tried to concentrate on the standardized-test-score statistics Clay was presenting to them, but her mind kept focusing on the man himself. He pointed to a graph on the wall and she thought about what nice hands he had. You could tell a lot about a man from his hands.

Clay had long, thick fingers and nicely trimmed nails. No rings. A classic gold watch. His hands practically shouted respectable and conservative.

Not the kind of man who would get involved with someone he supervised. Someone fifteen years younger.

She hadn't realized she'd sighed until she looked up to find everyone staring at her. "Is something wrong, Miss Lewis?" Clay asked.

She sat up straight, aware of the hot flush of embarrassment creeping across her cheeks. "No. Everything's fine."

"*Some* of us are very interested in these issues." Alyson gave her a withering look, then turned to Clay. "I think we should make improved test scores the main focus of our teaching."

"You can't just teach the test," Sara Stafford, the sophomore biology teacher, countered. "What happened to a well-rounded education?"

Everyone started debating ideas then. Mindy slumped in her chair, trying to follow the conversation, uncomfortably aware of Clay's eyes on her. He wore a puzzled expression. Who could blame him? He probably wondered what she was doing here. She was beginning to wonder that herself.

After what seemed like hours, the meeting adjourned and everyone began to file out. Mindy was last in line, reluctant to leave. This wasn't working out the way she'd planned. She hadn't had a chance to say one word to Clay.

He looked up just then and caught her eye. "Mindy, do you mind staying for a minute? There's something I need to discuss with you."

Her stomach sank to her ankles. Was he angry she'd let her mind wander? Was he going to ask her to resign from the committee? "Y-yes. What is it?"

He went around the table, collecting leftover papers, not looking at her. "I'm curious. Why did you volunteer for this task force?"

Because I wanted to be close to you. But of course, she couldn't tell him that. "I thought it sounded interesting."

"You didn't appear too interested tonight."

She flushed again. "I'm sorry, I—"

"No need to apologize." He looked up, smiling. "I didn't mean that as a reprimand. Frankly, I find these things incredibly boring myself. And I know I'm not the world's most scintillating speaker."

Scintillating. How many men did she know who used words like scintillating? None. Well, one. Clay. The other men she'd dated didn't even know what the word meant. There she went, letting her mind wander again. "I'm sorry. I guess I just have a lot on my mind."

He looked concerned. "If it's anything I can help you with, I hope you'll come to me."

That's the whole problem, I can't come to you. She lowered her gaze. "Thank you. I—I appreciate the offer."

"In any case, I wanted to thank you for signing up for the committee. It's refreshing to have someone with your youth and energy and enthusiasm to keep the rest of us on our toes."

Oh, no, he'd called her young. Did he think she was too young? That he was too old?

He turned away and her heart sank. She hadn't had a chance to say any of the things she'd rehearsed in front of the bathroom mirror last night. "Wait...I—"

He turned around, eyes alert. "Yes?"

"I—I do have some good ideas for the committee." She took a deep breath, searching for courage. "Maybe we could get together to discuss them. Over lunch or...or dinner?"

His smile could have melted chocolate. "I'd like that. When?"

When? She hadn't thought this far. She hadn't dared think he'd even be interested. "Wh-when would you be available?"

"Next Friday is a teacher's work day. Everyone goes home at two. Perhaps we could meet for a late lunch or an early supper."

A meal together would be a good start. "Okay. Next Friday. Supper. That would be nice."

He picked up his briefcase. "Let me walk you to your car. It's already late."

They walked slowly, as if neither was in a hurry to leave. She kept glancing at him out of the corner of her eye and was surprised to find that he kept looking at her, that same puzzled expression in his eyes she'd noticed earlier. When they reached the front doors of the building, he paused, his hand on the bar that opened the door. "Can I ask you a personal question?"

She swallowed. "I guess."

"Are you, um, seeing anyone?"

"Seeing anyone?" *As in, a doctor? Or a psychiatrist. Oh, God, did he think she needed professional help?*

"Are you dating anyone? I know it's none of my business, but—"

"No. I mean no, I'm not dating anyone." *Are you?* But she couldn't bring herself to ask that.

He nodded and opened the door and held it for her. She walked past him, scarcely breathing. Did he have a particular reason for wanting to know if she was dating anyone? Was he—maybe-going to ask her out himself?

"Isn't that Taylor Reed's car over there?"

She blinked at the sudden shift in the conversation and followed his gaze to the familiar Honda Civic. "That *is*

Taylor's car.'' She frowned. ''What's she doing up here this time of night?''

About that time, Taylor herself appeared, walking across the parking lot with a tall, handsome man. The closer they got, the more…disheveled they looked. The man's shirt was untucked and…was Taylor's hair wet?

''We'd better find out what's going on,'' Clay said. He took her arm and tugged her across the lot, toward her friend and the mysterious handsome stranger.

TAYLOR DIDN'T PROTEST when Dylan put his arm around her. No one was here to see them and, besides, it felt too good in his arms. She told herself she should enjoy this while she could.

''I've been thinking,'' he said.

''Oh?'' She glanced up at him, suddenly wary. Had he been thinking about them? Was he about to say something about his feelings for her or the things they'd been doing? She didn't want to hear anything that would take them out of the fantasy world they'd re-created, into a more treacherous territory of feelings and emotions and consequences for the future. ''I've been thinking, too,'' she hastened to add. ''About your running for school board. I definitely think you should do it.''

''Really?'' He looked down at her. ''Why do you say that?''

''You were so good with the kids tonight. I know you'd keep their best interests in mind and that's exactly the kind of person who ought to be on the school board.''

He nodded, his expression thoughtful. ''I'm supposed to give my backers a decision tomorrow.''

''What will you tell them?''

He grinned. ''If you think I'd do a good job, then I

think I'll tell them yes.'' He patted her shoulder. ''Your opinion means a lot to me, you know.''

There he went, talking about feelings again. Feelings she wasn't ready to explore. She searched her mind for another distraction, but one was provided as they turned the corner of the building. She was surprised to see several cars still in the lot.

''Is something going on here tonight?'' he asked.

She shook her head. ''Not that I know of. But it could be some group or other meeting.''

She straightened and moved out of his arms and said a silent prayer that no one would come along and see them like this. She thought her prayer had been granted when they stopped beside her car and she took out her keys. ''Good night,'' she told Dylan and started to unlock her door.

''Good night.'' He touched her arm, stopping her and making her look up at him. ''And thanks. For everything.'' He grinned. ''For inviting me to meet the kids *and* for the shower.''

She felt herself blushing. ''Thank you, too.'' She couldn't stop looking at him and she couldn't stop smiling. She felt seventeen again, her insides turned to warm applesauce by his mere presence.

''Taylor! Hey, Taylor!''

Her heart climbed into her throat as she whirled to see Mindy striding toward her, followed closely by Clay Walsh. Mindy grinned and stopped in front of them. ''What are you doing here this time of night?'' She cast a questioning look at Dylan.

''Taylor, is everything all right?'' Clay stopped behind Mindy, his forehead creased in a frown.

''Everything's fine,'' she said, a little too brightly. ''Um, this is Dylan Gates.'' She nodded to Dylan. ''Dylan, this is my friend and fellow teacher, Mindy Lewis, and our principal, Clay Walsh.''

''Pleased to meet you.'' Dylan shook hands with them both, his warm smile and easy manner betraying no hint of the nervousness and panic Taylor felt.

''Um, Dylan and I were working on a special project.'' She fought to keep from blushing farther. ''That is, the students and I are thinking of studying a book Dylan's father wrote about the civil rights movement in Bee County. Dylan came to talk to us about his father.''

''That's really nice of you.'' Mindy's smile brightened a few watts and she not-so-subtly checked him out.

Clay was still frowning. ''Why is your hair wet?''

Taylor wished a sinkhole would open in the asphalt and swallow her up. Now. She put a hand to her damp hair. ''I, uh…''

''We fell in the pool.''

She stared at Dylan. His eyes met hers, telling her she should just go along with him. ''Uh…that's right. I, uh…Dylan went to school here and he wanted to look around, so I was showing him the new pool that was put in a few years ago. I guess I wasn't paying attention to where I was walking and I slipped and fell in.''

''So, of course, I had to jump in after her.''

Clay however, was still frowning. ''But your clothes are dry.''

Dylan's smile faltered for half a second. Then he brightened. ''Microfiber.''

''Microfiber?'' Mindy looked as if she was trying hard not to laugh.

''Dries like that.'' Dylan snapped his fingers. ''Amazing stuff, huh?''

''Oh, it's amazing all right.'' Mindy's smile was a full-fledged smirk now.

"Well, we'd better be going." Taylor faked a huge yawn. "Big day tomorrow, you know." She jabbed her key into the lock and opened the car door. "Good night."

"Good night." Dylan was already backing away. Mindy and Clay stared at both of them as if they weren't sure who was craziest. They were still looking like that when Taylor started the car and backed out of her parking space. She waved and smiled and managed to drive somewhat sedately all the way to the street before dissolving into uncontrollable laughter. It was either that or give in to panicky tears.

9

TAYLOR'S GRANDMOTHER had always told her that if she had an unpleasant chore to take care of, to get it out of the way first so that it didn't ruin the rest of her day. So Taylor was waiting outside Grady Murphy's office the next morning when the head of the English department showed up for work. "Good morning, Taylor. To what do I owe this pleasure?" He grinned and unlocked the door.

"Good morning, Grady." She followed him into the office, *A Ranger Remembers* cradled in her arms. "My class has selected a book for their semester project, but it's not on the preapproved list."

Grady shoved his briefcase onto his desk and flipped on the desk lamp. "Now the whole point of having an approved list is so teachers will use *those* books in the classroom. There are plenty of good titles on there to choose from. I don't see why we need to even consider others."

Well, of course Grady wouldn't see. He'd made an art of upholding the administration's policies, no matter how shortsighted they were. She forced a pleasant, and she hoped persuasive, smile to her lips. "The students felt like this book would be an important one for them to study. And I agree."

"What do they want—*Catcher in the Rye* again? You'd think Salinger invented teenage angst."

"No, they've decided to go with a local author. And nonfiction."

He raised one eyebrow. "That's a new one on me. What did they choose?"

She held out the book, watching his eyes for his reaction. "It's called *A Ranger Remembers,* by Samuel Gates."

He took the book, frowning. "This is Dylan Gates's father, isn't it?"

"Yes." She braced herself for some crass comment.

He opened the book. "I remember some kind of controversy about this. What was it?"

"I believe some people were upset because they thought the book portrayed an unflattering picture of the town's past."

He nodded and thumbed to the section of photographs in the book's middle. "It's about the Civil Rights struggle, right?"

"Yes. He was a Texas Ranger here during that period."

He shut the book and handed it back to her. "I don't believe it's merely a coincidence you picked this particular book. It's all over town you're seeing Dylan again."

She shrugged. "Believe what you want. The students chose the book, not me."

Grady leaned against his desk and crossed his arms. "I hear Dylan's been asked to run for school board. This wouldn't be a ploy to garner a little extra publicity, would it? Play up the old 'local boy makes good' angle?"

Did he practice that smug look in the mirror? "This has nothing to do with that. If anything, some of the old objections to the book might surface, which could be a bad thing for Dylan's campaign."

He shook his head. "I don't know. Seems like studying this book now is asking for trouble."

She'd known he wouldn't say yes right away. The sole reason Grady accepted the position as head of the English department was to take his own little power trip. Riding herd on a bunch of English teachers wasn't exactly leading the Wild Bunch, but when you were a paunchy, fading former football star, it was something. "Grady, do you remember when we were in school and you and some of the other football players whitewashed every jockey statue in every front yard in town—including the one in Superintendent Peterson's yard?"

He grinned. "Peterson came out to go to church Sunday morning and just about had a heart attack." He chuckled. "My dad made me string barbwire fence all summer as punishment, but it was worth it to see the look on Peterson's face."

"The thing is, a lot of statues stayed white after that. And the rest of them quietly disappeared. You may have gone about it the wrong way, but you sent the right message." She gave him a long look. "Are we educating our students to do the right thing—or only the safe thing?"

He studied the toes of his boots. "I hear what you're saying." He nodded. "Let me think about it."

She didn't smile until she was out of his office and halfway down the hall. Painting Grady Murphy as a champion of civil rights had been a stretch. She had a hunch the jockey-painting idea had originated with Dylan and Grady had tagged along after him, as they all had in those days. Dylan was the star they followed, a rare leader at an age when they all wanted desperately to belong to the pack.

When she walked into her classroom, she was startled to find Mindy seated at her desk, riffling through the center drawer. She cleared her throat and Mindy looked up.

"You don't keep anything incriminating in here, do you?" Mindy said, her cheeks a deep pink.

"What exactly are you looking for?" Taylor laid the book on the corner of the desk.

Mindy closed the drawer. "For starters, something that will tell me what was really going on with you and Dylan Gates last night. Who is, by the way, a definite hottie." She fanned herself.

"What do you mean?" She pretended great interest in a stack of papers in her In box. "He came by to talk to my students about his father."

"Uh-huh? So what was with that bogus 'we fell in the pool' story?"

Taylor felt the hot flush creep up her neck. "Maybe it didn't happen exactly like that."

Mindy leaned forward, her voice low. "Your clothes were dry and your hair was wet. If you were in that pool, you had to have been *naked*."

Taylor winced and glanced toward the classroom door. It was early yet; the students were still gathering in the hallways. She looked back at Mindy. Maybe it would be a good idea to confide in a friend. Maybe Mindy could help her sort out her confused feelings. "We were in the shower," she said.

"The shower!" Mindy squealed and clamped a hand over her mouth.

"Shh-hh! I don't want everyone to hear."

Mindy uncovered her mouth, revealing a huge grin. "What were you doing in the shower? Or should I guess?"

Taylor checked the doorway again. Still empty. "Back when I was in school, there was this rumor that Dylan and I got caught showering together in the boys' locker room," she whispered. "It wasn't true, but lately... Well, since the reunion... He and I have been, um, re-creating some of those old rumors.''

''Re-creating?'' Mindy's eyes widened. ''You mean, you're doing now what everyone thought you were doing then? Why?'' She giggled. ''Not that you need a reason for having hot sex with a guy like Dylan....''

Taylor gripped the edge of the desk. ''I know it sounds crazy, but I thought... Well, I realized I've kind of had a crush on Dylan all these years and I thought this would be a good way to get him out of my system.''

Mindy pursed her lips and tapped her chin with one finger. ''Let me see if I understand this. You realized you're still crazy about Dylan after all these years. He comes back to town and you think this 'crush' as you call it, is a bad thing? Explain how you arrived at this conclusion, please?''

Taylor frowned. ''Consult your Webster's. I think you'll find 'crush' defined as 'an immature infatuation' or something along those lines. It's not anything lasting or real. It's just like you said—I've been stuck in high school, carrying around this unrealistic image of the 'perfect man' and it's ruined me for all other relationships.''

''So screwing your brains out with this gorgeous guy is going to 'cure' you?'' She shook her head. ''That's like telling me I'll lose ten pounds on a diet of cheesecake and Deluxe Danny Burgers.''

Taylor looked away. When Mindy put it that way, her ''experiment'' with Dylan didn't make any sense. If familiarity was supposed to breed contempt, if spending more time with him was supposed to make her see his faults and flaws more clearly, then so far it wasn't working. But one thing hadn't changed—the real reason she and Dylan weren't going to ever move beyond ''immature infatuation.''

"I'm still going away to Oxford after Christmas. Dylan is settling down here. He's even running for school board. This is his home."

Mindy frowned. "And you can't make it your home, too? Nobody says you *have* to go to Oxford."

"Oh, sure. Go to Oxford for dream year spent studying Shakespeare and possible future dream job or stay in small Texas town and continue to be outsider with risque past. What kind of choice is that?"

Mindy sat back, arms folded across her chest. "Try this one—run away to Oxford to avoid dealing with past or stay in small town and risk finding true love and acceptance."

Taylor felt as if someone was tightening a tourniquet around her heart. "For a math teacher, you aren't very logical," she said. "Dylan and I agreed to a short-term fling. This doesn't mean anything more to him than it does to me."

"You haven't convinced me that it doesn't mean anything to you."

She had a sudden memory of Dylan tenderly drying her body with the gym towel, wrapping the thin terry cloth around her and pulling her close. He'd made her feel so cared for. So safe. So…loved. The band around her heart tightened another notch and she shook her head to rid it of the image. It was just part of the fantasy she'd conjured. The feelings she had for Dylan—whatever they truly were—couldn't possibly last. "I'm going to Oxford in January. That's where I belong. Dylan is staying here, where he belongs. Right now, we're just having a nice time together."

"The last part I believe, at least."

Time to change the subject. She leaned toward Mindy. "What were *you* doing walking out to the parking lot with

Clay Walsh last night? Are you two finally getting together?''

Mindy frowned. ''Not really. We were at the task-force meeting and he offered to walk me to my car. I thought maybe he was going to ask me out, but nothing happened.''

''Maybe he just needs a little encouragement. A little push in the right direction.''

She uncrossed her arms and smoothed her hands down her thighs. ''We're having supper next Friday. I told him I wanted to discuss some ideas I had for the task force, but really I'm hoping we can talk about *us*.''

''I think you should be up-front with him. Come right out and tell him how you feel.''

Mindy chewed her lower lip. ''What if he doesn't feel the same way about me? I'd be so embarrassed, I'd have to quit my job.''

''You won't have to quit your job.'' She smiled. ''I think Clay would be really pleased to know you're attracted to him. It could be that because you're younger and under his supervision, he's reluctant to make the first move.''

''I'll think about it.'' She stood. ''I guess I'd better get to class. I'm giving a test today.''

''Good luck.'' When Mindy was gone, Taylor sat at her desk and tried to focus on the day's lesson plan. But her advice to Mindy pricked her conscience. Here she was advising her friend to be honest about her attraction to Clay and Taylor herself hadn't been completely honest about her feelings for Dylan. She had to admit she couldn't think of him any longer as just a sex partner. Now that they had renewed their friendship, her feelings for him were a lot more complicated. She would have liked to explore those emotions more fully, but there wasn't time. All she could do was keep things on a superficial level and hope she could avoid being hurt too badly when the time came for them to part.

She opened the top left-hand drawer of her desk and took out the packet of information from Oxford. The front of the folder was embossed with a line drawing of the university. She smoothed her hand over the picture. When she'd gotten this information she'd been so excited. It had been the middle of summer then and the thought of a year in cool, green England, devoting herself to studying poetry and playing tourist, had seemed like paradise.

Only now, as the date of her departure loomed closer, did she think of another side of the picture. She was going to a country where she knew no one, to live alone in a rented flat. Would she be any more at home there than she was here in Cedar Creek? At least here she knew people, some of whom she'd even miss when she was gone.

There was a knock on the door and Clay Walsh leaned in. "I stopped by to see if you're all right after last night," he said.

"Yes, of course." She set aside the folder and forced a smile. What did Clay think about last night? Had he drawn his own conclusions and come here now to voice his disapproval? She braced herself to take the reprimand she probably deserved. She and Dylan had been crazy to do what they'd done on school property. At least she could count on Clay to keep their secret. The principal wasn't one to gossip.

"Grady Murphy stopped by just now and told me about the class project you're working on." He stopped and tapped the copy of *A Ranger Remembers* on her desk. "He wanted my opinion before he gave his approval."

She relaxed a little. Maybe Clay wasn't going to say

anything about last night, after all. "And what is your opinion?"

"I think it's a good idea. Something the students will benefit from. And the community, too."

"Does that mean I have approval, then?"

He nodded. "I think it does."

Her smile was genuine now. How nice to work for a principal who supported his teachers and trusted their judgment. Clay was good man. He deserved a good woman in his life, as well. "You just missed Mindy Lewis," she said, just to gauge his reaction.

He blinked and looked back over his shoulder, as if to catch a glimpse of the young teacher. "You and she are good friends, aren't you?"

"Yes, we are. Mindy's a pretty special woman, I think."

"Oh, I'm sure you're right." He drummed his fingers on the book, his expression thoughtful.

"She tells me the two of you are having supper next Friday."

"She told you that?" He looked surprised. "Yes, she said she had some ideas for the task force. I'm looking forward to hearing them."

Taylor smiled. "I'm sure you'll have a great time. Mindy's always fun to be with."

He looked uncomfortable, his gaze darting around her desk top. Finally he spotted the packet from Oxford. "You must be excited about the teaching fellowship," he said.

She nodded. "Yes. It's very exciting."

"We're all very proud of you, you know? It isn't every day a teacher from a small school like this wins such a prestigious appointment."

"Thank you."

"We should plan some sort of formal send-off for you. A reception or assembly."

"That really isn't necessary...."

"No, we really should do this." His expression brightened. "I'll ask Mindy. She'll know what to do."

"You do that." But he was already out of the room. She stared after him. Now that she was leaving, people wanted to make a big fuss over her? It didn't make any sense.

She shoved the packet back into the drawer. All she'd ever wanted was to blend in, to be accepted. Obviously that was never going to happen in a place like Cedar Creek.

BETWEEN SETTING UP his practice and running for office, Dylan had plenty of work to do. Unfortunately his brain refused to concentrate on anything but erotic memories of Taylor—in the shower at the gym, in the front seat of his truck, on the sofa in her living room. Not to mention less-erotic images of her smile, her laugh or the way she tilted her head to one side when she was thinking.

If his brain had been a TV, it would have been tuned to the All Taylor, All the Time network. And where his brain went, his body followed, so that he spent all his time with a hard-on. Not exactly good conditions for getting anything constructive done.

He couldn't remember ever obsessing over a woman this way and he didn't like it. He didn't like that even when he wasn't with her, she was still controlling his thoughts. He'd never thought of himself as a man ruled by his sex drive, but that's what he felt like now with Taylor. He'd left her only a few hours ago and he was ready to be with her again.

He was on edge not only from desire, but from his

chaotic emotions. Was Taylor his friend? His lover? A passing fancy or an enduring flame?

Determined to get something done, he pulled out a case file and forced himself to concentrate on a question of real estate law. Within a few minutes he was scribbling notes on a legal pad, plotting his defense of the case. He paused to pull a book from his shelf. When he opened it, a sheet of paper fluttered to the ground.

He retrieved the paper from the floor and found himself staring at a letter his father had sent while Dylan was in law school. Characteristic of his father, it was short and to the point.

Dear son,
I hope you're doing well. I'm sure you'll find some use for the enclosed check. Everything here is the same. The book is out and my publisher tells me they are pleased with sales. A few local folks have made a fuss, but I guess that means they are reading the thing, which is good. Your mother sends her love.

Love,
Dad.

The sight of his father's familiar handwriting made him catch his breath. He could almost see his dad, seated at the old desk in his study, scribbling these few lines to his son. *A few locals have made a fuss,* he'd written, reducing to a few words the irate letters to the editor, public protests at city council and school-board meetings and the banning of his book from the school library. How much that public derision must have hurt his father, a quiet, private man who had spent his life giving to the community, only to have his most personal gift thrown back in his face.

How much the memory hurt his son now. Dylan refolded the letter and replaced it in the book. If nothing else, he owed Taylor a debt of thanks for re-introducing his father's legacy to a new generation. Not that the move surprised him. Taylor had always put personal freedom ahead of public opinion. When rumors had circulated that a certain male student was gay and possibly suffering from AIDS, Taylor had made a point of going up to the boy in the lunch room and kissing him on the lips. Dylan had stood in the crowd that day, watching her, heart pounding. He'd been awed by her bravery and more than a little jealous that he wasn't the one she was kissing.

No wonder people were willing to believe she'd do all the wild things credited to her and Dylan. From what he could tell, she hadn't changed that much over the years. In public, perhaps, she was a little more reserved, but in private, she held nothing back. She sought and gave pleasure with equal abandon. When he was with her, he felt he really knew her, and himself, in a way he never had before.

He sank into the chair, lost once again in memory and fantasy. Maybe he'd have to wait until Taylor left the country before he got any real work done. A deep ache blossomed in the center of his chest at the thought. He didn't want her to go, but he was powerless to stop her. Going to Oxford was her dream, just as coming back to Cedar Creek had been his. No one had the right to steal someone else's dream.

He stared at the phone, wishing he could call her. Hearing her voice right now might make it easier to get through the day. But she was working right now. Teaching. He couldn't interrupt. What would he say, anyway? *I called just to talk?* Even as a besotted teenager he hadn't been that pathetic.

He sighed and picked up the legal pad again. Nothing like a riveting real estate law case to take your mind off a woman. Not.

Half an hour later the phone rang. Grateful for any distraction, Dylan lunched for it. "Hello?"

"Dylan, it's me, Taylor."

At the sound of her voice, it was as if someone cut a cord that had been wrapped too tightly around him. He relaxed into his chair, smiling. "I was just thinking about you."

"You were? Imagine that." Her voice was a sexy purr.

"I don't think I'll ever look at a shower the same way." He picked up a pencil and began turning it, end over end, in his hand.

She laughed. "It's safe to say I won't, either. I called to tell you our class project with your father's book has been approved."

"That's great. Dad would be happy."

"Are *you* happy with it?"

"Yes, I am." He laid aside the pencil. "I'll come speak to your class whenever you're ready."

"I'll have to look at my schedule and get back to you. I just thought you'd want to know it's a go."

He thought she might hang up then, and hurried to stop her. "Wait. When can we get together again?" He took a deep breath, telling himself to slow down. "I mean…you must have quite a few more rumors in that diary of yours."

"Hmm. I seem to recall a few more. There's no rush, though."

No rush. Except that he wasn't going to be good for anything if he didn't see her again. Soon. "No reason to waste any time, though."

"Unfortunately, I'm judging a speech tournament next

weekend. And I have some sort of meeting every night next week.''

''You couldn't take to your bed with a sudden cold?'' *And a certain school-board candidate to keep you warm?*

''We can get together next Friday evening.''

A week away. He drummed his fingers on his desk. Was she putting him off to send a message—reminding him she didn't intend to get too involved with him? ''All right. What time should I pick you up?''

''I'll meet you. You remember the old drive-in?''

''Didn't they close it down years ago?''

''It's been for sale for five or six years, but everything's pretty much the same, though deserted. Meet me there about eight o'clock.''

''We're not going to run into Pete Alavero again, are we?''

She laughed, a low, throaty chuckle that sent a bolt of heat straight to his groin. ''It's Friday night. Everyone in town will be at the football game. No one will bother us.''

''I'll be there.''

''See you there. And, Dylan?''

''Yes?''

''Better take your vitamins.''

10

MINDY STUDIED HER reflection in the mirror. The leather miniskirt and low-cut black sweater clung to her like shrink-wrap. Her new black satin Miracle Bra gave her cleavage where she'd never had cleavage before and the three-inch stiletto pumps and black silk stockings made her legs go on forever. She dared Clay Walsh to take one look at her and not think of her as a woman first and a teacher a distant second.

She smoothed the skirt over her hips and tucked an errant strand of hair behind her ear, then turned away from the mirror. She'd spent every moment of the past week anticipating this afternoon. If this didn't work, she was never going to be able to return to school again. She'd be so embarrassed she'd have to leave town, change her name and become a waitress or something. She'd never have the guts to face Clay again if she threw herself at him and he turned her down.

"Think positive," she told herself, reaching for her purse. "He's a man. You're an attractive woman. Nature will take care of the rest." She opened the little black handbag and double checked to make sure she had the essentials: vamp-red lipstick, breath mints, credit card, condoms. Everything she needed for an evening of seduction.

She locked the door behind her and picked her way down the gravel drive to the curb, where her car sat waiting, freshly washed and waxed, the top down. The red Jetta convertible was her one true extravagance. He hadn't said anything about her car when he'd walked her to it the other night, but then, they'd been distracted by Taylor and Dylan. She hoped Clay would think she was as wild as a red convertible implied.

He'd offered to meet her at a restaurant, but she'd insisted on picking him up. "There's a great place I want to take you," she'd said. "We can talk on the drive down."

Clay lived in a new complex west of town, in a nice but unremarkable town home. The kind of place a man lived when he was old enough to be tired of an apartment, but not yet ready to commit to owning a house, she thought. A house meant home and family, so maybe Clay was still looking for those things. She hoped so. The idea made her heart flutter.

She parked at the curb and walked up to the front door, her high heels tap-tapping on the brick pavers. Her stomach felt as though someone had let loose a hive of bees inside her. She rang the bell, then stepped back, trying to look calmer than she felt.

Clay was smiling when he opened the door, but the smile dropped off his face when he saw her. He stared, mouth slightly open, his gaze shifting from her chest to her legs, back to her chest and finally, reluctantly, settling on her face. "Mindy." He shut his mouth and swallowed. "Hello."

She pressed her lips together, holding back a smile, and managed to nod. "Hello, Clay. Are you ready for supper?"

He nodded, mute. She turned and led the way back to the car, conscious of the exaggerated sway of her hips in the tight skirt, aware of his gaze fixed on her. She walked around the car to the driver's side and slid in.

"Nice car," he said, settling into the passenger seat.

"When I saw it, I couldn't resist." She fit the key in the ignition and started the engine. "My motto is, 'life's too short not to have what you want.' In truth, she'd just made that up. But it sounded good, didn't it?

She pulled into the street and headed west, out of town. Clay shifted in the seat, as if he couldn't get comfortable. "So, how are your classes going this year?" he asked.

"They're going well. I have some really good students. A few problems, but nothing I can't handle." She shifted smoothly as they hit open highway and eased the gas peddle up to eighty. Wind whipped around them, making conversation difficult. That was okay. She wanted Clay to have plenty of time to look. To think. She shifted and the skirt rode higher up her thighs. She didn't bother to smooth it down. Anticipation hummed through her, in time with the throbbing of the car's powerful engine.

She glanced at her passenger out of the corner of her eye and found his gaze focused on her thigh. He wore a slightly dazed expression and was breathing heavily. Her smile widened. Why hadn't she thought of this approach before?

After about twenty minutes, Clay came out of his trance for a moment and looked around. "Where are we going?" he asked, raising his voice to be heard over the engine noise.

"I found this great little restaurant out in the country. We'll be able to talk in private there." The Hilltop Café was owned by a French chef who had once worked for the finest restaurants in Houston. His wife ran the attached bed-and-breakfast cottages, one of which Mindy had visited yesterday afternoon and reserved for tonight. She only hoped she hadn't wasted her hundred dollars.

Clay opened his mouth as if to protest, then closed it and sat back in the seat, staring out at the countryside. She hoped he wasn't having a crisis of conscience. After all, they hadn't done anything to feel guilty about—yet. *She* had no intentions of feeling guilty about anything they did. If only she could convince him to adopt the same attitude.

Ten minutes later she guided the car into the shaded drive of the Hilltop Café. Purple petunias and orange marigolds spilled from window boxes lining the front deck and larger urns of flowers flanked the doorway. "This looks great," Clay said as they exited the car.

"The man who owns it used to cook at the Four Seasons in Houston. He retired here and opens the place on weekends now."

An elegant woman in a black dress greeted them and showed them to a table by the window. It was almost six, early yet for dinner, so they had the dining room to themselves. Clay held her chair for her and she took her time settling in and arranging her napkin over her lap, aware of him standing over her, watching.

She picked up the wine list. "Why don't we order some wine?"

He frowned. "I don't know."

"Oh, it'll be all right. After all, we're off the clock now." The words sounded as reckless as she felt. She was going for broke here and why not? She'd tried being subtle and that hadn't worked. Maybe Taylor was right—some men required a more direct approach.

When the waitress came, she ordered a bottle of Pinot Grigio and the herb-roasted chicken. Clay chose the peppercorn fillet. "So," he said when they were alone again.

"What are some of the ideas you have for the task force?"

"We can talk business later." She gave him her warmest smile. "Why don't we enjoy a nice meal first?" She didn't want Clay to think about business or school tonight. She wanted him to focus on her. To look into her eyes and see her feelings for him.

"Oh. All right."

She sat back and looked out the window at the view of green countryside and flowers. "It's nice to get away from school for a while, isn't it?" she asked. "To get out of our roles of teacher and principal and be just two people, having a nice supper."

He didn't answer and she turned to find his gaze fixed on her, his eyes half closed, his expression unreadable. She leaned toward him, wanting to touch his hand, but hesitating. "I'd really like to get to know you better," she said.

"I'd like that," he said and those three words made her feel as if she could levitate out of her chair.

The waitress brought the wine and poured them each a glass. Clay raised his in a toast. "To friendship," he said.

She touched her glass to his. "To friendship." *And more,* she silently added. She smiled at him over the rim of her glass. "So tell me about yourself. How did you end up as principal of Cedar Creek High School?"

Over the next half hour, as they ate salad and crusty bread and drank wine, she learned that he was from Corpus Christi on the Texas coast, that he had majored in history at the University of Texas and taught in Houston for ten years before moving to Cedar Creek to take a job as assistant principal and eventually principal at the high school.

"That must have been a big change for you, moving from a big city to a small town like this," she said.

He shrugged and stabbed at his salad. "After my divorce, I was ready for a change of scenery."

The arrival of their meals allowed her to hide her shock at this revelation. But of course, it wouldn't be that unusual for a man his age to have been married before. "Do you have children?" she asked, half afraid of the answer.

"Two boys. They live with their mother in Houston. I see them in the summer and one weekend a month."

Two boys. Oh, wow. She'd never dated anyone with children before. What would that be like? But she would handle it. Of course she would. She smiled. "Tell me about your sons."

By the time their plates were cleared, she knew all about Brian, who was twelve, and Josh, who was fourteen. She knew that Clay was a football fan, that he'd once been a rodeo team roper and even had a silver belt buckle he'd won at a Fourth of July rodeo. She knew that his parents had a ranch near Corpus Christi, that he enjoyed his job but sometimes missed teaching and that he was allergic to strawberries—he asked they be left off the cheesecake he ordered for dessert.

She knew everything about him but the one thing she most wanted to know—how did he feel about her?

"You've let me do all the talking," he said, stirring cream into his coffee. "Tell me something about Mindy Lewis."

"There's not a lot to tell." She tore the end off a package of artificial sweetener and watched the white powder drift into her cup. "I'm twenty-four, single. I teach algebra, like to ride my bike or swim, love dogs but can't have one in my apartment." She shrugged. "Not terribly exciting, I'm afraid."

He looked at her for a long moment, not saying anything. She felt warmed by that gaze. What would he do if she leaned across the table and kissed him? Would he think she'd gone crazy? "You said the other night you aren't seeing anyone," he said. "Mind if I ask why?"

She swallowed. "Have you checked out the staff of the high school lately? Not a lot of eligible bachelors there. And that's about all the men I meet."

He nodded. "But there are other single men in town. Parents of your students…"

She made a face. "That would be…complicated. Don't you think?" She pushed aside her coffee cup and leaned toward him. "There is one man who interests me, but I don't know if he even notices me."

The lines around his eyes tightened and he pressed his lips together as his gaze dropped to her cleavage once more. "I don't think you're the kind of woman who goes unnoticed by men. Not unless they're blind."

"He's not blind." She wet her lips, eyes locked to his. "But we come from different backgrounds."

"I wouldn't think that would make much difference these days."

The waitress brought the check and he turned away from her, reaching for his wallet. "No, I invited you," she protested. "I'll pay."

But he was already counting money out of his wallet and rising. "We'd better go," he said.

He walked out of the restaurant, leaving her standing by the table. She stared after him, her confusion quickly overcome by anger. What was *wrong* with him? How dare he walk out on her like that!

She stalked to the door, stopping at the ladies' room on her way out. She took her time, using the toilet, washing her hands, then combing her hair and touching up her makeup. She studied the results in the mirror. She looked hot! Clay Walsh ought to be thanking his lucky stars she wanted to spend the evening with him. He ought to be doing everything in his power to prolong the encounter instead of cutting her short that way.

She turned on her heel and stalked out of the rest room, intending to give him a piece of her mind.

She found him by the car, leaning against the front fender, arms folded over his chest, gaze fixed on the door of the restaurant. When she came out, he straightened but didn't alter his irritated expression. She walked up to him, stopping only a few inches away. To move, he'd have to push her out of the way. "What was that all about?" she asked.

"What was what all about?"

"You walking out like that, in the middle of our conversation."

His gaze slid away from her. "I didn't think we had anything else to talk about."

"Maybe you didn't, but I did."

"Look, I'm sorry." He spoke the words through clenched teeth. "But I don't think I'm qualified to give you advice on your love life."

"Oh, yeah? Who says I was asking?"

He frowned. "In there…I thought…"

"Dammit, Clay! You think too much! Why don't you try just *feeling* for a change?" She put her hands on either side of his face and stood on tiptoe, pulling his lips to hers. She put everything she had into that kiss—anger, passion, hurt, and the longing she'd carried inside of her for months. She wanted him to remember this moment. Even if things didn't work out between them, he would never forget that kiss.

For a split second they stood frozen in time in an awkward embrace, lips together. Then whatever lock he'd put on his emotions broke and he put his arms around her and gathered her close. His lips parted, deepening the kiss, his tongue sweeping across hers, sensuous and skillful.

She molded her body to his, feeling the hard planes of his chest, the muscles of his thighs, the thick heat of his erection. Blood pounded in her ears as she struggled to be closer still.

His hands were everywhere, smoothing down her back, squeezing her buttocks, caressing her breasts. He trailed kisses down her throat, along her collarbone, each touch of his tongue and lips sending a searing wave through her. He kissed the top of her breasts, then pulled at the sweater, revealing the lace-trimmed satin of her bra. He slipped his hand beneath her skirt and cupped her bottom. "Do you know how many times I've watched you walk down the hall and fantasized about seeing you naked?" he murmured. "When I saw you standing on my doorstep in this outfit, I thought I would lose it, right there in front of you. It was all I could do not to drag you into the house right then."

"You should have." She arched against him, shock waves of arousal spreading through her as he slid his thumb under the edge of her bra and began to fondle her nipple.

"I should have. Then we wouldn't be looking at a forty-minute drive back to my place." He unsnapped the front hook of the bra, freeing her breasts. "Frankly, I don't know if I can wait."

Any answer she could have made was replaced by a low moan as his mouth closed over her nipple. If he'd laid her back across the hood of the car and taken her right then, in the deepening dusk, she wouldn't have cared.

With a groan, he dragged himself upright once more and gently pulled her sweater back into place. "We'd better go," he said. "Before we embarrass ourselves even more."

She smiled and took his hand in hers. "We don't have to go."

"Yes, we do."

She shook her head, then reached into her purse and fished out a key. "I have a room."

His eyes widened. "Where?"

"Here." She nodded toward the row of cottages behind the restaurant. "Number six."

He grabbed her hand and pulled her toward the cottages. "Let's go."

She laughed. "Slow down. I can't walk fast in these heels."

The next thing she knew, he'd swept her into his arms and was carrying her toward the cottage. She pressed her head against his shoulder, holding back laughter. An incredible feeling of happiness welled up in her, almost too much to contain. *Thank you, Taylor,* she thought. *I hope you're having as wonderful a time this weekend as I am.*

FRIDAY AFTERNOON, Taylor decided to stay at school to grade the essays her students had turned in. She had four hours to kill before she met Dylan at the drive-in. She told herself grading papers would make the time pass faster, but that proved a lie. With the quiet of the empty school wrapping around her, she was reminded of the night she had been here with Dylan, sneaking through the darkened hallways to the boys' locker room. She smiled at the memory, a warm buzz of arousal humming through her.

Thoughts of that encounter led to anticipation of her

plans for tonight. She could hardly wait to see Dylan's reaction when she told him what she had in mind. Even she couldn't believe she was going to be so daring.

With a sigh, she forced her attention back to the papers. She had work to do and she couldn't let thoughts of Dylan keep her from it. Hadn't she purposely stayed away from him for the past week, in an attempt to get her life back on an even keel? When she'd come up with the idea of reenacting all those old fantasies, she'd never imagined it would be so...distracting.

After slogging her way through four papers in an hour, she was ready to give up. Maybe she should call him and suggest they meet earlier....

A knock on the door startled her. She looked up and thought for a moment her imagination had gotten the better of her. Dylan was standing in the doorway, dressed in a blue suit, his tie loosened at his throat, a briefcase in his hand. Her heart raced and she smiled and rose from her chair. "Dylan!"

His smile hit her with one hundred watts of sex appeal. Her knees went weak and she had to sit down again. She remembered now why she'd been avoiding him. When he was around, she couldn't think clearly. Not a good sign when the whole point was to keep their relationship casual.

Or as casual as it could be considering they were having the most mind-blowing sex of her life. "Dylan, hello. What are you doing here?"

"I need your help with something." He sauntered to her desk and set the briefcase alongside her student papers. "I have to come up with a slogan for my campaign posters. I thought—you're an English teacher—you're good with words. And I'm desperate."

She laughed. "How many times did I hear those words

when we were kids? You were always desperate for help with your homework.''

''And you were always willing to help.'' He grabbed a chair, pulled it alongside her desk and sat facing her. ''Come on. If you don't help, I'll be stuck with the slogan Troy Sommers came up with.''

''You asked Troy Sommers before you asked me?'' She faked a hurt look.

''Troy's my campaign manager. But he sucks at slogans.''

''So what did he come up with?''

A pained look crossed his face. ''Do It With Dylan.''

She choked back laughter. ''Oh, my—that's really bad.''

''Troy thinks it's young and hip. I tried to tell him it's just stupid. He challenged me to come up with something better, but so far, I've failed.''

''Maybe we should focus on the issues. What platform are you running on?''

He frowned. ''I just want to do the best job I can for the kids, but Troy convinced me we have to have something the public can latch on to, so we settled on the idea that in my administration I intend to focus on the educational needs of the students—a focus on fundamentals with more money in the budget for libraries and computer labs, as well as some freebie things like public recognition of students' contributions to the community and appointment of student liaisons to work with the school board.''

Taylor let out a low whistle. ''Ambitious.''

He grinned. ''Not too much, I hope.''

''No. I like your ideas. A lot of voters will, too.'' She shifted into a more comfortable position. ''One exercise I do with my students is brainstorming.'' She opened a desk drawer and took out a legal pad. ''We write down whatever comes to mind. It doesn't matter how silly it is, the idea is to come up with a lot of material to work with.''

''At this point, I'm willing to try anything.''

She picked up a pen. ''Okay, so 'Do It With Dylan' is out. How about 'Dylan Gets It Done'?''

''Or 'A Done Deal With Dylan.'''

'''Dylan Does It Right.'''

He nodded. ''Or 'Dylan Does It Left,' depending on your political views.''

'''Don't Delay—Vote Dylan Today.'''

'''Decide On Dylan.'''

'''Dylan For Destiny.'''

He made a pantomime of sticking his finger down his throat. ''I'm beginning to hate my own name.''

She studied the sheet of paper. ''We could go with your last name. 'Get With Gates' or 'Go With Gates.'''

He made a face. ''Worse.'' He craned his neck to study the paper. ''Maybe I'll give Troy a list and let him choose. 'Dylan Gets It Done' doesn't sound quite as horrible as the rest.''

She laughed and pushed the paper away. ''I can see neither of us has a future on Madison Avenue.''

''That's all right.'' He leaned back in the chair, relaxed. ''I'm happy to stick it out in Cedar Creek for the next fifty years or so.''

Her throat tightened at this reminder that he would be staying here while she was going away. No matter how much she tried to live in the moment, some reminder of the future always intruded, didn't it? ''Are you getting settled in downtown?''

''Finally. I hired a secretary and that's helped.''

''Oh? Who did you hire?''

''Anita Brandtley. She used to be a clerk in the judge's office, so she has legal experience.''

"I had Anita in my class my first year teaching here. She's a very nice girl. Very smart, too."

He nodded. "I think she'll work out. And I'm starting to get a few cases, so I guess I won't starve."

"Speaking of starving…" She glanced at the clock, startled to find it was already five-thirty. "I didn't have lunch. Would you like to go somewhere and get a bite to eat?"

"Sure. We can go out to dinner, then swing by the drive-in. There's no need to take separate cars."

She hesitated. Her idea to spend as little time with him as possible wasn't working out. But really, there was nothing wrong with two friends having dinner together, was there? "Let's go in my car. I'll bring you back to your truck later."

"All right. I'll let you chauffeur me around."

She stood and gathered up the student papers and some other work she needed to take home. "Where do you want to go?"

"I saw a place last night, out on the highway. Mama Lena's?"

She nodded. "I've been there before. It's good."

It had been a while since she'd been to Mama Lena's however, and she'd forgotten how blatantly romantic the little Italian bistro was. From the private booths and red-shaded candles to the soft violin music playing in the background, Mama Lena's was a classic "date" restaurant. This being Friday night, it was packed with couples eating out before the big game.

As they stood in the foyer, waiting for their table, Taylor was aware of dozens of eyes focused on them. No doubt everyone was speculating what the teacher and the lawyer were up to. She raised her chin and focused her eyes straight ahead. Let them wonder. Their wildest imaginings couldn't come close to the truth this time.

"Hello, Dylan. Taylor."

"Good to see you, Dylan. You, too, Taylor."

"Good luck with your campaign." People greeted them from all sides as they followed the hostess toward an empty booth. Dylan smiled and shook hands while Taylor held back. Was this sudden friendliness because of Dylan or merely because people were curious?

She settled herself across from Dylan in the booth and opened the menu. "No one would know you've been away ten years," she said. "People still love you."

"I've renewed a lot of old friendships since I came back."

Did she imagine the significance of the look he gave her? She looked down at the menu, not really seeing anything listed there. "I think you're a shoo-in to win the election."

"Nothing is certain in politics or so they tell me." He closed the menu and set it aside. "I'm excited about the election, though. It's what I've always wanted—to come back here and be involved in things. I couldn't really do that in L.A. Things are on too large a scale there."

"It is easier to be a part of things in a small town." She took a sip of water. "But it can be harder, too. Once you're labeled as a certain type of person—a troublemaker or a do-gooder or whatever—it's difficult to break out of that mold."

He frowned. "Is that why you're leaving? Because you think you've been labeled?"

"I'm the Wild Woman. The California Girl." She shrugged. "I'm not even saying I don't deserve the reputation."

"Of course you don't deserve it." The vehemence in

his voice startled her. "Besides, you're not a girl anymore. You're a talented woman. A teacher. Someone with a lot to offer this town."

His praise made her feel soft inside. Vulnerable. She looked away. "I'll admit, people have paid a lot more attention since I was awarded the fellowship to Oxford. There was even a write-up in the paper."

"That's important, isn't it? For people to notice you? To respect your accomplishments?"

"Everyone likes to be thought well of."

The waitress came and took their orders. When they were alone again, Taylor studied Dylan through veiled lashes. What would he do after she was gone? A man as handsome and charming as him wouldn't be alone for long. Which woman would he end up with? Would he do with her the things he did with Taylor?

She reached for her water glass, wanting to drown out the thoughts. Sadness dragged at her and sudden tears stung her eyes. Why had she ever taken that path? Time to think of happier thoughts. "Have you been out to the old drive-in since you got back in town?" she asked.

He shook his head. "No. Until you told me, I figured it had been torn down." He grinned. "I'm looking forward to seeing it again tonight. With you."

She leaned toward him, her smile purposely seductive. "I've got very special plans for us tonight. Something you'll like, I promise."

"I'd like anything with you, Taylor. You ought to know that by now."

His words were an arrow, piercing her heart. She squeezed her eyes shut. *No,* she thought. *Don't get all serious and romantic now. I can stand anything but that.*

11

AS SOON AS THEY were in the door of the cottage, Mindy fell onto the bed with Clay, their bodies entwined. His kisses left her dizzy. Delirious. She grabbed at his shirt, pulling it free of his pants. "You're wearing too many clothes."

"So are you." He shoved the sweater up over her bra, then shoved the bra down, framing her breasts in fabric. Cupping her in his hands, he kissed first one breast and then the other, licking and suckling, teasing her distended nipples with his tongue until she was incoherent with need.

She grabbed at his tie, tugging vainly at it, trying to loosen the knot. He raised his head and jerked it loose, then sent it sailing across the room. It was followed quickly by his shirt, the starched white cotton billowing and floating like a kite before settling to the floor.

She wrapped her arms and legs around him, pulling him close, savoring the feel of her breasts against his chest.

He rolled them over onto their sides and glided his hand up her leg, up under her skirt and across her thigh, coming to rest between her legs. "You're soaking wet," he growled.

"Maybe you should do something about that." Eyes locked to his, she raked her fingernail up the length of his zipper, watching as his eyes dilated and darkened with arousal.

With a grunt, he rolled away from her and stood. With a few swift movements he stripped off socks, shoes, belt, pants and underwear, until he was standing in front of her, naked. She lay back against the pillows, sighing with satisfaction. He was gorgeous, in the way a man should be—all hard planes and muscle. There was nothing flashy or phony about him, but he was one hundred percent sexy male.

She rolled over onto one hip and lowered the zipper on her skirt. He watched, mesmerized, as she stripped out of shoes, hose and shirt. "I can see my fantasies didn't do you justice," he said, kneeling beside her.

"So you were fantasizing about me? But you never let on."

"I didn't think a young woman like you would be interested in an old man like me."

"You're not old."

"I'm fifteen years older than you. And I'm your boss."

"If I cared about that, I wouldn't be here now."

He sat beside her, one hand caressing her hip. "Now probably isn't the best time to bring this up, but you do realize us being here together could cause problems."

Her breath caught. "What kind of problems?"

"People might think I was granting you special favors."

She let her gaze rest on his impressive erection. "I'm hoping you'll grant me lots of special favors."

"Besides those."

She looked him in the eye again. "I don't see why either one of us has to behave any differently at school than we do now."

He frowned. "What are you saying?"

"I'm saying, there's nothing wrong with keeping our relationship to ourselves." She stroked her hand down his arm. "Cedar Creek is a hotbed of gossip, so why open ourselves up to that? We can still see each other. We just need to be…discreet."

"You mean, we'll have to sneak around."

"It could be…exciting. Don't you think?"

He shook his head. "I don't know what to think."

She slid her hand up his thigh and came to rest around his penis. "Then don't think anymore. Just feel."

He reached for her, but she pushed him back. "Wait. Get my purse."

He retrieved her purse from the bedside table and handed it to her. She opened it and took out the condom.

"You think of everything." He slid down to lie beside her. "That's a big turn-on, you know? A woman who takes charge."

"I'll have to remember that." She pulled him to her and they kissed again. A long, deep, searing kiss she felt with every part of her body. It was a kiss that telegraphed urgent need, but spoke of a willingness to wait. To drag out their pleasure to its most satisfying end.

She broke the kiss and smiled at him. "So you like a woman who takes charge?"

He nodded.

She pushed him onto his back. "Like this?" She straddled his thighs, her legs spread wide, exposing herself completely to him.

He looked up at her, eyes dark with passion, focused on her swaying breasts. "I could get used to this."

She bent and kissed his chest, circling his nipple with her tongue, feeling it tighten against her mouth. She did the same to the other nipple, his breath hard and fast in her ear. She stroked her hand down his stomach, the muscles tightening at her touch, and trailed her fingers to his hot, hard shaft.

When she touched him, he groaned, the blatant need in the sound sending melting heat through her. She wrapped her hand around him, sliding up and down, feeling him pulse in her hand.

With her other hand, she found the condom and tore the packet with her teeth. Carefully she sheathed him, already anticipating him inside her.

He grasped her hips and helped guide her over him. She moaned as he filled her, feeling herself tense around him, caressing him. Then they were both moving, thrusting and withdrawing, their movements no longer languid and in control. She planted her hands on his chest and rode him hard, driving herself onto him, desire ripping through her, spiraling upward.

She screamed as her climax took her and he grasped her bottom and drove into her once more, letting out a guttural cry as he came. She collapsed onto him and they clung together, panting, dazed and sated.

She closed her eyes and smiled. What did it matter if they had to keep their relationship secret, if they had this?

"I CAN'T BELIEVE they haven't torn this place down," Dylan said as Taylor guided the car across the rutted lot of the old drive-in.

"It's been for sale for a number of years. There's talk now of preserving it as some kind of historical landmark."

"It's a landmark, all right." He looked around, at the leaning speaker stands and the faded screen stretching to the sky in front of them. "I had a lot of fun times here. When I was a kid, my parents would load all of us into the back of my dad's truck with a bunch of pillows and quilts. We'd play on the playground until the movie started, then pile up in the truck to watch the show. When I was little, I'd be asleep before the first reel ended.''

"And when you were older, did you come out here with girls?''

He raised his hands. "I plead the fifth on that one.'' He glanced at her. "What about you? Did you come out here with boys?''

She shook her head. "No one ever asked me.''

Her voice was matter-of-fact, but his chest tightened as she said the words. *I should have asked you,* he thought. *Why didn't I?*

She pulled the car to a stop in the front row, a few feet from the remains of a rail fence that separated the area directly under the screen from the rest of the lot. She shut off the engine and unfastened her seat belt.

"Now what?'' He turned toward her, anticipation setting his nerves on edge. Whatever she had planned for them, he had no doubt it would be enjoyable.

She took her diary from her purse and handed it to him. "Read the page I've marked.''

He reached up and flipped on the map light, then opened the diary to a page she'd marked with a few inches of ribbon. "*December eighth.* Is that the right entry?''

She nodded. "Read it out loud.''

He squinted at the page and cleared his throat. "*I swear, the people in this school must be on drugs or something. How else do they come up with such crazy ideas? When I got to my locker today, Alyson couldn't wait to ask me how I liked the show Saturday night.*

"*'I'll admit, I fell right into her trap. 'What show?' I asked.*

"*'The movie, silly!' She punched my arm. Actually punched my arm! She's lucky she didn't draw back a nub!''* He laughed and glanced at her. "You were a feisty thing, weren't you?"

"Only in my thoughts." She nodded toward the diary. "Keep reading."

He found his place on the page again. *"'Of course, you didn't really see much of the show, did you?' Alyson said. Then she doubled over in that awful laugh of hers. It sounds like she inhaled a broken accordion. 'Everyone else got to see the show* you *put on, didn't they?'*

"I told her she wasn't making any sense and walked away, but of course, that wasn't the end of it. The minute I sat down in history class, Evan Stevenson and his buddies, Mark and Steve, started nudging each other and laughing.''

He glanced at her again. "Those three stooges always were losers."

She nodded. "But they were football players, so they were still popular."

What could he say to that? It was true. In a town where football was king, playing on the team automatically made you somebody. He turned the page and continued reading. *"Finally, I couldn't stand it anymore. I whirled around in my seat and glared at them. 'What is so funny, you morons?' I said.*

"They just laughed all the more. Then Alyson took her seat across from me. 'Don't you know everyone saw what you did Saturday? You only thought everyone had gone home. But lots of people stayed around to see what would happen and they saw you.'

"'I was home Saturday night,' I told her. 'I'm always home on Saturday night. What else is new?'"

Guilt pinched him again. Where had he been that Saturday night? Out with friends? With another girl? Whoever it was, likely he'd really wanted to be with Taylor. Why had he been so stupid back then?

"Go on," she prompted.

He nodded. *"She just smirked and shook her head. 'You're a lousy liar. Ricky Anderson told me himself that he saw you standing up there in front of the drive-in screen, big as life, taking off all your clothes while Dylan sat in the car watching.'*

"I stared at her. I tell you, I was seconds away from leaping out of my desk and ripping that smug look off her face with my fingernails when Mrs. Solis walked in and said it was time to start class.

"After first period, I told the nurse I was sick and called my mom to come and get me. How in the world am I ever going to go back and face those morons?"

"That's enough." She reached out and closed the book.

She had a funny look on her face. Maybe hearing those words again had brought back all the old pain of that time. She could pretend the old taunts didn't bother her anymore, but if that was the case, why were they even here, attempting to banish those old demons? He reached for her. "I wish I'd known they were saying all those things to you. I guess I was pretty stupid and oblivious."

She shook her head and gently pushed him away. "We were kids. We didn't know anything."

"Still, I hate thinking they were so cruel." He frowned. "And I was cruel, too, for doing nothing."

"Hey, I didn't come out here to beat you over the head with past mistakes." She smoothed her hand down his arm. "I came here to have a little fun with what might have been."

A shiver crept over him as he stared into her eyes and remembered the words in her diary. "A striptease?" he asked.

She nodded and fingered the top button of her blouse. "Do you want to watch?"

The words sent white heat lacing through him, along with a kaleidoscope of erotic images. He wet his lips and nodded. "Yeah. I'd like that. A lot."

She pushed against his chest, pressing him back against the seat. "Then sit back and relax. I think we'll both enjoy this."

SHE WAS A LITTLE NERVOUS at first, standing out there in the open. The lot was empty, leaning speaker stands dotted across the gravel like bizarre shrubs. The only sounds were the pinging of the car's cooling engine and the rattle of cicadas in the trees by the broken-down concession stand. She looked up at the stars scattered across the sky like silver glitter. She felt small against all the vastness. Vulnerable.

The trick was to take that vulnerability and to turn it into strength. To take her nakedness and turn it into power. Wasn't that the whole point of this—to take a bad time in her life and turn it into something good? To learn how to risk a little in order to gain so much more?

She looked toward the car. In the darkness, she could only see the outline of Dylan as he sat in the passenger seat. She reached for the top button of her shirt.

"I can't see you," he said.

She hesitated. "You could turn on the headlights, but I think they'd blind me."

"We need something else for light. Do you have a flashlight?"

Why hadn't she thought of that before? "There might be something in the trunk."

He got out of the car, keys in hand and walked around to open the trunk. A moment later he emerged with a heavy-duty light, the kind they used on boats. She vaguely recalled her father giving it to her. She didn't think she'd ever turned it on.

Dylan balanced the light atop the rail fence and aimed it at her. It cast a halo of yellow light around her. "There you go, madame." He executed a stiff bow, then strode back to the car.

Take two. She faced the car again, trying to center herself, to get into the mood. Dylan had seen her naked before, after all—though not quite so well-lighted. Suddenly she was aware of every flaw in her body. Would he notice? Would he care?

She wished she could see him. Then again, maybe it was better if she couldn't. She could use her imagination, the most powerful aphrodisiac of all.

She kicked off her shoes, then reached up and began to unbutton her blouse. She moved slowly, focusing on the way the slight breeze puckered her nipples and raised the hair on her arms, on the fullness in her groin and the humming of blood in her temples. She felt the power of her sexuality moving through her, making her heart race and her spirits soar.

Music burst into the silence, startling her, then she smiled. It was an exotic, Irish air, one of the CDs from her own collection. Why hadn't she thought of music before? It helped to have some rhythm to move to, something to help set the mood.

She began to sway, turning all the way around, arms out to the side, her open blouse flaring, then falling to her side, giving glimpses of her lacy bra. She concentrated on paying attention to the way her body moved, the interplay of muscle and skin, the sensation of cool air on bare flesh, of fabric brushing against her.

She stopped turning and faced forward again, looking

toward the shadowy interior of the car. Imagination was a powerful thing. She had no trouble imagining Dylan watching her, his eyes dilated with desire, his mouth slack.

Leaving her blouse on, the front open, she turned her back to him and eased open the zipper of her skirt. Bending forward, she slid the skirt down over her buttocks, moving slowly, revealing herself to him inch by inch.

"You have the most beautiful ass." His voice drifted to her, disembodied. "I get a hard-on watching you walk down the hall."

She was instantly wet, tension building between her thighs. With an exaggerated swivel of her hips, she faced forward once more and let the blouse slide off her shoulders. She focused her eyes where she thought he might be, imagining how he must look, letting him see how much she wanted him.

She began to sway again, shimmying, each movement sending the blouse sliding farther toward the ground. It fell, leaving her in her bra, garter belt and hose, black silk thong. It was underwear designed to seduce. Wearing it, she'd felt incredibly sexy.

She reached back and unfastened the bra and slipped it off her shoulders. Her breasts fell free, swaying slightly. They felt heavy and tight, the nipples swollen, aching. A slight breeze brushed across her, arousing her further.

She turned her back to the car once more and slid her thumbs under the edge of the thong. She bent over, butt in the air, and slid the scrap of silk toward her ankles.

"Spread your legs."

She did so, feeling the breeze over her clit like a lover's breath. She wondered what he was doing while he watched her. Was he touching himself? The thought aroused her further.

"Turn around again," he said. "I want to see you."

She did as he asked and reached up to touch her aching breasts, holding them. She heard the sharp intake of his breath. She closed her eyes, telling herself not to think about anything, to just feel. Do what feels good. She covered her breasts with her hands, brushing her palms across her aching nipples.

"Yesss," he hissed.

Continuing to sway to the music, she reached down and unsnapped one garter. She propped her foot on the rail fence, the makeshift spotlight aimed directly at her sex. With agonizing slowness, she rolled down the stocking, her skin paper-white against the black silk. The musk of her arousal mingled with the scent of dusty sage.

She changed position and removed the other stocking, then stood and unsnapped the garter belt. When she straightened, she was completely naked. She grew still, hands at her sides, waiting. "Come here," she said.

The door of the car thrust open and Dylan emerged, removing his shirt as he walked toward her, kicking off his shoes. She helped him out of his pants and briefs, stripping them down his muscular legs, aware of his erection pointing at her.

He pulled her close, wrapping his arms around her, bending her head back with the force of his kiss. One hand on her breast, he reached the other down between her legs, parting the folds, sinking his finger into her, stroking, caressing, driving her mad with wanting. "I'm going to make you come until you scream," he whispered, his lips against the corner of her mouth.

She nodded and all but whimpered, arching against his hand. He grew still, his finger still inside her, and lowered his head to her breasts. She moaned, weak-kneed with wanting, barely able to stand.

"Turn around." He put his hands at her waist and turned her back to him. "Put your hands on the hood of the car."

She did as he asked, bracing herself with her palms flat against the car hood. He nudged her legs farther apart with his knee, then put his arms around her. He caressed her breasts, rolling her nipples between his thumb and forefinger. She pressed her back against his chest, his erection nestled against her buttocks.

He wrapped his arm around her waist, holding her tightly against him, and slipped two fingers of the other hand into her once more. She groaned, straining against him. "Dylan, please!"

"Shh, just a minute. Don't move." She felt cold as he moved away from her and began to shake from more than the chill in the air. She was so close to coming she felt the breeze itself might send her over the edge.

Dimly, she was aware of the sound of the condom packet being torn, then she felt the head of his penis nudging at her. He reached around to caresses her breasts, lightly pinching her nipples. He slid into her and she tightened around him, smiling at the different sensation created by this new angle.

He began to move and she braced herself against the car once more, surrendering to wave after wave of desire washing over her. He thrust deep within her, then withdrew slowly, his hands caressing her breasts, until every nerve was on fire for him.

He leaned forward and began to kiss the back of her neck, the tenderness of the gesture sending her over the edge. A scream tore from her throat as her climax crashed through her, going on for what seemed like minutes. She was dimly aware of him following her, the force of his thrusts pressing her against the car. Then he slipped out of her and turned her to face him once more, holding her tightly against him, his face buried against her neck.

"Th-that was incredible," she gasped.

"You're incredible," he murmured, crushing her to him. "I..."

She put her hand to his lips, afraid of what he might be about to say. She didn't want to talk about feelings now. She didn't want to talk about anything. She wanted to close her eyes and savor the moment, to pretend there was nothing before, or after, to worry about.

12

MONDAY WAS A DAY of revelations for Taylor. At times she wondered if somewhere between going to bed Sunday night and arriving at school to begin a week of classes, she'd slipped into an alternate universe, one where no one behaved the way she expected them to.

It started with Grady Murphy stopping by her classroom before first period. "I just wanted to let you know I've approved Dylan's dad's book for your class project," he said.

"Thanks." Of course, Clay had already given her this news, but as department head, Grady had every right to deliver it himself. "My class will be excited to hear it."

Grady lingered, rocking back and forth on his heels, sliding one hand along the edge of her desk. She braced herself for some probing question or cutting remark about her relationship with Dylan. "Is there something else?"

"Yeah." He picked up the blown-glass paperweight her mother had sent for her birthday and examined it, then put it back down. His eyes met hers. "I wanted you to know—I think you've got a lot of guts taking on a project like this."

Her mouth dropped open. "Y-you do?"

"Yeah." He folded his arms over his chest. "I've thought a lot about what you said the other day, about what we're really supposed to be teaching these kids."

He shook his head. "Sometimes in the middle of all the paperwork and politics, we lose sight of that."

"Yeah." She stared at him, as if seeing him—*really* seeing him—for the first time. The man in front of her wasn't a loser or an ex-jock who was still clinging to his high school glory days. He was a teacher, like her. Someone who cared about his students and his job. The revelation shook her. "Yeah, I guess we do."

He straightened. "Anyway, I wanted you to know, I'll back you up if you get any flack from any parents or any of the people in town."

"Thank you, Grady. I—I really appreciate that."

"Yeah, well, that's my job, isn't it?"

The first bell rang, breaking whatever spell had been cast over them. Grady rolled his shoulders and was transformed to the Grady she knew. Or thought she knew. "I'd better get going. If I'm not there those junior boys are liable to break into my desk and steal a copy of next week's test."

When he was gone, she sank into her chair and stared after him. What had just happened here? Had she glimpsed the real Grady Murphy or only a mirage? Could she have been wrong about him all these years?

Her second world-tilting moment came after third period, when Alyson stopped her in the hallway outside the library. "Hello, Taylor. Did you have a nice weekend?"

For a moment Taylor was back in high school, standing beside her locker while Alyson asked this familiar, loaded question. She stared at her older but eerily unchanged former classmate, looking for the poison barb she was sure was waiting on the other side of her answer.

But the snideness she remembered from high school was gone from Alyson's voice now and her heavily made-up eyes held no guile. "I had a nice weekend," Taylor said. "Those Friday afternoons off are always a welcome change." Especially considering how she'd spent her Friday afternoon and evening.

"You're still seeing Dylan, right?"

Here it comes, Taylor thought, stiffening. "Yes? What about it?" Had someone seen them—seen her—at the drive-in and reported the news around town?

"Hey, I didn't say there was anything wrong with that, did I?" Alyson shifted her clipboard to her other arm. "I was wondering if the two of you would be interested in chaperoning the Homecoming Dance weekend after next? I need another couple of adults."

"The Homecoming Dance?" Taylor had forgotten that one of the high school's social events of the year was fast approaching. She'd purposely put it out of her mind. She'd spent her own homecoming making fudge and watching old movies, trying not to think about Dylan at the dance with another girl.

"So, will you do it?"

Alyson's question pulled her back to the present. Go to homecoming with Dylan? Why not? She smiled. "I'll have to ask Dylan, but I think so."

Alyson smiled. "Great. Let me know soon as you can."

She turned to leave but Taylor stopped her. "Alyson?"

Alyson looked back over her shoulder. "Yes."

"Thanks. Thanks for asking me."

"Sure. I thought the two of you would be perfect." She grinned. "Just like old times, huh?"

But this time, the familiar comment didn't have the sting it had before. Had Alyson's attitude changed over one weekend—or had Taylor's? Had being with Dylan transformed her somehow, so that she was seeing the people around her through different eyes?

She was eating lunch at her desk when Mindy came in.

The normally bubbly blond looked dazed, her hair un-styled, dark circles beneath her eyes. Taylor rose to pull a chair over to the desk for her. "What happened to you?" she asked. "Did you have a rough weekend?"

Mindy sank into the chair and flashed a weary smile. "Sort of. But in a good way." She blushed to the roots of her hair.

Taylor sat again and leaned toward her friend. "What happened?" Then she remembered Mindy's plans for the weekend. "Did you have supper with Clay on Friday? Tell me what happened. And don't leave anything out."

Mindy tucked her hair behind her ears and smoothed her skirt over her thighs. "I did what you suggested. I came right out and told him how I felt." A sly smile stole across her lips. "Or I guess you could say I showed him."

"What?" Taylor's heart raced. "What did he say? What did he do?"

Mindy pleated the fabric of her skirt with her fingers. "I—I kissed him. And…one thing led to another…." She giggled. "It was incredible. He's incredible."

Taylor leaned over to hug her close. "What did I tell you? I'm so happy for you."

Mindy nodded. "There's only one thing. We have to keep this a secret. No one can know. It might reflect badly on Clay."

"Reflect badly on him?" Taylor frowned. "In what way?"

"He doesn't want people to think he's showing any favoritism toward me."

Taylor sat back in her chair. "Give me a break. You're both adults. You can still work together."

"I know, but Clay wants to be careful. You know how people around here are." She smiled. "It's sweet, really. I think he's trying to protect me."

Taylor crossed her arms over her chest. "I don't know. It doesn't seem right, you two having to sneak around."

"It'll be all right. Once summer gets here, we won't have to be so secretive. By then...well, maybe it's too soon to get my hopes up, but if we married..."

"It's that serious?"

Mindy nodded. "I think it is. I know we just started seeing each other, but..." She sighed. "Everything seems so...so right when we're together, you know?"

Taylor didn't know. Sure, she'd had moments with Dylan when she'd felt more complete, more content, than she ever had with anyone else. But that didn't mean they were meant to spend the rest of their lives together. Did it?

"What about you and Dylan?" Mindy asked.

Taylor blinked. At first she thought Mindy was asking if she and Dylan had plans to marry. "I don't think—" she began.

"I thought you were going to see him Friday," Mindy said.

"Oh. Oh, yes. I saw him."

"What did you do?" Mindy grinned. "Or is that a secret?"

"No secret. We went to the old drive-in."

Mindy raised her eyebrows. "Was this another fantasy?"

Taylor nodded. "Another wild rumor that circulated about us in high school."

Mindy laughed. "Don't you two ever feel like making love in a bed?"

Taylor stared at her friend. Before now she hadn't realized that she and Dylan had yet to have sex in any conventional setting. Maybe a bed was too...real. Too everyday. They were re-creating fantasy here. Something wonderful and not made to last.

"What about Saturday? Did you see him?"

She took a drink of her soda. Dylan had asked to see her Saturday, but she'd refused. Friday night's encounter had been so powerful, so…moving. She'd needed time to absorb those feelings. "We've agreed not to see too much of each other. It makes things too…too complicated."

Mindy frowned. "I think you're falling for him and you don't want to admit how hard it's going to be when you leave for England."

She looked away. Maybe that was part of it. All the more reason to back off as much as she could now. "I knew what I was getting into when I started this," she said. "I can handle it." Though she'd never imagined the emotions she felt when she was with Dylan would be so powerful.

Mindy leaned over and put her hand on Taylor's. "You don't always have to be so tough, you know." She smiled and stood. "Thanks for listening. I'd better go get something to eat while I still have a chance."

When Taylor was alone again, she tried to finish her lunch, but her stomach was in a turmoil. What did Mindy mean, she didn't have to be so tough? Of course she did. She never would have made it this far if she hadn't learned to look out for herself and to protect her feelings. It was the only way to survive life relatively unscathed.

DYLAN SPENT HIS LUNCH hour Monday dropping off ads at the newspaper and arranging for five thousand leaflets to be printed and distributed by Friday. He had barely fifteen minutes for lunch but decided to stop by his house for a sandwich rather than swinging by Danny's or one of the new fast-food joints at the south end of town. One of the benefits of being your own boss was that you could be late returning from lunch and no one made much of a fuss. He didn't have any appointments this afternoon and his new secretary, Anita, would handle the phones.

He unlocked the back door and let himself into the kitchen, the quiet of the house descending around him like a cloak. The clock above the stove ticked loudly and the ice-maker rattled as it dumped a load of fresh cubes. The silence seemed out of place here. When he was growing up, Dylan was sure the house had never been like this.

Maybe he'd get a dog. A Lab or a golden retriever who would run to greet him whenever he arrived home.

He made a sandwich and carried it and a glass of milk into his dad's old office. Dylan's office now. A card table filled in for the desk he hadn't bought yet, though the rest of the room was substantially unchanged from the days his dad had lived here. The ten-point buck he'd shot in South Texas still hung on the wall over the built-in book-cases that held his dad's collection of Zane Grey novels and bound issues of *Texas Highways*.

Dylan sat on an old kitchen chair behind the card-table desk and sorted through his mail. Junk. Junk. Bill, flyer, junk. He took a closer look at the flyer and grinned. "Elect Jes Ramirez for School Board Position Six," it read.

"Let the games begin," he said, thinking of his own flyers that would go in the mail at the end of the week.

He told himself it didn't matter if he won this race or not, but a voice in his head immediately named him a liar. So, okay, he really wanted this. He wanted the people in this town to know his name. To think of him as some-body. To say, "There goes Sam Gates's son. His father would be proud."

Sam would have been proud to see Dylan's name on a

ballot. He'd have been first in line to cast his vote, too. Dylan could be thankful for that certainty. He knew too many men, and women, too, who shriveled with regret when their parents were gone, because they hadn't mended fences or had drifted apart. Dylan and his father had remained close their whole lives together.

Dylan's only regret was that his mom and dad hadn't lived longer, to see everything their children had become.

Donna was living in Houston, married to a petroleum engineer, with a beautiful little boy and another one on the way. Debby taught elementary school in a Dallas suburb and was engaged to a doctor.

Then there was Dylan, the oldest and still unattached, living in the house they'd grown up in, where every room seemed to be waiting for a family to fill it.

Of all the things he'd come back to Cedar Creek to find, family was key. The family of his past and the family of his future. Here, he was sure he'd find a woman and settle down to raise his children. Someone who had roots as deep as his own. Someone who could make his home her home.

And then Taylor had sauntered into their class reunion and shattered that idyllic vision with one look from her brown eyes. She didn't want a home. She wasn't interested in settling down. She didn't fit at all with his picture of the future, yet when he was with her, none of that mattered.

He wanted her with him. Yesterday. Today. Tomorrow. Next year. The fact that it couldn't happen didn't make him want it any less.

Worse, he was afraid Taylor had ruined him for anyone else. Would a woman who married him and settled down to raise his children do a striptease at a deserted drive-in, then let him take her from behind on the hood of her car?

Would the kind of woman who devoted herself to local politics and small town life strip naked in the front seat of his truck or leave him trembling with need in a high school shower? Could any ordinary woman make him feel the extraordinary things Taylor had made him feel?

He pushed aside the remains of his lunch and leaned back in his chair. He was screwed any way he looked at it. And not in a good way. Taylor had messed with his body and now she was messing with his mind.

He could ask her to stay, of course. But no, he couldn't do that. She deserved her happiness more than anyone and if she thought she couldn't find it here, she was probably right. Hadn't he always thought she was too wild and exotic for this dusty old town? She needed something more. Something even he couldn't give her.

He felt weighed down with sadness at the thought, but he determined not to show it. As long as he and Taylor were together, he'd squeeze every last drop of enjoyment from the moment and give every bit of pleasure he could to her. He'd have time for mourning later, when she was far away, where she couldn't see what she'd done to him.

THE NEXT AFTERNOON, Taylor stopped by Dylan's office. She told herself she was here on business, to discuss his plans to speak to her class. But she could have done that over the phone. Deep down, in a part of herself she didn't want to examine too closely, she wanted to see him again. Four days apart was too much. She wanted to see his eyes light up when she walked into the room, to bask in the warmth of his smile, to feel his arms around her.

She found the office easily enough and stood on the sidewalk, admiring the gold lettering on the front door: Dylan M. Gates, Attorney-At-Law. Inside, she found a simply decorated office with a few potted plants, leather chairs and wildlife prints on the wall. The office was subdued and masculine, like the man who worked here. A smiling Anita Brandtley stood to greet her. "Ms. Reed, it's so good to see you again."

"Hi, Anita. Dylan told me he'd hired you." She gave her former student a hug. "Are you enjoying the job?"

"I love it. Dylan's so easygoing. Let me tell him you're here." She reached for the phone.

"I don't want to disturb him." In fact, now that she was here, she was wondering about the wisdom of visiting Dylan in a place so closely tied to his public identity. Seeing this side of him added too much information to her picture of him. The more she knew about him, the more difficult it was to keep him confined in her mind to the role of fantasy lover.

"It's no bother. I know he'll want to see you."

While she waited for Dylan to come out, she studied the pictures on the wall. In addition to the wildlife prints, he'd hung photographs of himself and his family. She admired what looked like an enlarged family photo showing Dylan and Sam standing on the end of a wharf, a string of fish between them. Dylan looked nineteen or twenty, a younger copy of the silver-haired man beside him, who must have been in his fifties. Anyone would have known immediately they were father and son, from the way each stood with hips slightly cocked, to the unabashed grin each wore.

She studied Sam's face more closely, noting the way lines fanned out from his eyes and the creases on either side of his mouth. Is this what Dylan would look like when he was older? Is this the face his wife would see across from her at the breakfast table every day? An invisible hand squeezed her heart at the thought.

"Taylor! What a nice surprise."

She turned and saw Dylan crossing the office toward her, arms outstretched. He pulled her close in a quick hug, then stepped back, the same grin she'd seen in the photo fixed on her now. "What brings you downtown this afternoon?"

"I wanted to see where you work." She looked around them. "Very nice."

"Come on back into my office. I've got something to show you." He put a hand at her back and steered her toward the room at the back of the suite. A massive desk took up most of the space, though there was room for a bookcase and two side chairs.

He strode to the desk and picked up a handful of bumper stickers and thrust one at her. "These just came in. What do you think?"

She looked down at the sticker and smiled. "'Dylan Gets It Done.'" She laughed. "It looks good. People will remember it."

"Let's hope they remember to write my name in on the ballot, too."

He dropped the stickers back on the desk and nodded to the stacks of paperwork there. "I can't believe how fast this is taking off. Troy has me booked to speak to every group in town, from the League of Women Voters and the Kiwanis to the Junior Leaguers and the New Neighbors Club."

"You'll wow them all with your charm," she said. "I hope you can squeeze me into your schedule."

He grinned wolfishly. "I always have room for you."

She looked away, suppressing a grin. "I was referring to my class. Remember, you promised to speak to them about your father and his book."

"I haven't forgotten. Just tell me when you want me and I'll be there."

Was it coincidence that he'd chosen those words? Or was it only her one-track mind that made her think of wanting him in a physical way? "How does Tuesday, a week from now, sound?"

He glanced at the planner open on his desk. "I have to speak to the Rotary luncheon that day. But Wednesday's open."

"Wednesday it is, then."

"How's the project going?" he asked.

"It's going great. I haven't seen students this excited about an assignment in a long time." She settled into one of the leather chairs across from his desk and he lowered himself into the other. "They've already come up with a list of places to film and people to interview. Dale will be the cameraman, Berk the producer, Jessica, Patrice and Owen Rodriguez were picked to be the on-camera re-porters, and Randy Padgett and Sue Hartsell are in charge of editing. Others in the class will help with promotion, write scripts and research background. I'm really proud of them."

"They sound like a great bunch of kids. I could use that kind of organization on my campaign."

"Hey, anytime you want help, just ask."

"How about next Saturday evening?" He picked up a handful of bumper stickers. "Troy wants to organize an envelope stuffing party. We need all the manpower we can get."

"I'll let the students know. I'm sure some of them will want to help."

They sat across from each other, both smiling, attrac-tion building in the sudden stillness like an electrical cur-rent. Taylor watched his eyes darken and shifted her gaze from the wanting she saw there. Her own eyes probably gave her away. She would have thought by now she'd be past this heated edginess she felt every time he was near. She wasn't an adolescent fighting raging hormones, but a grown woman who had plenty of other things to think about besides sex.

Except when she was with Dylan. Then she was never far from anticipating being in his arms again.

"I see homecoming is next Friday. Are you going?"

The question startled her into looking at him again. "Funny you should ask. Alyson Michaels stopped me in the hall yesterday and asked if the two of us would like to chaperone the Homecoming Dance."

"For real?" He grinned. "I'd love that. At least I think I would. What does a chaperone do, exactly?"

"We have to go to the dance and be on the lookout for troublemakers—you know, any students who might be drinking too much or doing drugs. The kids aren't allowed to leave the dance and come back in, so we watch for that." She smiled. "It's a pretty tame crowd, really. It's considered a plum duty."

He nodded. "I'd love to take you to the Homecoming Dance." His voice softened. "I never got the chance before."

Did you want to? He sounded as if he had, but that led to the question of why he hadn't asked her to the dance when they were both students. She was working up the courage to voice this question when the intercom buzzed. "Mr. Sommers is here. He says he needs to speak to you about the campaign," Anita said.

Dylan stood and punched the intercom button. "Send him in."

Troy burst into the room, waving a sheaf of papers. "I've got you booked all over town, buddy," he crowed. "There won't be anyone in town who doesn't know you're running for school board and once they meet you, they're all going to want to vote for you." He stopped short in front of the desk. "Well, hello, Taylor. How are you?"

"Fine, Troy. And you?"

His grin broadened. "Great. I guess you heard I'm heading up the campaign here for our boy."

Behind Troy's back, Dylan winced. Troy turned to him. "I stopped by the printers and they're already at work on those flyers. We'll do this mailing and then an even bigger one closer to the campaign. We'll need to round up some volunteers to stuff envelopes."

He nodded. "I can do that." He shoved his hands into his pockets. "Who's paying for all this? Mailings are expensive."

"Don't worry. You've had a number of donors come forward to help out with the costs." Troy winked at Taylor. "Dyl is too modest. He doesn't understand how many people *want* to see him succeed at this. And this is only the first step." He dropped the papers onto the desk. "Today the school board. Tomorrow—U.S. Senate."

Hearing this proclamation about anyone else, Taylor would have been skeptical. But she had no doubt Dylan could go as far as he wanted in politics—or anything else. Who wouldn't vote for a smart, handsome, honest, hard-working man like him? Though it was sexist to say so, he'd get any number of female votes on the basis of his smile alone.

"Not everyone is thrilled that I'm running for office." Dylan picked up the latest edition of the *Cedar Creek Clarion* and folded it back to the editorial page.

Troy snatched the paper from his hand and frowned at it. "I'd hardly call one letter to the editor an outcry against you. And consider the source."

"Who is it? Let me see." Taylor reached for the paper.

A letter headed. "Gates Campaign A Cheap Publicity Ploy?" was signed by city councilman Darrell Spivey. She pictured the aging city councilman. He'd been a fixture in town politics for so long he'd become both a symbol and a caricature of Cedar Creek government. "Why should he care whether you run for school board or not?" she asked.

"Spivey has his knickers in a twist because he heard about your class's plan to study Dylan's daddy's book," Troy explained. "There are some things in that book that aren't very flattering to Spivey's old man."

Taylor's stomach churned. "Dylan, I'm sorry—"

He took the paper from her and tossed it aside. "It's not your fault. He's just a bitter old man. I can ignore him."

"Believe me, most people will," Troy said. "Now, there are a few more things we need to go over…"

While Troy and Dylan discussed campaign strategy, Taylor fidgeted in her chair and fought the sadness knotting in her chest. She could see Dylan succeeding in the years ahead, but she was missing from that picture. She'd be in England or California or somewhere far away, living her own life.

What kind of life would she have? Would her "experiment" to get Dylan out of her system be successful? Would she finally find the right man for her?

Or was the right man standing here with her now? Was the reason she hadn't been able to get him out of her head all these years because he was the one she was supposed to spend her life with?

The thought sent a surge of panic through her. The feelings she'd had for Dylan all those years ago had been a silly teenage crush. And what she felt for him now was simply a more mature version of that crush, undoubtedly fueled by the best sex she'd ever had. You didn't build a future on those kinds of feelings. Surely you didn't.

She pushed herself up out of the chair, anxious to be out of this room, away from Dylan. "I'd better go," she said. "It was good seeing you again, Troy."

"Wait," Dylan said. "I'll only be another minute."

"Don't leave on my account," Troy said.

"No. I really do have to go. I have work to do." She nodded to them, managing to keep a smile on her face, then hurried away as fast as she dared, scarcely nodding to Anita as she passed. She had to get away, somewhere where she could think more clearly. She'd go home and take out the folder of paperwork for Oxford to remind herself again why she had to leave Cedar Creek and move on with her life. A life that didn't include Dylan Gates.

13

AFTER SURVIVING SPEECHES to the Rotary Club, the Lions, the Kiwanis, the Junior League and the Happy Homemakers in his first two weeks of campaigning, Dylan considered himself a public speaking pro. But the thought of standing up in front of a classful of teenagers made his stomach do backflips. "I don't see how you do this every day," he told Taylor before the start of class.

"They're just kids." She smiled. "Relax."

"I *was* one of those kids once. I remember how brutal they can be."

She laughed. "Don't worry. They're going to love you."

Do you love me? The thought popped into his head, unbidden. He watched her walk to her desk and bend over to consult her grade book. She was so graceful. So beautiful. He was starting to care for her so much.

Too much. He looked away, down at his hands, which he'd unconsciously formed into fists, as if trying to hold on to something as elusive as the time he and Taylor had left together.

Any fool knew you couldn't stop time, anymore than he could stop Taylor from going away and leaving him.

The first bell sounded. "Get ready," she said. "Here they come."

As students filed into the classroom, he glanced at her again. He couldn't hold on to her, but he could make the time they had left the best it could be. He'd make sure she had special memories to take with her, memories that would stay with her the rest of her life, the way he knew his feelings for her would always be a part of him.

"Hey, Mr. Gates! How's it going?" Dale walked up and shook his hand.

"We've got some most excellent footage for our movie." Berk joined them at the front of the room.

"That's great. I can't wait to see it."

"Everybody take your seats and we'll get started," Taylor said. "You all remember Dylan Gates. His father wrote the book we're working with, *A Ranger Remembers*."

She nodded for Dylan to take the floor. He stepped into the middle of the room and cleared his throat. "Thank you for inviting me here today. I know my father would be very pleased to know you're studying his book. I remember he worked very hard, researching it and writing it. He wasn't a very demonstrative man, but I know the book was always very dear to his heart."

The door at the back of the room opened and he was startled to see Grady Murphy, Alyson Michaels and Clay Walsh file in. He glanced at Taylor. She raised her eyebrows and shook her head. Great. As if he didn't have enough to be nervous about.

"Don't let us disturb you," Clay said as he and the others took seats at the back.

Doing his best to ignore them, Dylan turned back to the students. "I thought I'd start by talking a little bit about my father and then you all can ask me questions."

He took some note cards from his pocket and referred to them, then told the class about his father's birth and childhood and how he became a Ranger. Researching the talk had transported him back to the days when he'd sit on the living room floor, playing, while his father talked to Dylan's grandmother and aunts about things that had happened when they were young. He'd spent a whole evening last week thumbing through old photo albums, laughing at pictures of himself and his sisters at Christmas or splashing in the stock tank in the summer.

"This is a photo of my dad at his first book-signing." He passed around the black-and-white shot that had run on the front page of the *Cedar Creek Clarion* eight years before. "I thought you might want to use it in your film."

"This is great." Berk held up the picture, a grin stretching across his face. "Thanks!"

When the time came for questions, the girl from the drive-in restaurant raised her hand. "Yes, Patrice," Taylor said.

"What did your father think about the book-burning that was held on the courthouse lawn?" she asked.

Dylan took a deep breath. "As you might imagine, he wasn't particularly happy about it. I was away in college at the time, but I heard later that he called Councilman Spivey, who started the whole thing, a number of names that aren't suitable to repeat."

"Why did Mr. Spivey want to burn your father's book?" another girl asked.

"I suppose he thought he had a good reason, though I don't know if there ever is one for actions like that. Mainly, there had been bad blood between Spivey and my dad for years. I don't really know what started it, though I know my father ran against Spivey for city council and my dad lost. And apparently, there are some things in the book which reflect negatively on Spivey's family."

"His father was one of those who were against segregating the schools," Berk said. "And he was rumored to be part of the Klan that was active in the county back then."

Dale grinned. "We've got a really cool reenactment of the Klan burning a cross in front of the school," he said. "We filmed it at night and everybody wore Klan robes. It looks awesome."

"It sounds like you've all done a lot of research. I can't wait to see the final product." He looked around the room. "Any other questions?"

Jessica raised her hand and he acknowledged her. "Is it true you and Ms. Reed are going to be chaperones at the Homecoming Dance?"

He glanced at Taylor and almost laughed out loud. Her cheeks were bright pink and she was unsuccessfully attempting to look indifferent to the question. "Yes, I believe we are. I'm looking forward to it." He directed the words at Taylor, hoping she'd know how much he meant them.

"Did the two of you go to homecoming together?" Patrice asked.

"I think that's all the time we have for questions." Taylor stood. "Dale, why don't you set up the camera and you can tape your interview with Dylan."

For the next half hour Dylan answered questions from the two "reporters" Patrice and Owen. It felt odd, sitting in the glare of the bright lights with the camera running, but he told himself he should get used to it. After all, if he was going into politics, he had to be prepared to spend time in the spotlight.

At last the bell rang and the students gathered up their books and left the room. Grady, Alyson and Clay came forward to shake his hand. "I see you're running for school board," Grady said. "Are you a glutton for punishment or what?"

"He certainly has *my* vote." Alyson didn't exactly bat her eyelashes at him, but she came close. Dylan bit his tongue to keep from laughing. Some things never changed.

"Thanks for agreeing to chaperone the Homecoming Dance," Alyson added. "That's one more chore I can mark off my list."

"Thanks for asking us. It should be fun."

"I have to get to my next class." Grady headed out the door. "Thanks for letting us sit in on this."

"I better go, too," Clay said. "Thanks."

Everyone filed out and at last he and Taylor were alone again. "I think that went well," he said, joining her at her desk.

"Are you kidding? You were fantastic."

He grinned at her. "I was, wasn't I?"

She grabbed his lapels and pulled him close. "Why don't we get together tonight and I'll show you fantastic?" she purred.

His body responded to her like gunpowder to a match, desire flaring, burning through him. He resisted the urge to pull her to him, to bury his face in her neck and feel the warm softness of her surround him. Instead, he took a step back and shook his head.

"No, I don't think so."

She blinked. "Why not?" Her expression turned coy. "I was reading in my diary last night and found where we supposedly went skinny-dipping out at the old gravel pit."

He swallowed, fighting the vision of her naked. And wet. He shifted and cleared his throat. "I think we should wait until Friday. Until Homecoming." The idea had just come to him. Not that he didn't want to be with her tonight. Right now. All the time. But he'd vowed to make things special for her. And what better way to heighten their pleasure than to add anticipation to the mix? He'd make her wait, letting the heat between them intensify until, by Friday night, they'd both be ready to burst into flame with a mere look or touch.

He was sweating now, his chest tight from the effort to breathe normally. Taylor frowned at him. "There's no need to wait." She moved toward him, her voice low, enticing. "We only have a few weeks left. I don't want to waste one second of it."

He swallowed hard, and put his hands behind his back to keep from reaching for her. "Believe me, this will be worth the wait."

She stopped, her gaze considering. "So you have something planned?"

He nodded. "Something special." He had no idea what that would be yet, but he'd come up with something. He had two days to think of a plan. Something worth enduring this slow torture of wanting her and not being able to touch her.

TAYLOR CHECKED THE CLOCK on her bedside table. Twenty minutes until Dylan would be here. She went back to fussing with her hair. Did the left side look too poofy? She kept trying to smooth it down, but it wouldn't cooperate. She hit it again with a blast of hair spray, then glanced at the clock again. Eighteen minutes until Dylan would be here.

The past two days had been torture. Dylan had resisted her attempts to get him to drive out to the gravel pit—or anywhere else—with her. Then he'd added to her misery by having his secretary call her to ask mysterious questions. What was her favorite flower? Red zinnias. Who did she think was sexier, Cary Grant or George Clooney?

Cary. No doubt about it. Which was more romantic, classical music or the Beatles? Close, but classical got the edge.

What was he up to? Half a dozen times she'd picked up the phone to call to ask, but had fought back the impulse. There was something to be said for waiting, even if it did mean she spent most of the week edgy with frustrated desire.

The doorbell rang and she jumped, her hairbrush clattering into the sink. Her gaze flew to the clock. He was ten minutes early. Did that mean he was as anxious as she was?

She replaced the brush on the shelf, smoothed her black cocktail dress over her hips and took a deep, steadying breath before walking to the door. All that carefully martialed composure was lost, however, the minute she opened the door and saw the man standing there.

Dylan was dressed in an exquisitely tailored black dinner jacket and trousers, a maroon paisley cummerbund emphasizing the slimness of his waist, a blindingly white shirt calling attention to his broad chest. Her mouth went slack. He looked good enough to eat. She had half a mind to lock the door behind him and drag him into the bedroom this instant.

He held out a small, square, plastic florist's box. "They didn't have zinnias. I hope red roses will do."

She scarcely glanced at the corsage of red roses and white baby's breath before dragging her gaze back to him. "You clean up very nice," she said. "I can guarantee you'll win more than a few female votes tonight."

"You look gorgeous." His eyes raked her, sending the definite message that he intended to take the dress off of her at the first opportunity.

Too bad they had at least four hours of chaperoning the

dance to get through before that would be possible. There were some times when adult responsibilities were a definite drag.

"Would you like me to pin it on?"

She blinked and stared at him, her one-track mind making it difficult to think about anything else at the moment.

"The corsage." He nodded to the florist's box. "Do you want me to pin it on?"

"Oh! Sure!"

She handed him the corsage and he moved closer to pin it to her left shoulder. She sucked in her breath sharply as he slid his fingers under the neckline of her dress. Her nipples contracted and she leaned toward him. She'd spent a week anticipating his touch. This brief contact wasn't nearly enough.

Corsage in place, she collected her purse and her wrap and followed him out onto her front porch. Once again, she was struck speechless when she saw what was waiting at the curb. Instead of Dylan's red pickup, a gleaming black stretch limo awaited them.

"A limo?" She searched his face. What *was* he up to?

"That's what all the kids do these days, isn't it? We might as well be as stylish as they are."

The driver opened the door for her and Taylor discovered firsthand how difficult it was to climb into a limousine while wearing a short, tight skirt. Inside, she arranged herself on the back seat as Dylan slid in next to her.

She looked around at the plush interior, aware that she was gaping like a schoolgirl but unable to stop herself. Everything about the interior of the automobile, including the roof and the wet bar along one side, was upholstered in quilted black leather. Discrete bars of light ran along the side and front and a blackout window separated them from the driver.

"I heard on the radio on the way over here that the Cyclones won the game. So this dance will be a real celebration." Dylan reached for the bottle that was chilling on the wet bar. "It's nonalcoholic champagne," he said as he popped the cork. "I figured it wouldn't look good for the chaperones to show up at the dance with alcohol on their breaths." He poured a glass, his dark eyes fixed on her. "But I do have the real thing for later."

Later. Her temperature climbed another notch and she shifted in her seat, trying to ease the tension between her legs. He handed her a filled glass, then leaned over and kissed her lightly, his lips barely brushing hers before he pulled away again. "I don't think we should arrive with your lipstick smeared."

She sipped her champagne and smiled. "Sounds to me like a good way to get a rumor started."

They joined a line of limos disgorging giggling couples under the portico outside the school gym. When they emerged from their car, squeals and more giggles greeted them. Taylor saw a few students pointing and waving at them.

"You two sure know how to make an entrance." Alyson rushed up to them. She was wearing a shirred white-satin minidress with an enormous bow balanced atop her butt. She looked as if she'd escaped from a Barbie doll convention. "Things are liable to be extra rowdy since the Cyclones won the game, so don't let those high spirits get out of hand. You know what to do, right?"

Taylor nodded, remembering the instructions Alyson had given her earlier. "Take our turn at the door, keep an eye out for suspicious behavior, quietly diffuse any troublesome situations and report any illegal or inappropriate activity to you and to security."

"You forgot one thing."

Taylor frowned, mentally reviewing the list. "What did I forget?"

"To have a good time." Alyson slapped her on the arm so hard she rocked back on her heels.

"We won't have any problems." Dylan slipped his arm around her.

In keeping with the homecoming theme, the gym was decorated with crepe paper streamers in the school colors of blue and gold, pom-poms and strings of colored lights. A local band occupied the stage at one end of the room where the DJ would spin records between sets. A concession stand in one corner offered soft drinks and snacks and there were tables and chairs set up along one side.

Taylor spotted Mindy near the door that opened into the school parking lot. Clay stood opposite her at the end bank of doors. The two were pretending not to notice each other and doing a poor job of it. While Taylor was watching, Mindy didn't even notice the parent who stopped to talk to her because she was too busy staring at Clay as he talked to another parent—a tall, buxom blonde in a too tight sweater. Taylor smiled. Mindy ought to know she had nothing to worry about. Every time she looked away, Clay's gaze fixed on her.

"Ms. Reed, you're lookin' good." Berk popped up beside them, making his own fashion statement in red high-top sneakers, black jeans, tuxedo jacket and red cummerbund.

"Hi, Ms. Reed. I love your dress." Patrice Miller looked decidedly un-bookwormish in a red sequined dress, her hair was upswept and pinned with sparkly clasps.

Taylor realized Patrice was holding Berk's hand and smiled. So, the class clown and the class brain had found something in common after all. "Thank you. The two of you look pretty nice yourselves."

Berk nodded to Dylan. "Some of us are coming to help out at your headquarters tomorrow night," he said.

"Thanks. I really appreciate it."

"No problem." The band began a new song and Berk waved as he dragged Patrice onto the already packed dance floor. Music throbbed through the room and the scents of perfume and aftershave mingled with the buttery aroma of concession-booth popcorn.

"It's warm in here, isn't it?" Dylan tugged at his tie.

"It is." She started to slip out of her wrap and he reached to help her. His fingers grazed the back of her neck, sending tremors of awareness through her.

"Why don't I get us something to drink?"

"That would be great. I'll go say hello to Mindy." At least a drink would give her something to do with her hands, when all she really wanted was to pull Dylan into some dark corner and touch him. All over.

She made her way across the room to Mindy. Her friend looked gorgeous in a green silk pantsuit that showed her figure to advantage. "You don't look like you're having a very good time," Taylor said.

Mindy glanced toward the other set of doors. "I'm hoping Clay will come over and ask me to dance, but I'm afraid he won't."

"Then you ask him."

"Believe me, if he doesn't come over here soon, I will." Her knuckles whitened around the door bar. "I just hope we don't spontaneously combust on the dance floor. We haven't seen much of each other for the past week."

Taylor sympathized. She and Dylan were in danger of creating their own firestorm. She craned her head, trying to see him over the crush of dancers. She thought she spotted him, surrounded by a group of parents. It had been this way in high school. He was so popular, he couldn't walk down the hall without being waylaid by people who wanted to talk to him. Whereas Taylor always breezed through the hall unimpeded, usually arriving at class early. She even developed the habit of walking quickly, nose in the air, as if she had more important things to do than talk to her classmates.

"So how are things with you and Dylan?"

"What?" She turned back to Mindy. "Oh. They're fine."

"Fine?" Mindy laughed. "Face it, Taylor, there are some feelings you can't hide. You and Dylan can't keep your eyes off each other." Her own gaze drifted to the opposite doors. "That's the same way I feel about Clay."

Taylor nodded. "I guess you're right."

"So, what are you going to do at the end of the year, when you have to leave?"

She shook her head. "I don't want to think about that right now." Tonight, she didn't want to think about anything…but tonight.

"I hope Coke's okay." Dylan had made his way to them, carrying three cups of soda. He offered one to Mindy. "You looked thirsty."

"Thanks." She smiled and accepted the drink. "If there was a vote, I'd say that you and Dylan are the best-looking couple here," she said.

He put his arm around Taylor. "I think that title goes to the Homecoming King and Queen." He glanced at Taylor. "Who is it this year, anyway?"

"Jessica Rawlings and Terence Duvall." She sipped her drink. "I remember you were Homecoming King our senior year."

He laughed. "I had to wear this horrible, cheesy crown."

"Who was the queen?" Mindy asked.

"Millie Stefanovitch. Her crown looked a lot better than mine."

Taylor gripped her drink harder. The *Cedar Creek Clarion* had run a picture on the front page of Dylan and Millie, on the football field at halftime, with their crowns and bouquets. She'd clipped the picture for her scrapbook and very carefully excised Millie from the photo.

Dylan set aside his empty glass. "Mindy, you don't mind if Taylor and I dance, do you?"

"Of course not." Mindy nodded toward an older couple making their way toward them. "In fact, my relief is here right now. I think I might go find my own dance partner."

Taylor and Dylan joined the crowd on the dance floor. As Taylor moved into Dylan's arms, she felt almost as if she were back in high school again, celebrating the team's victory at the homecoming game and all the joys of being young.

But that was as much of a fantasy as the rumors she and Dylan had reenacted. She'd never been to a homecoming dance, never been a part of the "in" crowd, at least not after she'd moved to Cedar Creek.

As if reading her thoughts, Dylan squeezed her hand and pulled her closer. She looked up into his eyes and felt her heart race. If she and Dylan *had* danced in high school, it wouldn't have felt like this. You had to live life awhile to know this complicated mixture of anticipation and regret, of longing to be alone together and dreading the time you would be apart.

She ducked her head and rested it on his shoulder. She didn't want to think about the future now. Or at least no farther ahead than a few hours from now, when the frustration she'd felt all week would come to an end.

He smoothed his hand down her back, the weight and heat of his touch as familiar as the caress of sun on a warm day, as tantalizing as the promise of chocolate on her tongue. Warmth spread through her, heating up as he slid his thumb down to rest in the small of her back, gently stroking the indentation at the base of her spine, sending a silent message her whole body understood.

He spoke softly in her ear. "I'm glad Alyson asked us to do this. I'm glad we finally get our homecoming together."

She smiled into his shoulder, but said nothing. This moment was too precious for mere words.

The song ended and they danced another. Then it was their turn to watch the door. During a period of inactivity, Taylor glanced across and saw Dylan watching her, his gaze raking over her, a half-smile on his lips. She caught her breath, then gave him a slow smile. If he wanted to watch, she'd give him something to watch.

Slowly, she traced her hand along the neckline of her dress, one finger dipping beneath the fabric to graze the top of her breasts. His eyes widened and he shifted his stance, buttoning his jacket. Lips parted, she slicked her tongue across her teeth, letting her hand drop slightly to graze her nipple. She hoped anyone looking their way would think the movement was accidental; she was sure Dylan would know it was not.

The door at Dylan's station opened, ending their little game. Taylor glanced out over the gym and spotted Mindy dancing with Clay. She smiled. She hoped the two of them *did* fall in love and marry. It was what Mindy wanted and it was nice to believe some people could have that kind of happily-ever-after in their lives.

Disturbed by this reminder of her own uncertain situation, she shifted her gaze, trying to spot students she knew. Instead, her gaze came to rest on a stack of gym mats right outside the door marked Boys Locker Room. She had to grab hold of the door to steady herself as she remembered sneaking past that stack of mats with Dylan. The boys' locker room had seemed a strange place for a romantic interlude and yet the memory of that shower still touched her, both physically and somewhere soul-deep.

She looked across at him again. He was talking to one of the football players who had his hand up, apparently describing a pass that had been crucial in tonight's victory. Dylan had been a football hero in high school. Was he reliving those days now?

She checked her watch. Only ten-thirty. Would midnight ever get here? Unlike Cinderella, the real party would begin for her at that witching hour.

They danced more, shared nachos from the concession stand, worked more door duty and at last, the dance was over. The students left in couples and groups, the band packed up their instruments and the weary group of chaperones gathered around Alyson. "Thank you all for coming," Alyson said. Somehow, she looked hardly wilted, though she'd spent hours racing around making sure everything ran smoothly. Taylor felt a grudging admiration. "Everything went great. I hope you all had a good time."

Murmurs of agreement went up from the group. "Do you need any help with cleanup?" Clay asked. He was standing next to Mindy, not touching her, but close enough that Taylor was sure no one was fooled by their pretense at being "just friends."

"That's okay," Alyson said. "The football boosters are taking care of that in the morning. So everyone, go home. Get some rest."

Dylan took Taylor's arm and whispered in her ear. "Rest isn't what I had in mind."

The limo was waiting for them. Taylor collapsed into the plush seat and slipped out of her heels. "Forget the gravel pit," she said, stifling a yawn. "Let's go back to my place." Tonight, she wanted something more comfortable than the front seat of a car.

Dylan took her hand and squeezed it. "I've got a better idea."

She glanced at him, a flutter of apprehension in her stomach. She glanced out the window and saw that the driver had turned onto the highway leading out of town. "Where are we going?"

Dylan slid closer, so that their bodies touched from shoulder to knee. "You'll see." He pulled her into his arms and kissed her forehead, her temples, the corner of her mouth. "You were the prettiest girl there tonight, did you know that?"

It wasn't true, she knew. No woman approaching her thirties was a match for a teen beauty queen. But that didn't matter, did it? What mattered was that, at least for tonight, Dylan thought she was the prettiest. Just as she had known he was the best-looking man. It was one of the wonders of biology or psychology or whatever—this selective vision two people who shared a powerful attraction had for one another.

She turned more toward him, offering her mouth for a kiss, but he held back, brushing his lips across her cheek instead. He caressed her hip and smiled into her eyes. "Right now, it wouldn't take much to make me lose control," he said. "Let's not hurry."

The thought of an out-of-control Dylan sent a rush of wanting through her. She squeezed her thighs together and hugged him closer, wondering if that rumored male trick of thinking of baseball stats really helped. Too bad she'd never followed baseball.

On the outskirts of town, the limo exited the freeway and pulled up in front of the Valley Grand Hotel. Taylor stared at Dylan. "A hotel?"

He grinned. "When we were in school, some kids rented hotel rooms after the homecoming dance, for parties." The driver opened the door and Dylan took Taylor's hand and helped her from the car. He pulled her close, his voice a sexy growl. "You and I are going to have our own very private party."

14

DYLAN TIPPED the limo driver and fished in his pocket for the key to their hotel room. He took a deep breath, trying to control his racing heart. Tonight was going to be a damn sight better than an interlude at the gravel pit—though he had no doubt Taylor would have made even that exciting.

But tonight would be special. He and Taylor would have all night to explore and discover each other.

They rode the elevator up to their room in silence, not touching. He glanced at her and found her staring at the floor. Her hair had fallen forward, shielding her face from him. *What is she thinking?* he wondered.

They stepped from the elevator onto the plush lavender carpet of the hallway. Their room was at the end of the corridor.

''The Bridal Suite?'' Taylor's voice shook as she stared at the gold plaque on the door.

''It was the best they had.'' He slipped the card key in the slot and opened the door. ''I wanted the best for tonight.''

She stared at him a moment, biting her lip. Then she brushed past him into the large sitting room. The drapes were open to a view of city lights. Two sofas faced each other across the velvet-soft beige carpeting, while a table and two chairs sat ready for an intimate dinner.

"It's very nice," she said, pausing to sniff the arrangement of lilies and roses on a side table.

"Are you hungry?" He picked up the phone on the wall by the bathroom. "I'll call room service."

She put a hand to her stomach. "I guess I am a little hungry."

"Yeah, those nachos didn't last long."

She walked over to the window and he joined her, slipping his arm around her back and tugging her close. He was surprised to find she was trembling. "What's the matter?" he asked. "You're shaking. Are you cold?"

She ducked her head. "Just nervous. It's silly, I know."

He rubbed her shoulders. "Why are you nervous?"

She shrugged. "It feels strange…being here. It's so…so formal."

"You mean, this doesn't revolve around one of the rumors in your diary." He frowned. Did she only want sex with him when it was casual and connected to their past?

"It's not that." She turned to face him, her hands resting on his chest. "I want to be with you. I just don't know why you'd go to all this trouble."

He slipped his arms around her and pulled her closer. "So far, whenever we've been together, it's been all about the past. We were re-creating old rumors to take away their sting. Tonight, I wanted to live in the moment. To enjoy what we have right here. Right now."

He kissed her, long and hard. They might not have much time together, but he wanted her to know how special she was to him now. How special she'd always be.

A knock on the door signaled the arrival of room service. The waiter carried the tray and ice bucket to the table and Dylan signed the check while Taylor went into the bathroom to freshen up.

When she came out, he'd arranged fruit, cheese and

crackers on two plates and opened the bottle of champagne. "To us," he said, offering her a glass.

"To us," she murmured, and touched her glass to his.

She picked up a strawberry and brought it to her mouth, then paused and smiled. "I've got an idea."

"Oh, yeah?" His heart pounded, recalling some of the more exciting ideas she'd had in the recent past.

"Why don't we feed each other?"

He grinned. "All right." He moved his chair around to sit next to her. "You go first."

Her gaze locked to his, she brought the strawberry to his lips. The fruit was ripe and sweet, juice bursting from it as his teeth closed around it. The nectar ran down her fingers and he hurried to capture it, sucking each digit into his mouth.

With growing pleasure, he watched her eyes darken, her lips part and her breathing deepen. He suckled each finger, tracing his tongue up along the underside, stroking the pads. When she pulled away at last, he was already fully aroused.

"My turn," he said, selecting a wedge of Brie.

The cheese was soft and fragrant, dissolving around her tongue. She followed his lead, taking his fingers into her mouth, sucking at the tips, exerting pressure with her lips as he withdrew. He slipped them in again, withdrawing slowly, mimicking the movements he would make later, his erection twitching with need at the pressure of her lips around him.

They ate peaches and grapes, crumbly crackers and more cheese, washing them down with sips of the wine. The taste of the food mingled with the taste of their flesh. They stared into each other's eyes as if attempting to read one another's thoughts, feeding on the raw wanting they found there as much as on the food itself.

When at last their plates were empty, they were far from sated. Taylor stared at the crumbs strewn across the table tablecloth. "I may never be able to eat a peach in public again."

Dylan stood and dropped his napkin on the table. "Why don't we get more comfortable?" He walked into the bedroom and returned with a wrapped gift box. "I thought you might like this."

"Oh-hh." The word was a sigh as she accepted the box. "You didn't have to get me anything."

He grinned. "You could think of this as a gift for me, too."

She undid the gold cording around the box and slipped her fingers under the edge of the foiled wrapping paper. As the paper fell away, she pried the lid off the box.

Her eyes widened as she folded back the red tissue paper. "Take it out of the box," he urged.

She set the box on the table and pulled out a froth of white satin and lace. "It's gorgeous!" she gasped, holding up a short gown. She took out the pair of matching bikini panties.

"Go on, put it on." He nudged her toward the bathroom door. "I can't wait to see you in it."

She left and he went into the bedroom to change out of his suit. His hands shook as he unbuttoned his shirt. He couldn't wait much longer to feel her lying beneath him. Anticipation was fine and good, but he was more than ready now for the real thing.

TAYLOR STUDIED HER reflection in the full-length mirror on the back of the bathroom door. The short, white-satin nightgown had strategic lace panels over her breasts and across her thighs that left little to the imagination. Yet somehow she felt more naked than she had when she'd been wearing nothing.

If the lingerie had been black or even red, she might have felt differently. But Dylan had chosen white. A color for brides. And he'd rented the bridal suite.

Why? He knew she could never be his bride. Was this night merely another fantasy, a time for imagining what might have been, instead of what never was?

A knock on the door interrupted her thoughts. "Is everything okay in there?"

"Yes. I'm fine." Taking a deep breath, she grabbed the doorknob and twisted it open.

She thought her heart might stop beating as she stared at Dylan. Dressed in black satin boxers, he was straight out of her most dangerous fantasies.

She brought her gaze up to meet his and the force of the wanting in his eyes made her knees buckle. She grabbed hold of the doorjamb, but Dylan was quicker, sweeping her into his arms, his mouth covering hers in a mind-numbing kiss.

She melted against him, eyes closed, lost to the sensation of his mouth pressed to hers, his tongue tangling with her own. He tasted of champagne and strawberries, reminding her of summer and romance.

She melted against him, tears stinging her eyes. She couldn't say if she wept from happiness or sadness. Everything he'd done had touched her so much and had frightened her, too. How would she ever be able to walk away from this man?

If he noticed the tears, he said nothing. Instead he carried her into the bedroom. A dozen candles glowed from every flat surface in the room, bathing the bed in golden light. The covers were folded back, revealing lace-trimmed sheets and feather pillows. "You're going to spoil me," she said as he lowered her to the bed.

"That's the whole idea." He leaned over to pick up a glass of champagne from the bedside table and offered her a sip.

She drank the wine and leaned back against the pillows, determined to forget her worries about the future and to do as Dylan had said—enjoy the moment. "Then I'm ready to be spoiled."

He sat beside her and cradled her face in his hands. He trailed his fingers down her neck, along her collarbone, outlining the shape of each satin-shrouded rib before coming up to circle her breasts. His eyes were closed, as if he was trying to memorize the feel of each part of her.

Her nipples rose to attention at his touch, pressing against the lace of the gown. Her breasts were heavy and aching. He squeezed her lightly in his hands, then brought his thumbs up to stroke her nipples. She closed her eyes and leaned toward him, her groin pulsing with each movement of his hands.

When he released her, she cried out and opened her eyes, but already his fingers were working new magic. He slipped his hands beneath her gown and stroked her stomach, then moved on to her hips, down her thighs then up again. He stroked the outside of her thighs and then the inside. She could almost feel her nerves vibrating at his touch.

He brought his palm to rest flat against her groin. She felt her own dampness against the heat of his hand and arched toward him, grinding against him, seeking relief.

Still, he didn't look at her face or speak. He focused on his hand, watching as he shifted to the side and slipped one finger beneath her panties. He pulled the slender band of fabric aside to expose her to the cool air.

She grunted with impatience. How much more of this slow torture could she stand? He smiled. "You're beautiful," he said. "I love watching you."

He moved up to lie alongside her. "I love watching you come." With these words, he slipped one finger inside her and then another.

She gasped and felt herself tighten around her. He bent his head to suckle her breast through the lace of her gown and her head fell back against the pillow.

Tremors rocked through her, days of pent-up desire seeking release. She clutched at the sheets, fighting the building tension, wanting this to last.

His mouth left her breast and moved down, across her belly, to that aching center. His fingers still in her, he began to stroke her with his tongue, hot and wet and insistent.

She lost all control, crying out and bucking against him. Almost immediately, he was reaching for a condom from the nightstand, tearing it open with his teeth as he stripped out of his boxers.

She struggled free of her negligee and panties, anxious to feel all of him, flesh to flesh. When he knelt once more between her legs, she reached for him, taking him in.

Objectively she knew that when it came to sex, the human body could accommodate a variety of sizes and shapes. But it seemed to her that no man had ever fit her as well as Dylan. Surely no one had ever satisfied her so completely or made her feel so capable of satisfying him.

She kept her eyes open, meeting his gaze, telling herself no matter what happened, she would remember every moment of this night, forever. Maybe that was what Dylan had meant when he said they should enjoy the moment. The moment was all you ever had, really. The past was gone and couldn't be lived over, no matter how hard you tried.

And the future...who knew what the future held?

He reached down between them to fondle her, at the same time driving deeper within her, increasing the pace of their rhythm. She recognized the familiar building tension and this time surrendered completely, rising up to meet each thrust, letting him take her over the edge along with him.

They collapsed together and lay very still for a long time, their breaths coming in gasps. She stared at the flickering shadows on the ceiling, gradually becoming aware of the dampness of the sweat on his back, the scrape of his beard against her cheek, the crushing weight of his body atop her own.

Gently she pushed him away. "Sorry," he mumbled, and slid off of her. "Didn't mean to smother you."

"It's all right." She snuggled alongside him and rested her head in the hollow of his shoulder. She felt completely drained, physically and emotionally exhausted.

What had just happened here? More than sex, surely. They'd had sex before and it had been wonderful. But this...this had been something else. Something more. Something moving and wonderful...and a little scary. What did it mean when you could lose track of yourself like that with another person?

What did it mean when you wanted to feel that way over and over again?

Her eyes drifted shut and, lulled by Dylan's own regular breathing, she fell asleep, the sound of his heartbeat, strong and steady, reassuring in her ear.

SHE AWOKE HOURS LATER, disoriented at first. Sometime in the night, she and Dylan had moved apart. She lay on her back in the unfamiliar bed and stared up at the ceiling. The candles had gone out, but light from a crack between the curtains showed the gold and lace bridal suite.

With a start, she realized this was the first time she and Dylan had ever slept together. Really slept together, instead of leaving one another after sex to go home to their own beds.

In fact, this was the first time they'd made love in a bed. Careful not to disturb him, she pushed herself into a sitting position and turned to look at him.

He lay on his side, facing her, one hand beneath his cheek, the other reaching out toward her. A lump rose in her throat at the sight and she covered her mouth with her hand to keep from crying out.

In that moment she knew she loved Dylan. Maybe she'd always loved him. Maybe she always would. They came from different backgrounds, they wanted different things, they had very different plans for the future, but that didn't change the fact that he'd stolen her heart. Or maybe she'd surrendered it willingly.

So, what were they going to do now? On shaking legs, she stood and made her way to the bathroom. She used the toilet and washed her face and studied her reflection in the mirror over the sink.

Dylan was running for school board. This was his home. He wasn't about to leave Cedar Creek to come with her to Oxford. She'd made a stab at town life and knew it wasn't for her. She'd tried, but she'd always be an outsider here. She couldn't go through life that way. Not even for Dylan.

Fighting angry tears, she reached for her clothes and dressed. She'd leave a note for Dylan and call a cab from the lobby. If she stayed until he woke, she was liable to say something, or do something, they'd both live to regret.

15

SOMETIME LATER that morning, the telephone woke Taylor from a restless sleep. She swam out from under the layers of sheets and down comforter and groped for the phone on the bedside table. "Hello?"

"Good afternoon. Don't tell me I woke you?" Mindy's voice was entirely too cheerful.

Taylor squinted at the clock. Was it really almost noon? She shoved her hair out of her eyes and struggled into a sitting position. "I got in late."

"Then I take it you had a good night?"

A good night. She frowned. "It was wonderful, but…"

"But what?"

She looked around the bedroom, searching for any excuse to get off the phone. It was too early to go into this, wasn't it? "I don't want to talk about it."

"But you're going to. Because you need to and I'm your friend."

"With a minor in psychology. How could I forget?" She sighed and plucked at the bedcovers, trying to get more comfortable. But she knew the tightness in her jaw and the churning in her stomach had nothing to do with lack of sleep or an uncomfortable bed. "I just think… things might be getting a little too…intense with me and Dylan. I only meant for this to be fun."

"Uh-huh. What happened last night?"

"He took me to the Valley Grand Hotel. To the Bridal Suite."

"Oh, Taylor!" Mindy's voice was a breathy sigh. "That's so romantic."

"It was, but..." She shook her head. How could she explain this to Mindy when she wasn't even sure she understood it herself? "Our relationship...what Dylan and I are doing...it wasn't supposed to be about romance. Just sex and fun."

"And you don't think those two things can lead to romance? Especially considering how long the two of you have known each other?"

"We hadn't seen each other in ten years before the reunion. And we never really had a relationship back in school. We were just kids."

"But you felt something for each other even back then, didn't you?"

Had she? What did a seventeen-year-old girl know about real, lasting love? "It was only a schoolgirl crush," she said.

"Don't be so sure."

"It doesn't matter what I felt back then." She pulled her knees up to her chest, bunching the covers around her. "I never intended for this to be anything more than a fun fling. I thought it would be good to get Dylan out of my system and move on."

"And now your plan has backfired." Mindy's voice lacked any sympathy. "What makes you think you can control someone else's feelings? Or your own, for that matter?"

"There's no point in going any further with this. I'm leaving. He's staying."

"Do you love him?"

The question stopped her heart and she struggled to

breathe. The knowledge that she *did* love Dylan was like a big, hairy monster that had been standing behind her for weeks. As long as she didn't turn around to look, she could pretend it wasn't there, even as she felt its hot breath on the back of her neck. "It doesn't matter if I do or not." She swallowed. "That doesn't change the fact that we're leading two different lives."

"Stop right there. I don't want to hear any more excuses. Who was it who told me if I wanted something I should go for it and not worry about the consequences?"

Taylor's shoulders slumped. "Maybe I'm finding out it's easier to say than do."

"You don't have to do anything right now. You don't leave for Oxford until the end of December. That's almost two months away."

"I guess you're right but—"

"But nothing. Now, what time should I pick you up tonight?"

"What?" She blinked at the sudden shift in the conversation.

"We promised to help with Dylan's campaign, remember?"

She put a hand over her eyes. The envelope-stuffing party! The last thing she wanted to do was to see Dylan, after the cowardly way she'd sneaked out on him this morning. But she knew Mindy wouldn't let her out of this. She'd tie her up and *make* her go if she had to and probably crow about how it was all in the name of love! "What time are we supposed to be there?"

"Six o'clock."

She glanced at the clock once more. Maybe in the next five hours she could find some small store of courage. "Then pick me up at a quarter til."

She started to hang up the phone, but Mindy's voice stopped her. "Taylor?"

"Yes?"

"Relax, okay? Stop worrying about what you think is going to happen and just…let things happen."

She nodded. Good advice. Again, not so easily followed. "I take it that's working for you?"

She heard the smile in her friend's voice. "Let's just say you weren't the only one who didn't leave the dance alone last night."

"WE MUST BE CRAZY to think we can get this all done tonight." Dylan looked around at the stacks of flyers, envelopes and labels to be assembled in time for Monday morning's mail. Reams of computer printouts jockeyed for space with bumper stickers, placards and T-shirts on folding tables arranged around the room. Already, volunteers, including some of the kids from school, were busy stuffing envelopes and assembling information packets. By next weekend, he'd be surprised if there was a single person in the Cedar Creek School District who didn't know about Dylan's campaign for the school board.

"What is this?" He reached into a box and pulled out a handful of six-inch flat rubber discs, each printed with the slogan "Dylan Gets It Done."

"Jar openers." Troy grabbed up one of the discs. "Every household needs one. I got them cheap at the print shop."

"So people are supposed to think of me when they're opening a stuck jar of pickles? Don't you think that's overkill?"

"There's no such thing as overkill in a political campaign." Troy clapped him on the back. "Relax. What's got you so jumpy this evening? Everything will be fine."

What had him so jumpy picked that moment to walk in the door. Though he hadn't seen Taylor since they'd fallen asleep last night, she hadn't been out of his mind all day and the sight of her now did nothing to cool the fever she'd left him in. He stared as she walked past the folding tables to the far end of the room, her head tilted to listen to something her friend Mindy was saying.

Dressed in simple jeans and a sweater, her hair loose around her shoulders, she looked better than any woman had a right to, especially when he was still pissed off at her for running out on him the way she had. The note she'd left had been brief and unrevealing.

Thanks for a wonderful time. I have to go now.

Fists clenched at his sides, he made a beeline for her, reaching her as she rounded the last table, trapping her in the corner. Mindy gave him a sympathetic smile and backed away, ignoring Taylor's silent plea for help. "Why did you leave this morning?"

She studied her manicure. The distracting image of those pink-tipped nails against his chest made his mouth go dry. "I—I had things to do. I—"

He put his hand on her shoulder, unable to keep from touching her any longer. "We never have lied to each other. Don't start now."

She nodded and raised her eyes to meet his. The sadness he saw in those chocolate-brown depths shook him. She wet her lips and it took all the strength he had not to lean down to kiss her. "Then the truth is…" She hesitated, cleared her throat, then went on. "I left because I was afraid."

He frowned. "Afraid of what?" Surely she didn't think he'd ever harm her?

Her eyes darted away from him, then back again. "Afraid that we're taking this too far. This was supposed to be a fun fantasy. Re-creating the past, having a great time. But now…'' She spread her hands in a gesture of helplessness. ''It's something more.''

He looked at her a long time, trying to read the message in her eyes. This had been about more than fun for him from the first. He'd started out wanting to correct old mistakes and quickly moved on to wanting to keep Taylor with him forever. Even though she'd make it clear that wasn't an option.

He took a deep breath. He'd said they shouldn't lie to each other, so he wouldn't. It was time he came clean about his feelings for her. No obligations, but she deserved to know how he felt. She deserved to know that he loved her.

''I know what you mean,'' he began. ''It is something more, for me at least. Taylor I—''

''Sorry to interrupt, Romeo, but I need you over here for a minute.''

Dylan frowned at Troy, who had come rushing up. ''Wait a minute—''

''Sorry, this really can't wait.'' He nodded at Taylor and took Dylan by the arm. ''I need you right now. We've got a little problem.''

''What's going on?'' Dylan asked, still annoyed at being pulled away from Taylor.

Troy nodded toward the door. One of the volunteers was attempting to keep three teenagers out of the room. ''You can't keep us out! We were invited!'' The biggest boy pushed into the room and headed for the pizza boxes set out on a table. ''We came to join the party!''

''Do you know them?'' Troy asked.

Dylan shook his head and hurried over to the group. Once he was close, it was obvious they'd been drinking. Their faces were flushed, eyes reddened, their voices slightly slurred. "You'll have to leave," he said firmly. "Now."

"Hey, we just got here." A kid with close-cropped red hair piled a paper plate high with pizza slices. "If they get to stay, we do, too." He jerked his head toward Berk and Dale, who had come to stand behind Dylan and Troy.

Dylan glanced at Berk. "Do you know these guys?" he asked.

Berk frowned. "They're troublemakers. You don't want them here."

"Who invited you?" Troy asked.

The biggest boy shrugged. "A friend. I don't have to tell you who."

"You can't stay." Dylan grabbed the big kid by the arm and shoved him toward the door. The kid was strong, but Dylan was stronger and had the advantage of being sober. "You've been drinking and you're underage. If you don't leave now, I'll call the police."

The boys glanced at each other, doubt edging out bravado. "Lemme go." The ringleader jerked out of Dylan's grasp. "We didn't want to hang out with a bunch of losers like y'all, anyway."

Dylan watched them swagger toward the door. They grinned at each other, as if they were getting away with something. "Wait!" he called, taking a few steps toward them.

The redhead turned toward him. "What?"

"Who put you up to this?"

The boy laughed. "Wouldn't you like to know?"

He turned and led the way out of the room, the boy's harsh laughter echoing behind them. Troy came to stand beside Dylan. "You think someone sent them here to cause trouble?"

Dylan nodded. "But I don't know who. Or why." He pulled his cell phone from his jacket.

"Who are you calling?" Troy asked.

"The police. If those boys are driving, they don't need to be out on the street. And maybe the cops can find out who gave them their beer and sent them here."

A dispatcher took his report and said they'd send someone out to look for the boys. Dylan slipped the phone back into his jacket and turned to look for Taylor. She was seated at one of the tables, stuffing envelopes and talking with Mindy, avoiding looking at him.

"Trouble in paradise?" Troy nodded toward Taylor.

Dylan looked away. "Why would you think that?"

"Maybe because you look like a hound dog that just lost his best friend."

He shook his head, but said nothing.

"Is it the election? Does she have a problem with politicians?" Troy shook his head. "Not that some people don't, but you don't have a criminal record—yet."

Dylan turned his back to Taylor, disappointment gnawing at him. How could she ignore him so easily when he'd been about to bare his soul for her? "I don't think that matters to her. She's going away to Oxford in January."

"Ah." Troy nodded. "And you don't want her to go. But you're too proud to beg."

"What good would that do?" he snapped. He picked up a flyer and began folding it, accordion style. "She's not a small-town kind of girl. She's never really fit in here."

"Says who?" Troy's eyebrows rose. "Seems to me she's made a pretty good life here—a good job." He looked around the room. "Everybody says she's a great teacher. She has friends. The students like her. How is that not fitting in?''

He shrugged. ''I guess she just doesn't feel…comfortable here.''

''Then maybe the problem isn't the town. Maybe it's her.''

Dylan glanced at his friend. What did he mean, the problem was Taylor? But before he could ask, Troy was called away to deal with a jammed copier and Sue Hartsell asked Dylan if he'd help her carry a box of information packets out to Troy's truck.

Three hours later, Dylan couldn't believe he was standing in the same room. Boxes of neatly sorted envelopes had replaced the random stacks of paper. Trash cans overflowed with empty pizza boxes, soft drink cans and assorted debris, but most of the tables were empty and a weary group of volunteers stood looking at the night's work.

''I can't believe we got it all done,'' Patrice said.

''We never would have made it without y'all.'' Troy went around the group, handing out Dylan Gets It Done! T-shirts. ''Thanks for all your hard work.''

''It was fun.''

''Anytime.''

''Good luck, Dylan.''

As they said their goodbyes and filed out into the night, Dylan stopped Taylor at the door. ''Let me take you home,'' he said. She started to protest, but he put a finger to her lips. ''We need to talk.''

She relaxed in his grip. ''All right.''

The car wasn't the place for the kind of talk they needed, so he retreated to safer topics. ''Do you know those kids who came by tonight?'' he asked.

''The three toughs?'' She nodded. ''I know the redhead

is Rudy Halberg. The big kid is Craig Derrazo. I don't know the third."

"Berk said they were troublemakers."

"Not downright delinquents. More the type to always be on the bad side of any situation." She glanced at him. "Why do you think they came by tonight?"

"I wondered if someone put them up to it."

"Someone who wants to discredit your campaign? But why send the boys?"

He shrugged. "Maybe because they knew I had other kids there tonight. Sending in a trio of underage drunks would look bad, don't you think?"

"Oh, no!" She turned toward him. "I hope that's not the case."

He turned onto her street just as his phone rang. He jerked it from his jacket and answered. "Dylan here."

"Dyl, it's Troy. I just got a call from the police. They picked up those three kids who were here earlier."

His stomach tightened and he let out a sigh. "Before they hurt anyone or themselves, I hope."

"They're okay. I'm not so sure about the rest."

The knot in Dylan's stomach squeezed tighter. "What's wrong? You sound worried."

"Apparently, those boys told the cops that *you* gave them the beer. That we had a bunch of kids here tonight and free drinks and a wild party."

"What the hell!" Dylan slammed his hand against the steering wheel.

Taylor jumped and stared at him. He pulled the car to the curb and shifted into park. "The cops didn't believe them, did they?"

"I don't know what they thought. All I know is, the shit has hit the fan, buddy. You'd better get down here. Now."

TAYLOR INSISTED ON GOING with Dylan to the police station. She didn't know what she could do to help, but one look at the anguish on his face told her he didn't need to be alone.

"If I find out who did this, so help me, I'll make sure everyone knows the kind of dirty games he's playing."

"But who would want to do this?" she asked.

His knuckles whitened on the steering wheel. "Maybe one of my opponents, though they both seem like decent folks. Or maybe Darrell Spivey. He's still making waves about my campaign."

"But why would he do something like this?"

He glanced at her. "Why do people hold grudges? You said yourself, people in this town have long memories."

She fell silent then, frowning. It was true opinions were slow to change around here, but she'd never imagined that judgmental thinking would haunt Dylan as it had her. He was the town's Golden Boy. The local man who had made good and come back to give to the community. How could anyone see that as a negative?

The normally quiet Cedar Creek police station resembled a Los Angeles precinct house on Saturday night. Half a dozen patrol cars were parked at the curb, along with the trucks and cars of a dozen citizens, including angry parents, other students, government officials and a trio of reporters from the local and county papers.

"Mr. Gates, what do you say to the accusations that have been made against your campaign?" A reporter thrust a microphone at Dylan as he and Taylor climbed the steps to the station entrance.

"Mr. Gates, is it true you threw a beer and pizza party to thank your campaign volunteers?"

"Mr. Gates! Mr. Gates! Mr. Gates!"

Taylor rushed up the stairs beside Dylan, grateful for

the brief respite that met them inside the station. A crowd milled around the front desk, but for the moment at least, no one had seen them enter. Dylan took her arm. His face was pale, his jaw set in a hard line. "Let's get this over with."

Troy turned and saw them first. He thrust a piece of paper into Dylan's hand. "I've written a statement for you to give the press."

Dylan handed the paper back to him without looking at it. "I need to find out what's going on first."

Troy glanced back toward the desk and lowered his voice. "It's like I told you on the phone. The cops stopped the boys for drunk driving. The boys said they'd been at your campaign headquarters, that you gave them the beer and were having a big party."

"And the cops believed them?"

Troy frowned. "They were wearing your T-shirts. I guess they swiped them from the tables when we weren't looking. And then one of the officers drove over there and found a bunch of beer cans in the trash we'd set out in the alley."

Dylan sucked in his breath. "It doesn't look good, does it?"

Troy patted his shoulder. "You've got plenty of witnesses who'll vouch for what really happened. Of course, it's still going to stink in the press."

Dylan glanced around them. "Has Councilman Spivey made an appearance?"

"I haven't seen him. Why? Do you think he had something to do with this?"

"He's pretty upset that my father's book is getting attention again. He accused me of 'digging up old garbage' to bolster my campaign. Considering how he hounded my father, I wouldn't put something like this past him."

Troy nodded. "I'll see what I can find out." He glanced at Taylor. "There's something else you should know."

"What's that?" she asked, uneasiness gripping her.

Troy leaned closer. "Apparently, people are saying you and Dylan came up with this idea of the party together. That you were the one who actually invited the students."

Anger surged through her in a red wave. She gripped Dylan's arm and stared at Troy, her throat too tight to speak.

"That's bullshit!" Dylan snapped. "Taylor had nothing to do with this."

Troy shrugged. "I'm only warning you what I heard." He thrust the statement at Dylan again. "Now, get out there and speak to the press before they make something up in order to meet their deadline."

He headed toward the door. Taylor started to go with him, but Troy pulled her back. "It'll be better if he goes alone."

She nodded, resenting the truth in his words. Now wasn't the time for Dylan to be seen with the known "party girl." After all, she might be all grown up now and a teacher, but a leopard didn't really change her spots, did she? And if word had gotten out about some of she and Dylan's recent *adventures*... She shuddered to think what the rumor mill would turn out from that.

She settled for standing in the shadows with Troy, watching Dylan deliver his statement to the eager crowd.

"The young people in question showed up tonight at my campaign headquarters, saying they had been invited by a person whose identity they refused to reveal. I did not know these young men before tonight and I had not invited them to attend our gathering. Nor did anyone involved with my campaign invite them.

"The purpose of tonight's gathering was to put out a

mailing for my campaign. We provided pizza and soft drinks for the volunteers. No alcohol was served and I would never condone such action. As soon as we had convinced these boys to leave, I notified the police. My only regret now is that I did not detain them and thus keep them from driving, until the police arrived.''

Refusing all questions, he ducked his head and strode past the reporters, back into the parking lot. Taylor watched him go, hurting for him, hating those who would do this to him. Why were people in this town always eager to think the worst of anyone?

16

By Monday morning talk of what came to be known as "the Dylan Gates campaign scandal" had edged out rehashing of the homecoming game and the latest increase in gas prices as the most popular topic of conversation around breakfast tables and coffeepots. When Taylor walked into the high school, no less than half a dozen people rushed up to get her story on what had happened. "You were there, weren't you?" Alyson asked, crowding in close and taking Taylor's arm. "Were those kids really there? Drinking?"

"They came by for a few minutes, but Dylan asked them to leave. They were drunk before they got there." She pulled away from Alyson's grasp and pushed past her. "I really don't want to talk about it anymore."

"You'll have to talk about it." Alyson rushed after her.

Taylor sent a silent plea for help to Mindy, who appeared at the door of the teacher's lounge. Mindy fell into step alongside her. "It's going to be a rough day," Mindy said.

Taylor nodded. A rough day. A rough week. A rough two months until she could clear out of here for good. The best she could hope for now was to do what she could to help Dylan get out of this with his reputation intact.

"Taylor, I'm sorry, but you have to know." Alyson put her hand on Taylor's shoulder, stopping her.

Taylor turned to glare at her fellow teacher, but found

only concern in Alyson's eyes. "A memo went out this morning. There's a school-board meeting called for tonight and you have to be there."

Taylor frowned. "Why do I have to be there?"

Alyson bit her lip, her gaze shifting away. "They're going to discuss what happened Saturday night. And the possibility of disciplinary action against you."

"No!" Mindy put her arm around Taylor and pulled her close. "Taylor had nothing to do with anything that happened Saturday night."

Alyson shrugged. "You were there. Some of your students were there. And, well, it isn't exactly a secret that you and Dylan have been seeing each other." She awkwardly patted Taylor's arm. "I'm sorry. I really am."

Taylor watched Alyson go, a sick heaviness in her stomach. Disciplinary action. That could mean anything from a reprimand in her personnel file to dismissal. She was leaving Cedar Creek, but she didn't want to go out on this note. Would that affect her acceptance to the Oxford program or her future chances to teach elsewhere? Did that even matter now?

"I was there Saturday and no one said anything about me," Mindy said. "Why should they single you out?"

Taylor shook her head. "You heard her—it's no 'secret' Dylan and I have been seeing each other." How much did people know about her relationship with Dylan? Did anyone know about the diary entries they'd been "reenacting?" If those things came to light, would they damage Dylan's reputation beyond repair? Had her attempts to put the past to rest stirred up trouble for the future?

"There's nothing wrong with a single man and a single woman going out together," Mindy said.

"Except that I've always had a bad reputation in this town. Why should that change now?"

She turned and headed for her classroom. "Taylor, wait!"

But she ignored her friend's cry. She didn't want to talk about this anymore, didn't want to think about it even. She was tired of defending herself and her actions to people who would always judge her as the person they thought she was, instead of trying to find out what she was really like.

In class, Berk, Dale, Patrice and Jessica gathered around her desk. "We heard about the school-board meeting," Berk said. "We're going to be there to tell people how it really was. Rudy and the others were out to cause trouble."

"That's very…kind of you to offer." She busied herself sorting papers, struggling to talk around a throat constricted by tears. "But I think you should stay home. Don't involve yourselves in this."

"But we can't sit back and not say anything!" Patrice's face was pale, her eyes wide with horror. "We have to let them know the truth."

"I'm sure this is just a formality and that nothing will come of it." Though she wasn't sure of any such thing. "Besides, it's really a moot point what happens, since I'll be leaving the district in January, anyway."

Berk stuck out his lower lip and hunched his shoulders. "We wish you wouldn't go. You're one of the few really cool teachers in this school."

She turned away, blinking back tears. "I'm flattered you think so. Now you really need to go to your desks. I believe we have a lesson on American Poetry to discuss."

Somehow, she made it through that morning of tedious poetry readings and halfhearted discussions of symbolism and metaphor. She ended by giving the students an assignment to write their own poem based on an emotion. She had no doubt she'd be reading her share of odes to anger and frustration in the coming days.

She was trying to decide what to have for lunch when her cell phone rang. It was Dylan. "I just heard about the school-board meeting," he said. "I'm sorry for dragging you into this mess." Frustration roughened his voice.

"It wasn't your fault." She cradled the phone to her cheek and closed her eyes, remembering his hand against her face there. "I'm the one who should apologize to you. I never should have approached you at the reunion and asked you to play these crazy games with me."

"It was more than a game to me," he said, his voice quiet, the words weighted with emotion.

She swallowed hard. "It…it was more than that to me, too," she whispered. "But now it's all turned out wrong.…"

"What happened Saturday night has nothing to do with you," he said. "I'll make sure the school board understands that. We should go to the meeting together. I can pick you up—"

"No!" She straightened, shaking her head. "We can't show up together. Let's not give them any more ammunition."

"What do you mean, ammunition?"

She swallowed, struggling to sound calm when she felt like screaming. "I can tell you exactly what's going to happen tonight. They're going to drag out my reputation as the wild party girl. All the rumors about us and the fact that we're seeing each other now will be rehashed."

"You don't know that."

"Oh, yes, I do. I've been here before. Remember?"

He was silent for a moment. She closed her eyes, waiting. Was he thinking of that other time, ten years ago, when they'd turned away from each other? She knew now he'd been trying to protect her then. Would he take her advice this time and protect himself?

"Taylor, whatever happens, I'm on your side this time." His voice was warm. Full of certainty and strength.

Fresh tears rose in her eyes and she leaned back against her desk as her knees threatened to buckle. "You don't have to sacrifice yourself for me, Dylan. After all, I'm going away. This is your home and you have to live here. You'd be better off distancing yourself from me as much as possible. At least you're one of their own. They'll forgive you."

"I think you've got it wrong. I think you've got more friends in this town than you know."

She shook her head. "Thanks for trying to cheer me up, but I have to go now." She clicked off the phone and let it dangle from her hand while she stared at the floor, willing tears not to fall. She had to stay strong. She could get through this. She'd survived before by herself. She could do it again.

TROY INSISTED ON accompanying Dylan to the school-board meeting. "We're in this together." He straightened his shoulders and puffed out his chest. "Besides, if it gets rough, you need someone to guard your back."

"It's a school-board meeting, not a gang rumble."

Troy shook his head. "Apparently you've forgotten how serious small towns take these things."

He began to see Troy's point when they pulled up to the administration building and found the parking lot almost full. Media trucks blocked the fire lanes and dozens of people, both locals and those from out of town, mingled around the entrance. Ignoring several reporters who crowded toward them, the two friends pushed their way through the door into the boardroom.

Dylan looked around at the people who filled every chair and lined the walls. His stomach was in a knot and he was ready to punch the first person who looked at him wrong. He saw Taylor with Mindy on the other side of the room. They were seated at one end of the front row, their heads together. He started to make his way over to them, but Berk stepped out, blocking his path.

"We're here to tell everybody what really happened the other night." Berk nodded to the other students gathered around him. "And to let people know what a big help you and Ms. Reed have been to us."

"Thank you." He looked at each of them. Had he been so young and earnest once? "Are you sure you really want to stick your necks out for us?" He looked around them at the sometimes hostile faces. "I don't think we're all that popular at the moment."

Jessica stepped up beside Berk. "One of the things we learned from your father's book is to do what's right, not what's popular."

He nodded, too moved to speak. *Did you hear that, Dad?*

"I call this meeting of the Cedar Creek Independent School District to Order." The board president, Sandy Ames, pounded his gavel and the audience settled into their seats. Dylan found a spot next to Troy along the wall while those who had signed on to address the board lined up behind a microphone in the center of the room.

The first speaker was a refined-looking woman who stated she was "appalled" at "this blatant corruption of our young people by persons responsible for the formation of their character." Subsequent speakers railed against young people being involved in politics at all, the arrogance of big-city lawyers who came into town and tried to change things and the questionable morals of some of those in the teaching profession.

Dylan ground his teeth together, hands clenched into fists. "These people would question the morals of Mother Teresa," he growled.

Troy put a hand on his arm. "Don't worry. Our side gets a turn, too."

Dylan watched Taylor. She sat stone-still, head up, facing forward, her skin the color of parchment. She scarcely blinked as angry parents and citizens called for her resignation. What was going through her head right now? Was she sorry she'd ever met him? Or only sorry that he wasn't beside her right now?

Grady Murphy stepped up to the microphone and cleared his throat. "I'm Grady Murphy, head of the English Department at Cedar Creek High. I've known Taylor Reed and Dylan Gates a long time, since we were all at school together. I think I know their characters pretty well."

Taylor jerked her head around to stare at him, eyes blazing. Grady continued speaking, his voice gravelly. "I have to say, Taylor Reed is one of the best teachers we've ever had. She has the rare ability to make her students want to learn. She teaches them, not just the subject matter of the course, but how to think and to use their minds." He cleared his throat again. "She's made me rethink some of the ways I teach myself. As for Dylan Gates…" He glanced over at Dylan. "He may have gone off to the big city, but he came home because he is a part of this community. He wants to give back to the place he calls home. I guess like anyone who's lived long enough, he's made his share of enemies. Maybe one of them had something to do with what happened last night, but I know Dylan is innocent, as is Taylor.''

As Grady moved away from the microphone, Dylan met Taylor's eyes across the room. She looked stunned, her cheeks flushed.

"I'm Clay Walsh, principal of Cedar Creek High School.'' Clay took Grady's place at the microphone. ''I want to second Grady's assertion that Taylor Reed is one of the top teachers on our staff. As some of you may know, Taylor was recently awarded a prestigious Oxford fellowship. It's quite an honor, though I've been doing my darnedest to convince her not to go. We need more teachers like her on the staff. I'm certain she had nothing to do with those students either drinking or being present at Mr. Gates's campaign headquarters that night.''

Mindy spoke next, about how Taylor had inspired her as a teacher and a friend. ''I was at Dylan Gates's campaign headquarters Saturday night,'' she said. ''Those boys came in uninvited and it was clear they'd been drinking before they ever walked in the door. Dylan and Taylor had nothing to do with their being there.''

Another teacher and a parent took their turn at the mike. Then Alyson stepped up. Taylor frowned and looked away. Dylan's shoulders tightened. What would Taylor's life-long nemesis have to say about her now?

"My name is Alyson Michaels and I teach physical education at Cedar Creek High School. I've known Taylor Reed since the first day she walked into that building as a student ten years ago.'' She grinned at the audience. ''She was a California girl who looked like she'd just stepped off a movie set and I was green with envy when I saw the way all the boys looked at her.''

Nervous laughter floated up from parts of the audience. Alyson looked at Taylor. ''But I don't think you can be jealous of someone unless you secretly admire them, too. And I always admired the way Taylor handled herself. She could be a little stuck up sometimes, but she was never mean. And I know as a teacher, she truly cares about her students. I think the board would be doing us all a disservice to take any action against someone like her, who has always given her best as a teacher.''

Alyson flashed her smile again and walked away, hips twitching. Dylan stared after her, then glanced at Taylor. She was sitting, head down, hand over her eyes.

''I understand we have a group of students who would like to speak,'' Sandy said.

''Yes, sir.'' Berk stood, followed by Dale, Jessica and Patrice. ''We're students in Ms. Reed's class, and we were at Mr. Gates's headquarters Saturday night.''

Sandy nodded. ''All right. You have five minutes.''

Berk shuffled to the mike and cleared his throat. ''Saturday night, we went to Mr. Gates's to help stuff envelopes for his campaign. We went because he'd been a big help to us with a class project we're working on and we wanted to pay him back.'' He looked at the others, who nodded.

''Anyway, while we were there, these three boys came busting in. Rudy Halberg, Craig Derrazo and Mike Palermo. It was pretty obvious they'd been drinking. Mr. Gates asked them to leave right away, but they wouldn't. They said they'd been invited.''

''Who invited them?'' the president asked.

''They wouldn't say.'' Jessica leaned into the microphone. ''They just kept loading their plates up with pizza.''

''We only had pizza and sodas,'' Patrice added. ''No beer. They brought theirs with them.''

"Mr. Gates and Mr. Sommers made them leave and that was it," Dale said. "Nothing happened."

"And Ms. Reed didn't have anything to do with it," Berk said. "She was over in a corner working on something when all this happened." He shoved his hands into his pants' pockets. "I just think y'all would be making a big mistake to try to blame any of this on her or Mr. Gates. Somebody screwed up, but it wasn't them." He nodded. "That's all."

"Thank you, son." The president slammed down his gavel once more. "If there are no more speakers..."

"Wait." Dylan pushed his way forward. "I'd like to address the board, if I may?"

The board members frowned and consulted one another. Dylan saw Maidy Sellers shake her head. Finally, Sandy turned to address him. "Your name is not on the list of speakers, but in the interest of fairness, I feel we should make an exception. You have five minutes."

"Thank you." He squared himself in front of the microphone. "I came back to Cedar Creek after some years on the West Coast because I knew that this was where I belonged. This town is a special place and I want to do my part to keep it that way. That's why, when a group of citizens asked me to run for school board, I agreed. I saw it as a way to give back to this community.

"About that same time, I renewed my old acquaintance with Taylor Reed. I've seen the fine woman she's become and how much she's done for her students. I was concerned and disappointed to see that anyone felt this meeting tonight was even necessary. Any accusations that have been made against her are entirely false."

"Of course you'd think that."

Dylan turned to see who was speaking and found himself staring across the room at Darrell Spivey. Though in his sixties now, the city councilman stood as straight and broad-shouldered as he had years ago when he'd railed against Dylan's father. "You're in an illicit relationship with the woman," Spivey continued.

"Councilman, you are out of order." Sandy slammed down his gavel.

"It's all right," Dylan said. "I'd like to address this, if I may." He nodded to Spivey. "I wouldn't call my relationship with Taylor Reed illicit." He looked at Taylor, willing her to meet his eyes. But she kept her head bent, forcing him to speak to her slumped shoulders. It didn't matter. She would hear what he had to say and know that he meant it.

He raised his voice, so that everyone else would hear it, too. "The fact is, I'm in love with Taylor Reed. I have been for a very long time." He focused his gaze on Spivey again. To think he'd once been intimidated by this man. "Do you know what that feels like, Councilman? I pity you, because I think you don't. I think you've let your bitterness over the past destroy any joy you might have in the future. I don't intend to let that happen to me."

He was dimly aware of the cheers that rose up around him, of hands patting his back and people jostling his side. Taylor still had her head down, her shoulders shaking, as if she were weeping. All the bravado he'd felt a moment before deserted him. What if Taylor didn't return his feelings? What if he'd just made a very public fool of himself?

He barely had the strength to push his way to the door. He needed air. As he shoved open the door, he heard Sandy Ames adjourn the meeting to an executive session to consider the matter at hand.

AS THE CROWD FILED OUT of the boardroom, Taylor slipped down the hall to a private office to hide. She was too overwhelmed by everything that had happened to face anyone right now. Not bothering to turn on the light, she sank into a desk chair and covered her face with her hands. Had people really said all those wonderful things about her—even Grady and Alyson?

She lowered her hands and stared out at the dimly lit room, Alyson's words replaying in her mind. Her comment about Taylor being "a little stuck up" hit home. Had her attempts to appear indifferent to others' opinions of her come off instead as aloof and unfriendly? Had *she* been guilty of judging too harshly?

Was Dylan right? Was she wrong about what people thought of her? Was her love life not the only part of her stuck in the past?

And Dylan. Oh, God, Dylan. She sank lower in the chair, heart beating so hard she thought it might burst. He'd said he loved her. That he'd loved her for a long time. Hearing those words she'd known they were true for her, as well. She'd loved Dylan Gates for ten years now. What had made her think she could purge herself of those feelings by retreating into fantasy?

She'd thought she could keep physical passion separate from emotional intimacy. What a fool she'd been.

What would she do now? She'd been wrong about so much. She didn't want to be wrong about this, too.

She put her head down on the desk and closed her eyes, willing her mind to empty, praying for direction.

She didn't know how much time passed before Mindy came to get her. "They're ready to announce their decision," Mindy said.

Taylor nodded and reached for her purse. "All right."

"Here. You'd better fix your makeup." Mindy turned on the light and handed Taylor a tissue.

She found a mirror in her purse and dabbed at her smudged mascara. "I look hideous."

"It'll be all right." She put a hand on Taylor's shoulder and squeezed.

Taylor looked up at her friend. "Thanks. For everything. I know I don't say that enough."

"I haven't really done anything."

"You're here with me now. That's something."

"You'd do the same for me."

But would she? Taylor wondered how good a friend she'd been to anyone. Was it too late to change that?

Together, they walked down the hall to the boardroom. Dylan was already there and when he motioned her over, she went to stand by him. She slipped her hand into his, holding on tightly, hoping that handclasp would tell him things she didn't yet have the words to say.

The board president, Sandy Ames, stood behind the lectern at the center of the dais, every line of his face deepened by the harsh fluorescent lights. She remembered seeing him in the grocery store he'd managed when she was a girl and thinking him old then, but he wouldn't have been over forty in those days. Funny how time changed all sorts of perceptions she'd had about people.

"Thank you for your patience at this late hour," he said. "Now, I'll make this brief." He consulted a piece of paper in his hand. "This board finds no grounds for disciplinary action in this matter."

Cheers went up around them. Taylor felt hands jostling her, congratulations echoing in her ears. She clung to Dylan. He put his arm around her, holding her up. "Come on." He spoke close to her ear, his breath warm, stirring her hair. "I'll take you home."

He led her out a back door, avoiding the press she was sure was waiting out front. She didn't bother to ask about her car; she didn't really care. She could think about those things tomorrow. There were too many other thoughts crowding her mind right now.

Neither one of them said anything until they were several miles away, past the turnoff to her house. "Where are we going?" She turned to look at him. His face was in shadow, but she thought she would have known the jut of his chin and the firm line of his brow anywhere, the way she knew her own profile in a mirror.

He didn't take his eyes off the road. "There's something I want you to see," he said.

Soon enough, she recognized the road leading to his parents' house. She hadn't been here in years, but little had changed. The same ranch property stretched on either side of the two-lane road. The same gas and grocery sat on the corner a mile above his place. "It's like time stood still out here," she said.

"There are a few newer houses," he said. "New families in some of the old ones. But mostly things are the same. I guess the developers don't consider this side of town attractive yet."

He pulled his truck into the driveway and parked by the back door. They entered through the kitchen, which smelled of fresh paint. Gloss-white cabinets reflected the glow of overhead floods, while a white granite island would have looked at home in a Los Angeles loft. "Everything looks great," she said, running her hand across the smooth countertop.

"I was able to keep a lot of the fixtures in the house, but this room needed updating." He opened a cabinet in the island. "Would you like a drink? Gin and tonic?"

"That sounds good." Anything to pull her out of the

numbness stealing over her. She could feel her senses shutting down from overload.

Drink in hand, she leaned back against the sink. "You've been really busy to get all this done in so short a time."

"The other rooms aren't this far along. Most of the paint is done and some of the floors. There's still plumbing and electrical." He looked around. "I'd have probably come off cheaper if I'd started over building a new place from scratch."

"But that's not the point. Those places wouldn't have been your home."

He settled against the island, facing her. "No. I wanted to be here, even if I didn't necessarily want it the same."

"Your parents would be proud."

A smile quirked the corners of his mouth. "It felt good coming back here. Right." He raised his eyes to meet hers, his gaze searching. "I know what that word means to me, but what does it mean to you?"

She set her glass aside and hugged her arms tight across her chest, digging deep for the right words. "I—I don't know. I think home is a place I'm still looking for."

"Do you think you'll find it in Oxford?"

"Before tonight, I might have said yes, but now..." She shook her head. "No. I don't think so."

"People meant what they said tonight about you. They respect you. They value your friendship." He set his own drink aside. "And I meant what I said, too. I do love you."

She nodded, her heart racing, her throat squeezing around her words. "I know you do." She sucked in a shaky breath. "And I think I love you, too."

He moved to her, wrapping his hands around her shoulders, pulling her close. She rested her forehead against his chest, trying to stop shaking. The words she'd said…the things she felt…why did they terrify her so? Was it because they seemed so fragile, something one wrong move would send shattering into dust?

He slid his hands down her arms and twined his fingers in hers. "Isn't that enough? Can't we take that and make our own future together?"

She looked up at him, into those brown eyes so full of trust. So full of faith in her. "I—I don't know. So much has happened tonight. So much to think about…" She closed her eyes and rested her forehead against his chin. "I'm tired. I don't want to think anymore. I just want to…*be*."

He cradled her face in his hand and tipped her chin up until her mouth found his. The kiss was gentle, but insistent, demanding an intimacy that both thrilled and frightened her.

He broke the kiss and looked into her eyes. "Stay here with me tonight." His gaze searched her, probing deeper. "All night."

She nodded. "All right." Maybe there was something to be learned from staying with him until the sun rose.

Wordlessly, he took her hand and led her from the kitchen, down the hall to a large bedroom. In the dim glow of one bedside lamp, she had an impression of heavy mahogany furniture and a blue-and-white quilt in a Texas Star pattern. He shut the bedroom door behind them, then turned and unfastened the top button of her blouse.

She reached up to help him, but he stilled her hand. "No. I want to undress you. All you have to do is relax…and *be*."

He worked swiftly, fingertips barely grazing her skin as he unfastened her blouse and skirt, letting the garments fall to the floor around her ankles. He undid the clasp of her bra and skimmed it back over her shoulder. She felt his gaze on her, as intense as any touch, and her nipples rose and tightened.

He helped her step out of her panties and panty hose, and now she was naked in front of him. He stepped back and looked at her, not speaking or saying anything. She fought the urge to cover herself with her arms. "What is it?" she whispered, not wanting to break the silent spell that held them.

He shook his head, his expression dark, unreadable. "I want to remember how you look, right now."

Then he began to undress himself. She watched, aroused by the play of light across muscle and skin. Every movement spoke of strength tempered by such tenderness. Her throat tightened and she had to look away.

Naked now, he took her hand and led her to the bed. "Lie back," he whispered, pressing her shoulders back against the sheets. "Close your eyes."

Eyes shut, she felt the weight of him settle beside her, smelled the musk of his arousal mingled with the fresh cotton of the sheets. His hand skimmed over her, the heat of him settling into her skin and she arched toward him, craving more.

He kissed her jaw, his tongue teasing the curve of her chin, tracing the column of her throat, outlining the bones of her shoulders. He feathered kisses around her breast, trailing his tongue in ever tighter circles toward her achingly taut nipple. She held her breath, anticipating, and gasped when he took the tip of her breast into his mouth.

He suckled and laved, his tongue teasing, torturing, relentless. She was soaking wet, writhing, wordlessly begging for release. He clamped his hand to her thigh, pinning her, opening her wide. Even the breeze from the ceiling fan across her aching center was too much.

She felt his erection against her thigh, heated and hard. She eased her hand down to stroke him and was rewarded with a muffled grunt. He tried to push her hand away, but she persisted. ''I like the way you feel,'' she whispered, squeezing him gently.

He responded by easing two fingers into her, probing deeply, then withdrawing, his thumb angling up to stroke her swollen clit. At the same time he renewed his attention to her breasts, overwhelming her senses. His hands and tongue claimed her, devoured her, left no room in her mind for anything but this incredible sensation of him awakening her to her own desire.

When she was drawn taut like a bow, on the very edge of reason, he knelt over her and plunged into her. He filled her and overwhelmed her, driving her higher still with each thrust, both demanding and giving more and more. There was no room for thought or reason here, only need and longing and being as she'd never known before.

She came with a keening moan and felt his own release quake through her. They clung to one another, eyes shut, gasping for breath, their hearts thudding in unison with the aftershocks of their lovemaking. Every nerve tingled with awareness and satisfaction. Was this what people meant when they talked of being loved completely—that they had been touched by something profound, even down to a cellular level?

After a long while—or maybe only a few minutes— Dylan eased off of her, though he kept his arm across her as he burrowed into the covers alongside her. His breathing grew more even and she wondered if he was asleep.

Careful not to disturb him, she rolled over onto her side and lay looking at him. His face was relaxed, unlined, the faint shadow of beard along his jaw giving him a rakish look. She smiled and gently brushed the hair back from his forehead. What was going on between them? Was tonight the last time they would be together or the beginning of a lifetime of such times together?

She took the fact that the thought didn't terrify her as a good sign. Maybe she was braver than she thought. She smiled and softly kissed his cheek. "I love you," she whispered, knowing he couldn't hear her. "Do you think we're brave enough to stay together? Forever?"

17

"WILL YOU GET AWAY from that window? You're making me nervous." Troy took Dylan by the arm and tugged him back from the front window of the campaign headquarters. "The media will see you and think you're anxious about the election results."

"I *am* anxious about the results." He picked up a computer printout of early polling results and laid it back down again. "We've still got two hours until the polls close."

"You're going to win. I know it."

Dylan glanced toward the front window again. School had let out an hour ago. Why wasn't Taylor here yet?

"She's going to be here," Troy said. "Maybe she went home to change clothes."

Dylan flushed. "How did you know what I was thinking?"

"I know all the signs by now." Troy laughed. "Why don't the two of you get married and get it over with, instead of mooning after each other all the time?"

Dylan ducked his head. "In case you haven't noticed, I've been a little busy. I don't think there's a group in this county I haven't spoken to lately."

"And it's going to pay off at the polls tonight." Troy tapped the computer printouts. "Tomorrow, people will be talking to you as the newest member of the Cedar Creek School Board."

The phone rang and Troy rushed to answer it. Dylan watched him, resisting the urge to reach into his pocket where the ring box made a hard knot against his hip. He and Taylor had carefully avoided the subject of her staying in the weeks since she'd spent the night at his house. He'd used the excuse of being busy with the campaign, but really, he was waiting for her to bring up the subject. Had she meant it when she'd said she realized she wouldn't find what she was looking for at Oxford? Did that mean she was willing to give things a try with him?

The front door opened and a group of students burst in. Berk led the procession, pushing a television on a trolley, followed by Dale with the video camera and half a dozen others. Taylor followed behind them, her face flushed with the November cold.

Smiling, he went to her and kissed her cheek. "Thanks for coming."

"I wouldn't miss it." She slipped out of her coat and draped it around an empty chair. "I would have been here sooner, but I had to stop and cast my vote."

"And who did you vote for?" He slipped his arms around her and pulled her close.

"This very handsome write-in candidate." She trailed one finger down his cheek, setting up an electric current that went straight to his groin. What was it about this woman that her mere touch could affect him this way? And how could he make sure these feelings never stopped?

"Is it okay if we set the TV up at the front of the room?" Berk interrupted them.

Reluctantly, Dylan moved away from Taylor. "Sure. What's the TV for, anyway?"

Berk grinned. "We finished our movie about your dad's book. We thought you'd like to see it."

"You bet I want to see it." He clapped Berk on the back. "I can't wait."

"We'll have it ready in a few moments for our first official screening."

The door opened again and Mindy entered, pulling Clay along behind her. "The polls are busy," she announced. "We had to wait in line. I was afraid we'd be too late to see the movie."

"I told her you wouldn't start without us." Clay helped Mindy out of her coat.

"We have a few other guests coming," Jessica said. "We won't start until everyone is here."

As if on cue, the door opened to admit Alyson, who was carrying a platter of cookies. "Who invited her?" Mindy wondered out loud.

"I did." Troy stepped forward to take the cookies. "I'm so glad you could make it."

"Oh, I wouldn't miss it!" Alyson fluttered her lashes. Troy grinned back.

"Must be something in the air," Clay muttered.

"What's that?" Dylan glanced at him.

Clay looked sheepish. "I think you started something with your romantic declaration before the school board." He reached out and took Mindy's hand. "It made me think I'd been a coward about my feelings for Mindy."

Mindy blushed and held up her left hand. For the first time, Dylan noticed the diamond solitaire glinting there. "Clay and I have decided to make it official," she said. "No more sneaking around."

"Congratulations!" Taylor hugged her friend close.

"Yes, congratulations." Dylan added his good wishes, even as the knot in his stomach tightened. How was it these two, who had been so shy about declaring their feelings, now found it easy to make this public commitment, when he and Taylor couldn't seem to get around to doing so?

He looked up, trying to catch Taylor's eye, but she was looking away, at the door, which had opened to reveal yet another visitor.

Councilman Spivey stood in the open doorway, back rigid, the lines of his face deepened in a scowl. "I'm here, Gates," he declared. "You've got five minutes to explain the meaning of this."

Dylan clenched his jaw. "I might have known he'd find a way to make trouble."

He started toward the door, but Patrice rushed past him to intervene. "Mr. Spivey, Mr. Gates didn't invite you here, we did." She took the city councilman's arm. "We wanted you to see for yourself the class project we've been working on. We have a chair reserved for you right here." She led him to a seat in the front row.

Dylan glanced at Taylor. She shook her head. Whatever the students were up to, they'd done it on their own. He turned and found Berk standing beside him.

"We're not trying to cause trouble," Berk said. "We just thought if he saw what we were really doing, he'd see it wasn't any kind of personal attack against him and his family." He glanced to where the councilman was accepting a cup of coffee from Jessica. "Besides, if he's here now, he can't say later there was anything out of order going on here tonight."

Dylan nodded. "Thanks. And maybe this will help."

Berk shrugged. "We figure it can't hurt."

"All right, everybody. Take your seats and we'll begin." Dale thumped a can of soda on a desktop as a makeshift gavel. "Somebody pull the blinds on the front window and we'll be set."

Blinds drawn and lights dimmed, Patrice walked to the

front of the room and stood in front of the television set. "You're about to see the movie our class made as our senior project. We chose to study the book, *A Ranger Remembers,* by Samuel Gates, who was a Texas Ranger in this county during the Civil Rights movement. He was also the father of Dylan Gates, who helped us a lot with the project. So, we want to start by thanking him for that help."

Applause and cheers went up from the partisan crowd. Dylan smiled and bowed.

"We also want to thank our teacher, Ms. Reed, for her help."

More cheers. Taylor beamed.

"We learned a lot about the history of our town and about the Civil Rights movement from this book," Patrice continued. "We also learned about things like research and art and filmmaking. And we learned that even one person who speaks up for what is right can make a difference. Not always right away, but eventually."

She stepped aside and Dale pressed the button to begin the movie.

The screen flickered to life with a still photo of Dylan's father as a young man, ramrod-straight in his starched khaki uniform, staring into the camera with clear eyes. More pictures followed, each added to the screen to form a collage: Cedar Creek circa 1960, the old high school, Sam Gates with his wife and children. Dylan stared at the image of himself as a five-year-old, clinging to his father's hand, and felt a rush of longing for his father.

More photos followed. Newspaper clippings telling the events of the day. The Texas Rangers escorting black children to school. Rows of black and white young people staging a sit-in at the corner drugstore.

The screen flickered again and shifted to live action.

Students from Taylor's class played the parts of the Rangers and the students and the townspeople protesting integration. Dressed in period fashions and hairstyles, they did a good job of conveying their impression of what things must have been like.

The next shot was of a timeline showing the chronology of the Civil Rights movement in the county. Students interviewed older adults who had been part of the movement in Cedar Creek and elsewhere.

Dramatic music blared from the speakers, then flames filled the screen. The camera pulled back to reveal a cross blazing on the lawn of the old high school. White-robed Klansmen marched around it. Flames crackled, music trumpeted and people shouted. The hair on the backs of Dylan's arms stood on end.

The scene shifted again to the present-day high school. Students of all races gathered in the cafeteria for lunch. Hip-hop blared from a group of cars in the parking lot. A black boy and a white girl danced together at homecoming.

Dylan's own face flashed on the screen next. He was talking about his father. "I think my father chose to write about this period of history because he knew it was important and because he had firsthand knowledge of it and because it had affected him deeply. He wanted people to see that civil rights had been a struggle, something they should never take for granted.

"I think he felt, because it hadn't been an easy fight, that made the victory that much sweeter. He wasn't naive. He knew there were still problems. There *are* still problems. But things are better than they were and can get better still if people remember. His book challenged people to remember, just as your class project does."

The screen went still again, with a last image of Sam

Gates, Texas Ranger. This was an older Sam, hair graying at the temples, lines radiating from his eyes. But he still stood straight as an arrow in a starched uniform, his eyes looking full-on at the viewer.

Dylan's throat felt tight. In those few minutes of film, these kids had captured the essence of his father. A man who wouldn't back down, who would tell the truth even if it hurt. As someone switched on the lights, he stood, applauding.

Others rose around him, until the room was filled with people cheering for the students. "My father would be very proud," Dylan said, raising his voice to be heard. "I'm very proud. Thank you for sharing that with us."

He shifted his gaze to Councilman Spivey. The old man sat hunched in his chair, staring at the black screen. As the crowd moved around him, he rose and turned toward the door. Dylan intercepted him. "You have to admit they did a good job," he said.

Spivey looked at him. "They took one of the ugliest periods in our history and reduced it to forty-five minutes of arty pictures and feel-good prose. A waste of taxpayers' money." He narrowed his eyes. "I suppose you see it as a perfectly good substitute for old-fashioned education."

"I think we learn in all kinds of ways. I've even learned a thing or two from you."

Spivey straightened. "What's that?"

"We're both after the same thing. We want to honor our father's memories and give back to the place where we came from. We don't go after those goals in the same way, but I don't think we necessarily have to."

"I don't have time to listen to this nonsense." Spivey pushed past him, out the door.

"Do you think the film changed his mind about anything?"

He turned and saw Taylor watching the departing councilman. "Probably not. But it doesn't matter. I'm through worrying about him." He put his arm around her. "After this is all over tonight, let's go somewhere. Just the two of us. I have something I want to show you."

She smiled up at him. "I was thinking the same thing. I have something I want to show you."

He raised one eyebrow. "Another rumor from your diary?"

She shook her head. "Something better."

What could be better? His stomach quivered with anticipation.

"Good news!" Troy rushed up to them. "I just got off the phone. The last polls closed ten minutes ago. The early tallies show you're ahead of Sellers and Ramirez by eight percent."

Dylan pursed his lips. "Not a very wide margin."

"It'll get wider. I have a good feeling about this." He handed Dylan a piece of paper. "You need to start practicing your victory speech."

Taylor slipped her hand into his. "Let's check out the buffet table. You can try your speech out on me."

"I'd like to try out a few things on you, but talking isn't one of them."

She gave him a coy look. "There'll be time for that later. I promise."

ANY FURTHER DOUBTS about Dylan's victory were erased at nine o'clock when Maidy Sellers called to congratulate him and to concede the election. Jess Ramirez followed suit shortly thereafter. When Troy made the announcement, cheers rocked the campaign headquarters. Someone helped Dylan to stand on a desk. "I want to thank every one of you for all the work you've put in to make this possible," he said. "I especially want to thank Troy Sommers, my campaign manager. I hope this is the beginning of many years of public service to the people of Cedar Creek."

The press snapped photos and people crowded around to shake his hand. Taylor watched, her heart feeling too big for her chest. She'd wanted this for him, because she knew how much he wanted it for himself. Only now did she realize she wanted it for *herself,* too. She could look at this victory and know all the fears she'd had about her reputation or image in town affecting the outcome of the election had been unfounded.

She was still adjusting to the idea that she might have been wrong about the people in this town. Ten years of looking at things a certain way didn't change overnight, but it was getting easier. She'd even eaten lunch with Alyson one day last week and managed not to grimace even once.

Dylan's gaze met hers across the room and warmth zinged through her. His caring and patience had touched her in ways she couldn't even name. But she'd been silent too long. There were things she had to say to him. Things she *needed* to say before the night was over.

An hour later, he found her by the buffet table, helping Alyson and Troy clean up the leftovers. He put his hand on her shoulder. "Are you ready to leave?"

She nodded. "I think so." She looked at Alyson. "Can you finish up here?"

"You go on." Troy patted Alyson on the back. "Aly and I will be fine."

Taylor waited until they were in the parking lot before she burst out laughing. *"Aly?"*

"I think my campaign manager might be smitten," Dy-

lan said, unlocking his truck. "Maybe Clay is right.
Maybe there's something in the air."

"Maybe so," she murmured. Once those two had made
up their minds, they hadn't waited long, had they? Why
was it so much easier for other people to have that kind
of faith in the future?

"Where to?" Dylan asked.

She laid her head back against the seat and stared out
at the clear, night sky. "The old gravel pit."

They drove in silence, the tires humming on the pave-
ment. The night was cool, so Dylan switched on the
heater. The warm air curled up around Taylor's ankles,
but a deeper warmth grew inside her.

"Why the gravel pit?" Dylan asked. "It's too cold to
go skinny-dipping."

She smiled. "I know."

He guided the truck up the rutted drive and parked beside the water-filled pit where generations of Cedar Creek
youngsters had splashed away the summers. Gravel hadn't
been mined there for fifty years, but people still referred
to the swimming hole as the gravel pit. Along with Inspiration Point, it was a popular make-out spot and, ac-
cording to Taylor's diary, the place where she and Dylan
had supposedly gone skinny-dipping.

He shut off the truck and turned toward her. "Listen,
I don't know if this is the right time or anything, but I
have something for you—"

"Wait. First, there's something I want you to have."
She unfastened her seat belt, then opened her purse and
took out a slim envelope. "Here."

He took the envelope and turned it over and over in his
hand. "What is this?"

"Open it." She reached up and switched on the map
light.

He fit his finger under the envelope flap and pulled out the single sheet of letterhead. Even from here, Taylor could see the familiar engraving depicting Oxford University. "'Dear Ms. Reed,'" Dylan read. "'We are sorry to hear that you are withdrawing from our program. We wish you well in all your future endeavors.'"

He looked up, gaze searching. "Then you really mean it? You're staying here in Cedar Creek?"

She nodded. "Yes. If you still want me."

He tossed the letter aside and reached for her, grasping her arms and dragging her to him. He stared into her eyes, stopping her heart with the intensity of his gaze. "You're a liar if you say I gave you any doubts."

"No doubts about you," she breathed before his lips covered hers in a drowning kiss. She surrendered to that kiss, giving up the last bit of fear that nagged her, losing herself in the power of her feelings for him.

When at last he pulled away, she felt drained of anything but happiness. He reached into his pocket and pulled out a small ring box. "I've been carrying this around for days, wondering when to give it to you."

With trembling fingers, she took the box and pried open the lid. A pear-shaped solitaire glinted in the glow of the map light. "Dylan, it's gorgeous!"

He took her hand in his. "Marry me, Taylor. We already wasted ten years. Let's not waste any more."

"Yes." She leaned forward and kissed his cheek, her voice choked with tears. "Yes, I'll marry you, Dylan. No more wasting time." He slipped it onto her finger and they kissed again. A leisurely tasting. *We'll have a lifetime of kisses like this,* she thought.

"Do you know what day it is?" he asked when he raised his head again.

She laughed. "Election day?"

He shook his head. "It's November tenth. Ten years ago today was the senior camping trip."

Her eyes widened. "The night the rumors all started."

He smoothed his hand down her back. "In a way, that's where it really began for us, wasn't it? If those rumors hadn't started, we might not have gotten together again to re-create them."

He bent to kiss her again, his hand sliding around to cup her breast. "Let's go back to my place," he said.

His thumb was tracing slow circles around her nipple, sending shock waves of arousal through her, making it difficult to think or speak. "N-not yet." With some effort, she pushed away from him and leaned down to pick up her purse. Sliding across the truck, she opened the door. "Come with me a minute."

"I told you it was too cold to go skinny-dipping," he said as he followed her toward the lake.

Offering no explanation, she took his hand and led him down to the edge of the water. Gravel crunched beneath their shoes and a chill breeze tugged at their clothes and hair. When they could go no farther without getting wet, she stopped and took the diary from her purse.

"Another rumor?" he asked.

She smiled and shook her head, then, reaching back, she lofted the diary. It sailed in a high arc over the water, tumbling end over end and landing with a loud splash. Icy droplets of water spattered them and waves lapped at the toes of their shoes.

Dylan stared at the ripples stretching out from the middle of the lake. "Was there anything in there we haven't done?"

"A few things." She shrugged. "It doesn't matter. I'm through reliving the past." She threaded her fingers through his, feeling the ring rub between them. "From now on, I'm more interested in the future.'' She turned toward him. ''Our future.''

He held her tightly, their bodies as close as could be while dressed. ''If it wasn't so cold out here, I suggest we start a few new rumors.''

''I like the way you think.'' She slid her hands up under his shirt, finding warm, bare skin. ''Next time we'll bring a sleeping bag.''

He kissed along her jaw. ''And some firewood.''

''Right now, let's go home and make our own bonfire.''

''I thought you'd never ask.''

HARLEQUIN®

Temptation

THE WRONG BED

What happens when a girl finds herself in the
wrong bed…with the *right* guy?

Find out in:

#866 NAUGHTY BY NATURE by Jule McBride
February 2002

#870 SOMETHING WILD by Toni Blake
March 2002

#874 CARRIED AWAY by Donna Kauffman
April 2002

#878 HER PERFECT STRANGER by Jill Shalvis
May 2002

#882 BARELY MISTAKEN by Jennifer LaBrecque
June 2002

#886 TWO TO TANGLE by Leslie Kelly
July 2002

Midnight mix-ups have never been so much fun!

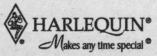

HARLEQUIN®
Makes any time special ®

Visit us at www.eHarlequin.com

HTNBN2

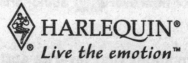

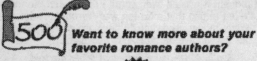

**If you're a fan of sensual romance
you *simply* must read…**

New York Times Bestselling Author

Carly Phillips

Simply

Sensual

Grace Montgomery has
been a good girl
long enough

The third sizzling title in Carly Phillips's *Simply* trilogy.

"4 STARS—Sizzle the winter blues away with a *Simply Sensual*
tale…wonderful, alluring and fascinating!"
—*Romantic Times*

Available in January 2004.

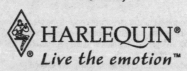

HARLEQUIN®
Live the emotion™

Visit us at www.eHarlequin.com

PHSSCP3

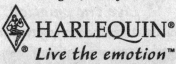

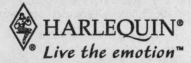